8 9 3

A Novel

893

A Daughter of the
Yakuza

Robert Cunningham

credo
house publishers

893: A Daughter of the Yakuza: A Novel

Copyright © 2014 by Robert Cunningham

Published in the United States by Credo House Publishers,
a division of Credo Communications, LLC, Grand Rapids, Michigan
www.credohousepublishers.com

ISBN: 978-1-625860-07-1

Cover design by LUCAS Art & Design
Interior design by Sharon VanLoozenoord

Printed in the United States of America

First edition

Contents

8 9 3

Background

Buddhist monks, according to legend, made up the first Chinese triads. They were intent on overthrowing the despised Manchus, who conquered China in 1644 and established the Qing Dynasty. The Manchus, however, managed to retain power for the next 300 years. Over this period this triad movement degenerated into a criminal underground, evolving into the Chinese mafia. In spite of their noble origins, triads over the course of time degenerated into the world's largest organized crime network.

Finally, in 1911, Dr. Sun Yat-Sen, along with his triad followers, established the Republic of China, centering their activities in Hong Kong and Shanghai. Chiang Kai-Check recruited followers from his Shanghai based triad and formed the famous Green Gang, which, in April of 1927, was responsible for slaughtering hundreds of Chinese Communists. In 1949 the Communists were finally successful in seizing power, forcing hordes of Shanghai triads to flee to Hong Kong, the nearest metropolitan haven, making that city from that point in time one of the world's headquarters of organized crime.

Currently there are four major triad societies in Hong Kong, with outposts in Beijing and Shanghai. The largest of these, Sun Ye On, is estimated to have 30,000 to 60,000 members. If the higher estimate of the total membership of the Chinese triads is taken as correct, this would involve one in 50 males (women are not allowed) in Hong Kong.

Triads are involved in numerous legitimate businesses, including hotels, cellular phone networks, nightclubs, karaoke bars, and airlines, and they make legitimate profits. Simultaneously, they also serve as a cover for their numerous illegitimate activities—brothels, smuggling illegal aliens, stolen cars, bootleg cigarettes, money laundering, protection, and drugs. Hong Kong has become the capital of the Southeast Asian heroin and amphetamine trade; from there the drugs are redirected to markets in the West.

Triads comprise the world's largest criminal fraternity. Membership brings solidarity, leverage, and connections, making it easy to find other criminal partners.

In Italy the mafia is known as the Costa Nostra. Literally "Our Thing," it refers to the alternative society that evolved in nineteenth-century Sicily and then emigrated to the eastern US, along with the waves of Italian immigrants, developing into the American mafia. In the Palermo dialect, *Mafioso* was associated with anyone who was bold, self-confident, or cool, and one credible theory claims that the word *mafia* evolved from this.

Like its Chinese counterpart, the original Italian mafia stereotype was almost completely positive, referring to an organization that existed to protect the weak from the excesses of the strong. The initiation ceremony involves pricking a finger, applying the blood to a wooden statue of a saint, setting it on fire and holding one's hand in the fire until the statue is consumed. Initiation ceremonies are considered permanent and cannot be easily nullified.

Another important mafia value is the vow of silence referred to as *omerta*; violate this vow and you become the target of one of its hit men. In modern times, with increased police scrutiny, such homicides are designed to look accidental.

A mafia of an entirely different composition also had its origin in noble purposes: to help powerless victims somehow achieve a sense of justice that would otherwise have been impossible. The Japanese *yakuza* is far bigger, controlling far more wealth and extending its influence to far more businesses than its American counterpart.

Oriental mafias maintain a covert and unofficial truce with the police; the police turn a blind eye to soft crime if there is a mutually understood assurance that harder crimes, such as homicide and kidnapping—ones that would blatantly disturb the peace and social order—will be avoided. This rather uneasy truce actually results in far better and more pragmatic controls on major crime in Japan than has ever been possible in America, with Japan having far fewer homicides and much less trafficking in heavy drugs.

The Japanese play a card game called *hanafuta* (flower cards), which they have enjoyed from the beginnings of their recorded history. Ancient decks of these cards with their elaborate artwork are eagerly sought after by collectors, and a set with good provenance brings high prices at an antiques art auction.

The hanafuta cards have numbers on the reverse side, as do most playing cards. One game played with them, called *oicho-kabu*, uses only three cards. When these three add up to the sum of twenty, they produce a score of zero, a losing hand. The worst hand one can possibly have is one with three cards with the numbers of eight, nine, and three, adding up to twenty.

In Japanese, when the first syllables from each of these three numbers (*ya-tsu, ku* and *san*) are joined together, the word *ya-ku-san* (8-9-3) evolves. Euphonic changes result in this being pronounced as *ya-ku-za*. Better known as the Japanese mafia, the yakuza resembles the hanafuta—it has a face side with a beautiful appearance, along with a reverse side with numbers—numbers that may comprise a losing hand, numbers that betray a dark and sinister reality lying just beneath the artistic surface.

Similar to the artwork on the hanafuta, a high number of the yakuza are artistically covered with tattoos (*irezumi* in Japanese). While the origin for the extensive tattoos on the torso, arms and legs of yakuza members is unclear, they are not entirely dissimilar to the artwork on the hanafuta, abundant in flowers and landscapes. Many of the themes of these tattoos are taken from classic Japanese woodblock prints. In Japan through the end of the seventeenth century tattoos were given to convicted criminals as a form of punishment. Some of these were later modified by adding additional decorations in order to conceal the original stigma.

Dragons, representing strength and virility, are popular as tattoo themes. It can take over one hundred painful hours to complete a large tattoo on the back. Such tattoos are indicative of machismo, courage, toughness and indifference to pain. Many yakuza members still elect to have their tattooing done the painful way, with a piece of sharp bamboo rather than an electric needle.

This body art allows for highly individualized expressions of uniqueness. Such traits are largely lacking and generally suppressed by the group culture orientation in Japan. A tattoo is a visible affirmation of one's ownership of his body. A respectable tattoo artist will not duplicate a single design but will always alter it sufficiently to create a unique piece of art for each client. Usually body areas that can be seen when fully clothed (upper neck, face, hands and feet) are avoided.

A fully tattooed person publically revealing his artwork can be intimidating. For this reason laws have recently been enacted prohibiting the public display of body tattoos in such places as *onsens* (Japanese hot spring baths) and public bathhouses. Due to some of the toxic ingredients used in tattoo ink, liver and allergy problems frequently develop among yakuza members with extensive tattoos. Sweat glands are also destroyed in the process, so the benevolent aspect of perspiration—the discharge of toxins—is largely nullified.

It is only when the reverse side of the hanafuta cards, the side with the numbers, is seen, that the true nature of the cards is known. A beautiful design on the front is in no way indicative of the number on the reverse side. You may have an attractive hand from the side others can see, but if the three cards add up to twenty you end up being a loser. In this light, the yakaza have chosen to call themselves The Losers—the 8-9-3—losers in the sense of being disengaged from the mainstream into an alternative society, of having to play an often challenging hand, a hand whose value is not evident from external appearance.

Encompassing perhaps as many as 2,500 families, the Japanese yakuza is currently estimated to have over 100,000 members. Japan's largest yakuza is the Yamaguchi-gumi (group or association), which formally began in 1915. Currently it alone has about 55,000 members, comprising about half of the total yakuza membership and having an active presence in 44 of Japan's 47 prefectures.

Two other prominent yakuza groups are the Sumiyoshi-kai (*kai* in Japanese means association or club, very similar in meaning to *kumi* or *gumi*) and the Inagawa-kai (in this context -*kai* and -*gumi* have the same meaning). The American mafia, in contrast, is estimated to have only around 3,000 members. In New York only five mafia families controlled the Eastern seaboard for decades. When adjusted for population, membership in the Japanese yakuza is proportionally 15–20 times greater than mafia membership in America.

The Japanese yakuza, when compared to the mafias of other countries, is relatively free of bloodshed. A noted exception occurred during the years following 1985, when the Ichiwa-kai, with 3,000 members, broke off from the Yamaguchi-gumi and succeeded in assassinating two of the Yamaguchi leaders, ushering in the Yama-Ichi war. Even so, the total number of yakuza-related homicides in Japan is usually below 20 cases annually, and in some years lower than 10.

Another yakuza attack occurred in 1990, shortly after the mayor of Nagasaki stated publicly that the Emperor bore some responsibility for WWII. The yakuza identifies with right-wing causes and almost all nationalistic movements. Another major assassination occurred in 1997 and yet another more recently when the mayor of Nagasaki, Iccho Itoh, was shot point-blank outside a train station on April 17, 2007, by Tetsuya Shiroo, a senior member of the Yamaguchi-gumi. This homicide originated from a personal vendetta that dated back four years to when Shiroo's car had sustained some damage from hitting a pothole while he was visiting a public works site.

Allowing a private matter—a personal grudge—to interfere at such a high level with gang business was, however, a violation of the yakuza code of honor. Normally such matters would be dealt with in a much more discreet and less public manner.

There is little room for individuality in Japanese society. "The nail that sticks up gets hammered down" applies more to Japan than to any other society. Japan's is a collectivistic society where the group to which one belongs provides identity and protection in exchange for uncompromising loyalty. In a country where group conformity and uniformity is valued above everything else, you have to keep the rules—or keep out.

An inability to fall in with the customs and trends of the times, along with opposition to conformity, has spawned sub-societies of outsiders throughout Japanese history. This frustration with a cookie cutter society is manifested not only in the 8-9-3, the yakuza, but also in the youth of modern Japan, who have but a few years between high school and college graduation to freely express their individuality.

When the casual visitor arrives in the Harajuku area in western Tokyo (one rail stop south of Shinjuku, the largest train station in Japan) on any evening and sees hundreds of Japanese youth dressed in black (some with white lace for emphasis) in the Goth-Loli fashion, they are usually surprised. These youth are adorned in the Gothic manner with crosses and crowns, even though these symbols carry little, if any, intrinsic meaning for them. Such young people provide another example of an alternative to the carbon copy society that characterizes their country. Membership in this case is informal and typically lasts until about the time of the first job interview, when neatness and conformity are mandated. Even in their nonconformity to society at large, these young people conform to a high degree to the dictates of this Gothic subculture.

Three hundred years ago a frightening and deadly sub-society emerged in Japan. Masterless, disfranchised *samurai* roamed the countryside, raising their swords against the rich, against thieves and dishonest businessmen, and against other corrupt samurai. They exemplified many of the traits of the *bushido*, the samurai code of ethics that included stoic endurance of pain, hunger and imprisonment. Because they helped the poor, their status in the public eye continued to improve until the early eighteenth century, when the elite and more established samurai began to curb their popularity.

Rejected by the masses and spurned by society, such marginal people sought a new home, a new place to belong. Castoffs, released prisoners, black sheep, orphans, and bastards all found acceptance and community by banding together and creating for themselves a sense of group identity.

Abraham Maslow is an American psychologist known for his famous "Hierarchy of Needs." The highest of his proposed five needs, self-actualization, is impossible to attain in a collectivistic culture such as Japan's, and even more so in the yakuza subculture. Maslow referred to those who settled for the routine and conformed to the limits and constraints of their subculture as "non-peakers," inadvertently an accurate description of the loser theme in the yakuza subculture. Such individuals have traded the high potential of their birthright for the immediacy of the temporary porridge that comes with belonging to an inclusive, although minority and fringe, subculture, one that demands loyalty as the price of the self-identity and protection it provides.

About the only manner in which individuality can freely be expressed is in body modification, especially in the form of extensive tattoos, which are usually concealed under one's clothing. Full obedience and conformity to one's *oyabun* (literally an individual in a yakuza who serves in a parent or boss role) is mandatory. Tattoos allow simultaneously for an extreme expression of individuality and full submission to one's oyabun.

There is much, in fact, about the melancholic Japanese personality that is drawn toward the dark side of the human condition, preferring the predictable and the pragmatic, even if this preference is expressed in a negative sense, as opposed to the mysterious and somewhat unpredictable nature of the process of faith, belief and self-actualization.

This is a major reason why the way of the Christian faith does not appeal to the Japanese. While admiring Christianity (some polls indicate that as many as 70 percent of Japanese highly respect it), they spurn belief in anything that would make them stand out as individuals. The Japanese do not inherently like to take unpredictable risks, including the risk of faith.

Koreans are different. They do not need to have all their ducks in a row before attempting something new. With approximately the same proportion of Christian missionaries and the same exposure to the gospel message, the Korean response to the Christian call to faith has been 100 times greater than that of the Japanese. Even the Chinese under communism have manifested about 50 times the response in following God's call when compared to the Japanese.

Yakuza groups in Japan reached the height of their power around 1960, when their numbers swelled to around 184,000 members—considerably more than that of the *jieitai* (Japanese self-defense forces) at that time. The jieitai currently numbers about 240,000, so it is now about twice as large as the yakuza.

Membership in a yakuza is somewhat inversely dependent upon the health of the economy; that is, the worse the economy, the more the recruits. The 11-year depression from which Japan is now emerging has resulted in an influx of new members who could not otherwise have found gainful employment or a significant employment group to belong to. While numbers have declined since the yakazu's peak to around 100,000, yakuza business endeavors have expanded and now encompass almost every thriving area of business in Japan. The American mafia, by contrast, has perhaps only 1,000 initiated members spread over approximately 25 families—about one percent of the number in Japan.

The Millennial Generation (those born between 1980 and 2000) and the steep rise in the NEET group (Not in Education, Employment or Training) have resulted in fertile Japanese soil for recruits. While many come from the lower classes, including the uneducated and school dropouts, they are inevitably headed by a boss, an oyabun, who is smart, savvy, capable and street-wise. Oyabuns do not fit the typical stereotype of the Japanese personality. They are usually decisive, talented in their own right, driven and possessing strong, authoritarian egos. Once they attain power they do not give it up—that is, until, in step with the rest of humanity on death's doorstep they are finally and reluctantly forced to make a handover to a successor. The successor typically carries on the wishes of the deceased oyabun.

Corporate extortion is one of the yakuza's tactics. In Japan this frequently makes the headlines as bribes, cover money and kickbacks (non-yakuza related activities), as well as in gambling in every form, including horse, bicycle and motorboat racing; and in loan sharking; drug dealing; real estate fraud; stock manipulation; pornography; protection; and tourist scams, all of which are yakuza activities. The yakuza is involved in almost all significant illegal activity and not far removed from most large-scale legitimate ones, especially those in the public sector (construction of roads, bridges, schools, etc.).

Ironically, Japan may be the only country in the world where even Christian charities (homes for the elderly, facilities for the handicapped, etc.) in almost all instances benefit from the yakuza. The low percentage of Christian believers (fewer than one percent—on any given Sunday in Japan only two to five people in one thousand will attend a Christian church service), along with the high level of financial commitment required to support the church, results in very little clean money being available for causes typically associated with the church.

This lack of available funding by believers, along with high overhead (property, utilities, salaries, etc.) within the church means that most significant Christian charities are dependent on yakuza donations given through neutral third parties, usually a quasi-government agency such as the United Fund.

Such worthwhile quasi-government agencies receive these donations and forward them to the charities in the form of passenger vans, monies designated toward improvements or alterations to buildings, assistance with heating costs, etc. This dirty money, used for clean purposes, has the indirect effect of silencing most voices that would otherwise speak against the yakuza's activities and vices.

The practice of using dirty money for clean purposes is not at all contrary to the philosophy of William Booth, the founder of the Salvation Army, who quipped that "the only trouble with tainted money is that there taint enough of it." Tainted money goes a long way, and it is highly probable that much of the economic infrastructure and social work in Japan would come to a screeching halt without it.

The sex industry is one of the yakuza's largest sources of revenue. In Japan love hotels (hotels that offer no food, and usually no overnight lodging) by far outnumber legitimate hotels. They cater to every fancy of the overworked, button-downed, salaried wage earner where a room is rented for a "two hour stay." The Japanese language, showing its adaptability to foreign words, uses the term *abeku*, adapted from the French *avec*, "to be with," to refer to such two- to three-hour liaisons.

A man typically brings his own female companion with him. Reflective mirrors on the ceilings, an Amazon jungle ambience, tranquilizers to relax the participants, erotic scents—all are intended to enhance the total sensory experience. Scandinavian pornography with blond subjects is popular; this type of porn was smuggled into Japan prior to the Internet. In recent years the yakuza, showing its marketing adaptability, has expanded into cyber porn.

Technically prostitution, according to the Japanese Anti-Prostitution Law of 1956, is illegal. However, as long as mutual consent is indicated by both parties, a liaison is looked upon as legal. Historically, Japanese culture is tolerant of sex. Shinto, the indigenous religion, doesn't regard sex outside of marriage as wrong. And Japanese Buddhism just doesn't have much impact or teaching on the subject. There is no "Seventh Commandment" in either of these religions.

For the Japanese, nature is ultimate and an integral part of nature is one's sexual desires. Both Shinto and Buddhist priests in Japan are well known for their various indiscretions, with many of them using donated monies to maintain mistresses, usually off but sometimes even on the temple grounds. There are also various loopholes in the law, coupled with very liberal interpretations as to what prostitution actually is, along with loose enforcement. So the yakuza operates in the *mizushobai* (literally "water of entertainment") industry with almost total impunity.

It isn't hard to spot a yakuza pimp. In any case, one doesn't need to—he'll spot them first. If you're a male without female companionship walking through the mizushobai area of town, you'll inevitably be approached by a young man, usually in his twenties;

often he will have his hair curled by a perm, wear pointed shoes and be dressed in a flamboyant manner. He carries with him a colored photo album with pictures and other information on his girls, including measurements so precise they come close to meeting Toyota's manufacturing standards. Females from nearby foreign countries are often flaunted, and additional data on them includes their background, hobbies and country of origin.

Recently the popularity of young, uniformed schoolgirls as sex objects has increased to the point of becoming a national obsession. Japanese girls engage in such activity for the extra spending money it provides. The yakuza also goes outside Japan to source young virgins from the Philippines, where impoverished parents, in order to feed the rest of their family, may sell off their daughter for a few thousand dollars.

In an attempt to control population, the Chinese have adopted the 4-2-1 policy, allowing for four grandparents, two parents and one child. If this one child is a girl, she is often unwanted and becomes a choice selection for the Japanese yakuza, providing some instant cash for an impoverished family. This in turn has resulted in a depleted population of eligible Chinese brides, resulting in much higher dowry prices for the ones that remain.

Methamphetamine (speed) was given to *kamikaze* pilots during WWII to help them remain alert during long suicide attack missions. Immediately after the war, markets in Japan were flooded with the excess methamphetamine until its addictive nature became known, at which time it was withdrawn from the public. Consequently, earlier laws dating from 1914 (the Harrison Act) were updated. The most extensive of these are the Boggs-Daniel Amendments (1956), by which methamphetamine, tranquilizers and LSD were added to the list. The first infraction can result in a prison sentence of 5–20 years, the second 10–40 years. Selling to a minor can result in a life sentence without parole, or even in capital punishment.

Today, tranquilizers are used legally in the country's network of private mental hospitals at a rate that would alarm many physicians in the West. Japanese patients tend to believe in the silver bullet and readily defer to the judgment of doctors with strong egos who tend to overprescribe medications. Some private hospitals even have their own pharmacies, so that the more medicine they prescribe the more money they make. Outside of these legally prescribed medications, the yakuza has almost total control, completely monopolizing the methamphetamine (*shabu*) market in the country. Recent years have seen a strong increase in the number of users between 14 and 18 years of age.

1

Alpha

"Hello *gaijin-san* [Mr. Foreigner]! Welcome to our company," mouthed the pretty receptionist, Rie Nakata, in nearly perfect English. Although she had studied abroad and was in the top one percentile of Japanese citizens with her command of English, she had nevertheless enrolled in Alfred B. Clark's company-sponsored English class.

"*Ha-ji-me-ma-shi-te* [Nice meeting you]," responded Alpha in perfect Japanese. Since his initials were ABC, the nickname Alpha, short for "alphabet," had been conferred on him by his middle school classmates. As nicknames go, this was one of the better ones; he didn't at all mind being called that, as the obsolete sounding Alfred was no longer a common or popular name.

As the English classes Alpha was offering were fully sponsored by Kyowa Shoji, the company employing him, sessions were free to all company employees. Eleven had enrolled—all but the senior management, who were too old, too proud to expose themselves to making frequent mistakes in pronunciation, or too busy (at least in their own estimation) to participate. Rie had the additional assignment of orienting Alpha to the company, introducing him to all the employees and accompanying him to all meals eaten during company time.

After the first class Rie, conscientious in the fulfillment of her new task, asked Alpha, "Got some time for dinner and a drink? I have a favorite hangout, a small mom and pop restaurant—nothing fancy—off the beaten path, about 10 minutes' walk from Kyowa Shoji."

This invitation evolved into Alpha's informal welcome party. In addition to Rie, four others from the class joined in—three young female employees and one male. All were single and most approaching 30 years of age. Marriage later in life is becoming customary in Japan, resulting in decreased birth rates. Due to high pollution, the sperm count of Japanese males decreases significantly as they age, making many of them infertile or nearly so.

Late marriages, along with infertility resulting in fewer children, is producing a serious decline in the Japanese population. There are now just over a million babies born annually—a poor showing for a population of 128,000,000. Nor does it appear that this trend toward reduced population, first manifest in 2006, will abate in the near future. Japan has become an aging society, "boasting" the largest percentage of elderly people in the world.

The Japanese do not typically date in the forthright manner of Americans; a small group activity like this dinner is par for the course. Even though the possibility of one-on-one intimacy is preempted, the young people can at least enjoy each other's company in the context of a small group.

The small restaurant was called the Paragon. Alpha smiled to himself, aware that the use of English and English names is more for embellishment and decoration than it is intended to convey meaning. The restaurant, while decent, clean, and fairly contemporary, was in fact anything but a paragon. The menu typified the Japanese version of Western offerings—spaghetti, curry rice, pizza, and sandwiches, including hamburgers. Alpha knew from his upbringing in Japan to avoid Japanese sandwiches. Their sliced meat often tastes like fish (which is used for animal feed), and the mayonnaise typically has a sharp, pungent flavor. "What would you like to eat?" Rie asked Alpha brightly. The first to order sets the tone for the rest. "I'd like some pizza," Alpha replied, "and an Asahi Lite." He thought this to be a safe bet and wasn't surprised by the kernels of corn and shrimp that had somehow found their way into this recipe for Japanese pizza.

All but two in the group ordered beer. Some wanted Sapporo, some Kirin, and some Asahi. The two who ordered Japanese tea instead, Alpha reflected briefly, might be within the 30 or so percent of Orientals who can't tolerate alcohol. Having a deficiency in one of the two liver enzymes necessary for its speedy breakdown, this subgroup experiences hyperventilation, rapid pulse, face flushing and nausea when they ingest alcohol even in small amounts. In fact, one reason alcoholism rates are about one-third lower in the Orient than in the West is simply that a minority of Orientals are genetically protected from drinking enough alcohol to become alcoholics. Nonalcoholic beer is just now beginning to catch on in Japan—the substance seems to the Japanese to be an oxymoron, an inconsistent entity like decaf coffee.

Sometimes Orientals, and especially the Japanese, in spite of their reputation for being reserved, ask some very blunt questions, particularly when stimulated by the synergy of a small group. No one seemed to feel the need for inhibition, and the queries flowed freely. "How old are you?" "Twenty-four." "Do you have a girlfriend?" "No." "No special friend back in the States?" "No." "What do you think of Japanese girls?" To this Alpha opted for a discreet reply, a noncommittal "No comment." "How did you become so fluent in Japanese that you can speak it with almost no accent?" Anticipating a lengthy response, Rie ordered three more beers—one from each of the big three Japanese brewers. Each beer drinker filled the glass of the person next to them.

Alpha began to explain: "Being in Japan isn't new to me, or to my family or ancestors. I am the fourth generation of the Clark family to have an extended and positive relationship with Japan. My great grandfather was in Japan more than a century ago and helped establish an agricultural school on the northern island of Hokkaido. It eventually developed into Hokkaido University. I think there's a statue of him somewhere near the clock tower in Sapporo."

As universities go in Japan, Hokkaido University is well established, with a good hospital and medical college, and has a reputation comparable to that of other notable Japanese universities. The hard part about attending college in Japan is just passing the entrance exam; once in, you're guaranteed to graduate. With fewer applicants due to a decline in the number of college age young people, some universities are for the first time in their history not requiring entrance exams. American teachers in Japan often have a crisis of conscience when expected to give a passing grade to a student who enrolls but seldom if ever attends their class.

This is in sharp contrast to the situation in America, where community colleges often have open enrollment, allowing students to get in without a qualifying entrance exam. Japanese companies look to the universities not so much for the knowledge and expertise to be gained there but for the lifelong connections to be established with fellow students. Thus a graduate from *Todai* (Tokyo Daigaku or University) may be hired strictly because the company that employs him can capitalize on relationships already made during the university years.

Alpha continued, "All three generations of my family since that time have spent at least part of their professional careers in Japan. My grandfather, working in Navy Intelligence during the war, helped draw up the 1944 Invasion Plan for Okinawa." As soon as he had divulged this fact, he realized he might have been wiser not to. "Sorry!" he offered. But no one had taken apparent offense. The generation born after the war carries no negative personal memories of the event. Alpha continued, "Grandfather played a major role during the Japanese Occupation, working until 1951 on various aspects of the Marshall Plan." Once again he checked himself. "Sorry about that!" This time everyone laughed. "Then my father worked as the vice-counsel in the American Embassy in Tokyo, in the Toranomon area." After the beer was finished everyone seemed satisfied, and the party broke up.

The employees from Kyowa Shoji welcomed Alpha into their

4

social network. To the Japanese, work and work relationships provide the basis for one's social life. Feeling himself to be genuinely accepted, Alpha was pleased to belong to a group of young adults who were optimistic about their future, hard working in the present and still idealistic about life. They seemed, in fact, to have a lot in common with him.

In spite of his rich bilingual heritage, Alpha remained a gaijin, a foreigner or "outside person"—someone who didn't have a single Japanese chromosome in his DNA. When he was three years old his family had moved to Japan to work at the US Embassy in Tokyo. He had attended a Japanese kindergarten and was then enrolled for two years at the local elementary school. Having spent most of his formative years in Japan, Alpha felt quite at home there. It was his appearance, not his upbringing or personality, that irrevocably defined him as a gaijin. In reality he was too individualistic to be Japanese—while too conscious of group values to be American.

Alpha walked, however, like an American. There was a forcefulness and directness, a high degree of self-confidence in his gait, that set him off from a typical Japanese person. If one could turn one's method of walking into sound, Americans would be much louder than Japanese.

Alpha was in fact a TCK. This term was originally coined to refer to a third-culture or transcultural kid, an individual who has spent a significant part of his developmental years in another culture, resulting in a syncretistic blend of both. Typical neither of their host culture nor of their native culture, such kids are sometimes referred to as global nomads. TCK applies to the children of business executives (business brats), diplomats, soldiers, and sailors (military brats), and missionary kids (MKs) who are raised in a foreign environment.

TCKs tend to manifest certain personality characteristics, such as being highly independent even to the point of being loners. They are self-reliant, which in a negative way can result in isolation, especially when they don't fully feel their need for strong social support. In contrast the Japanese, uncomfortable in unpredictable contexts, inevitably try to take their culture with them when they go abroad. They possess a state-dependent orientation, learning, working, and even existing in a defined social state along with other Japanese. They like to carry at least a part of that social state with them when they travel abroad. Unlike their Japanese counterparts, TCKs can never really go back home in a physical sense; in a very real way they have no physical or geographic home to go back to.

In spite of having American parents, Alpha didn't consider America to be his home, although he did consider being an American as his primary identity. At least his passport testified to the fact that he was American. No physical place can meet the criteria for a physical home for a TCK, as frequent changes in geographic locations often occur while they are growing up. TCKs often have no roots embedded in geography, especially when they have been raised in several cultures.

Instead, TCKs find their roots in relationships, the deepest of which tend to develop with others of similar experience—other TCKs. Otherwise, they gravitate to other bilingual or trilingual people whose world-and-life-view has been broadened by their learning and who share some of the same personality characteristics. They don't necessarily look at their own culture as being normative but see value in other cultures as well, enjoying the challenge of relating to people with other worldviews.

On the positive side, as they mature TCKs can make good leaders with their ability to make appropriate and timely decisions and to exercise effective leadership. In contrast to the Japanese, they tend not to be overly influenced by group think in their decision making, although they remain aware of group mores as they participate in social interactions, especially in unfamiliar contexts. As the world gets smaller, TCKs may be the best-equipped people to become the cultural brokers of the future.

On the negative side, there will remain in the background of every TCK an inherent tendency not to fully trust people, to be suspicious of almost everyone and everything. They find it difficult to remain blissfully ignorant, often defaulting to their detached, observant and inquisitive attitude. If unsuccessful, they can become cynical and sarcastic much more quickly and with much less provocation than a non-TCK.

Another day at work, and another invitation out. This time they were going to eat *o-ko-no-mi-ya-ki*, Japanese pancakes with shrimp and vegetables—one can select his own ingredients and cook his own cakes on the grill in front of him. This time the group dwindled to six, again including Rie. Curiosity would provide another night of interesting conversation.

At this early stage of his employment, Alpha didn't fully anticipate the emotional impact of the fact that he would be alone, socially isolated, without the abundant support of friends and family he had enjoyed growing up. Once home in his small apartment, his only companion was a small LCD Japanese TV. Television in Japan lacks the sophistication it enjoys in American. It seemed to him that the Japanese, unable to act freely in everyday life, used TV not so much for entertainment as for a safety outlet from the pressures of living in a country with so high a population density.

This made him all the more thankful for the social relationships that were developing from working and teaching at Kyowa Shoji. And he was especially thankful for Rie. Her timely assistance and helpful nature didn't seem forced or calculated. On the other hand, her caring for him didn't appear to be based solely on obligation. He sensed that her looking after him might have more than mere friendship overtones, and he didn't mind at all. If he was reading her cues correctly, she was playing the game just right, letting him glimpse a mild interest and an availability but never forcing the issue by becoming overbearing or obtrusive, and certainly not indicating that she was there for the taking. She evidently understood that men enjoy and appreciate a challenge.

Living in a foreign culture amplifies personal experiences. No significant experience impacts a vulnerable person in a neutral manner—good experiences become better and bad experiences worse. As the days went by, for Rie and Alpha everything was becoming increasingly good—in fact, very good. They enjoyed spending time together, and their friendship quickly deepened. He tried holding her hand for the first time during the third week at work. Rie didn't withdraw it immediately but gave a subtle Japanese smile in return before moving it beyond his reach.

Alpha didn't know how much to read into that enigmatic smile. Nobody, in fact, can accurately and consistently interpret what a Japanese smile means. What he did know is that inappropriate smiling is for the Japanese often a sign of discomfort. Yet Rie's suggestive smile seemed genuine, as if to say "I'm here for you. If holding my hand is pleasing to you, then please do so—just not here or now."

Alpha didn't yet know how to read Rie's emotions, but at the same time he didn't pick up any negative feedback. He knew that Japanese women through the centuries have developed perhaps the most subtle nonverbal communication skills in the world. They can be faultlessly modest and still covertly—and even sexually—alluring while appearing withdrawn. Just the right gesture—an inscrutable smile, a touch that feels like a caress from the wind—seems to be a part of the Japanese female DNA. Alpha couldn't have put it into words but somehow sensed that Rie was genuine in her response—a minimal threshold response that was still in a positive direction. Perhaps it's only Japanese women who can somehow flirt with you on a covert level while making you believe it's *you* who is taking the initiative.

In order to survive expensive rental costs in the Tokyo area, Rie shared an apartment with another older but single employee at work. Erika, already 34 years old, was on her own career path and didn't want marriage to slow her down. As a result of her hard work she traveled abroad twice a year, usually to Europe and usually in February and August. The Japanese call these two months 2-8, or *nip-pachi*, referring to the slowest times in the fiscal year and thus the best times to take a vacation.

For most companies the fiscal year ends in March, and a month prior to that the pace is invariably slow. And August 15 marks *Obon*, the time when the Japanese return to their ancestral homes and celebrate the end of summer. Rie and Erika didn't see much of each other except on an occasional Sunday.

Rie and Alpha developed a routine that evolved naturally. Most of the employees would go out for a drink after work. Initially Alpha and Rie joined them but hung around together and ordered a meal, after which Alpha walked her home.

Alpha's desire to be with Rie grew, and he found himself pleasantly surprised when he realized he was falling in love with her. Her feedback still seemed deliberately elusive. It was never overdone; in fact, it was at times so barely positive that it seemed to indicate that, if he wanted the relationship to progress, she wouldn't oppose or resist that development. If Alpha's perceptions were accurate, the feeling of developing love might be mutual.

Rie lived in a second floor apartment, down a narrow street where there was no room for cars. On the fourth night he walked her home, the street looked deserted. As Rie opened the door to her apartment he gave her a quick kiss on her left cheek. It was more of the teasing type of peck, the kind that says "I'm letting you know I like you." The gesture, while not forceful, would still have allowed Rie to pull back and say in effect, "Thanks, but that's enough for now." Rie, in the manner in which Oriental women can be so maddeningly skillful, neither pressed forward nor explicitly retreated. Her alluring dark eyes remained as imperturbable as they were impenetrable.

Usually fully in control, Rie blushed a little, fumbled for words and came out simply with "Good Night. Be careful going home." Words that contain both an "r" and an "i" are the most difficult for the Japanese to pronounce correctly, and Alpha thought he detected a more pronounced mispronunciation than usual. Before she closed the door a short enigmatic smile formed on her lips as though to indicate "There will be a tomorrow."

During the walk to the subway Alpha felt fully alive. Great spontaneous pulses of energy, of joy, resonated throughout his system. To have his existence, his very being, validated and honored by someone like Rie—he didn't know how to describe the sensation other than by the word poets have used for centuries: *LOVE*. Still plagued by uncertainty, Alpha was nonetheless wisely aware that he didn't know the extent of her true feelings, something the Japanese call *honne*. If there was any congruity between her *tatemae*, the external appearance or façade the Japanese present to the outside world, and her honne, Alpha wanted confirmation. He assured himself, "I'll find out soon—maybe by tomorrow, if possible."

The next day began in the accustomed manner. The *chorei*, a morning gathering at which the manager exhorted everyone to do their best for the company, proceeded as usual. This was followed by about 10 minutes of group physical exercises, accompanied by NHK—Japanese public radio. Nothing about the day was atypical, except for the fact that Alpha found the time dragging.

He wondered, as was becoming his habit, how Rie was feeling, whether his latest advances were truly welcomed or would be politely and discreetly rejected in a way that would save face for both of them. If rejected, this development could make his work environment at Kyowa Shoji somewhat tense. Rie maintained her professional attitude and poise, revealing nothing to those around them. If anything, she seemed a little cooler toward Alpha, who thought she might be putting him off. A knot developed in his stomach, and 5:00 was still more than three hours away.

When at last closing time came around, Alpha suggested casually, "Let's go back to your hangout." He knew Rie felt comfortable at the Paragon, and she readily complied. They were ushered to a small table for two in the corner. Ordering two glasses of Cabernet, he observed that Rie seemed a little tired and on edge. The evening was still young—it was just after 7:30—when they walked to her apartment. Probably not an auspicious sign.

No other soul was in sight, and Erika was still out. Rie inserted her key into the lock and, without opening the door, turned around to face Alpha, at the same time tilting her head ever so slightly to the right and standing there for an instant of vulnerable silence with her lips slightly parted. Alpha needed no more than a split second to seize the opening. Their hands met at the same time their lips touched, and at once he knew.

What Alpha hadn't realized, however, was how much information could be compressed into one kiss. Such soft lips, such fragrance: the more their lips touched the more he felt the great gift of being welcomed into the soul of another. This was not a kiss intended to open the door to further physical contact. Quite to the contrary, it was a kiss of grace, of gratitude, of affirmation, a kiss of great respect. Never before had he kissed a girl with that degree of passion, and yet her response was so honorable in it in no way invited an advance in the direction of personal lust.

It occurred to Alpha even in this moment of passion that what one really loves one honors and treats with great respect. Rie was to him like a bottle of costly wine—to be drunk moderately and politely, to be savored over a long time. The core of his being ignited as though on fire, burning with pure ecstasy. He was still himself and yet somehow a thousand times more alive; simultaneously, he was in some way becoming more than himself. The universal language of love, when two hearts beat as one, needed no translating, interpreting or explaining.

Rie turned the key in the lock, gave Alpha another subtle smile, mouthed "Good night," and closed the door.

Fire in a man's heart cannot long be hidden, and the other employees at Kyowa Shoji soon caught on to the relationship between Rie and Alpha. No one either censored them or openly encouraged their relationship. In compliance with the unwritten norm that work is to remain ever professional, everyone maintained a noncommittal demeanor. Some of the other office girls were secretly envious, but not in an overly negative way.

These girls were happy for Rie, although they would never have expected someone like her, with so strong a will, to find someone she could willingly follow throughout life. While the relationship between Rie and Alpha might not have been fully predictable from a rational standpoint, it made sense to the two of them. As the great French philosopher Pascal once said, "The heart has reasons the mind does not know." Rie and Alpha were in the process of finding that out.

Alpha was pleasantly surprised to find in Rie such an outgoing personality, combined with a degree of confidence and poise that was balanced by her being in no way obtrusive, forceful or obnoxious. She quickly became the antidote for his loneliness. He found himself in love in a way he had never known before or even imagined possible. Never before had he felt so lonely and isolated, and never before had he experienced that someone could fill that void in the way Rie did. Never before had he been able to commit with full abandon to another person with the assurance that the vulnerability that came with the territory wouldn't be taken lightly but highly prized and honored.

Even though Alpha was also independent in nature, he was aware that such independence without the positive input of a loving relationship could easily develop into a negative and sardonic type of isolation. He felt, perhaps counter-intuitively, that his single commitment to Rie was resulting in more freedom and less isolation. By that very commitment he was becoming more fully alive and free.

Most Japanese people don't make a public display of their emotions. Around the company, Rie and Alpha appeared as nothing more than two congenial employees, each with their own tasks to accomplish. As 5:00 approached each day, Alpha's thoughts gravitated toward Rie in anticipation of being together without interruption.

Walking the crowded streets savoring the warmth and comfort of her hand and her affirming presence beside him meant for Alpha that everything else in life would somehow work out. For both, a deeper sense of confidence was evolving. The more deeply their love blossomed, the more spontaneity and fun found a place in their relationship. No longer did they need to plan the evenings ahead of time—something enticing to do together always developed without their having to work at it.

Walking hand in hand through the crowded streets and sidewalks of Tokyo is perfectly acceptable in Japan, even if one of the two is a foreigner. Both Rie and Alpha wanted the world to notice that they were in love. The masses, the *hoi polloi*, however, passed by in indifference. But that didn't matter to them. They had each other, and that was all the affirmation they needed.

A high percentage of Japanese eat out regularly since they spend so many hours at work. Or perhaps away from home would be a better description. Long commutes, unofficial overtime, semi-mandatory stops at watering holes after work—all results in a long workday. As long as high-end establishments are avoided, meals eaten out are quite reasonable in price, especially in consideration of the time required to cook for oneself. Lunches eaten at the workplace are typically subsidized by the company, with any remaining amount deducted from one's salary. Tipping is not customary, so an adequate, fixed menu meal can often be found for around 10 dollars.

Alpha's responsibilities at Kyowa Shoji were to be available to assist with private tutoring; proofread documents translated into English; and teach English conversation twice weekly, or more, as demand would dictate. The trading company, being small, required that its receptionist, Rie Nakata, also work as an interpreter/translator to the best of her ability when not busy with the switchboard. Her translations into English would be proofread by the new *gaijin-san* [outsider]—none other than Alpha. This provided the two another opportunity for regular contact.

Both were careful to maintain professional appearances at Kyowa Shoji. Such behavior comes naturally to the Japanese, who maintain a tatemae that always appears positive, agreeable, and controlled. This is one reason for the ready Japanese smile.

Teaching English to Japanese students has its challenges, even for a native English speaker. As hard as they might try, for example, most Japanese never learn to say "Thank You" correctly. Their attempts tend to come out as "Sank You." And the Japanese language lacks a true "i" or "r" sound. Especially for someone with the entrepreneurial tendencies most TCKs exhibit, teaching English isn't a satisfying occupation for the long term. It's too repetitive, too predictable, and it doesn't present the challenge personal entrepreneurial endeavors do.

Teaching English does, however, make a decent short- or midterm transitional job, even for TCKs. What Alpha wanted at this stage was to test the waters, to try to determine whether he could make it in Japan in business for himself. He remembered that an Oriental sage had once said "Do something you like, and you will never work a day in your life." Teaching English didn't quite ascend to that level, although he enjoyed the interaction with his students.

The Japanese have rather thick barriers to their social groups. If one doesn't have some means of permeating these barriers—of which teaching English is one—admission to a group may not be possible. Once in, however, few barriers exist. Once an individual earns their trust, the Japanese are surprisingly open with their inner thoughts and feelings. The Japanese psyche is weak in an individual sense, requiring exposure to a small group in order to be solidified, confirmed and integrated.

After just three months Alpha felt reasonably connected, and his thoughts began to gravitate in the direction of self-employment. He thought seriously about setting up his own interpreting and translating business. The initial opportunity came when a classmate from the East-West Department at the University of Hawaii emailed him, asking whether he knew of any jobs in Japan open to gaijin. Without other culturally relevant skills (such as speaking good Japanese), the mandated choice is typically that of teaching English.

With a generous endowment from the cash gifts Alpha and Rie anticipated receiving at their wedding, Alpha decided to hand over Kyowa Shoji's position, if he were allowed, to his friend. The planned engagement would occur during the upcoming holiday—Golden Week. The wedding was just over two months away, and this would provide the opportunity for a new start. The Japanese customarily avoid giving sums at weddings that are easily divisible; this is thought to imply that the new union might be vulnerable to its own disillusion. Even numbered sums give place to odd numbered ones.

So sums such as 20,000 yen ($200) and 40,000 yen ($400) are avoided. The latter also has the dubious distinction of containing the number four, pronounced the same as the word for "death" (*shi*), so it is avoided for two reasons. An acquaintance may give 10,000 yen ($100), a business associate or close family friend 30,000 yen ($300) and others as much as 50,000 yen ($500). Presents that cut—knives and scissors—are studiously avoided, as it is surmised they could sever the relationship.

2

The New Entrepreneur

Boarding the train for Shinjuku, Alpha was soon to be dissolved into the anonymous sea of humanity of a Japanese rush hour train. In such contexts physical proximity in no way implies social nearness. The train arrived, and he noticed an oddity: the car immediately in front of him was assigned to "Ladies Only, 7–9 a.m." Those in the know realize that this is an attempt by the Japanese Railway to deal with the frequent pinching that goes on during rush hours when a female's butt, surrounded by a group of sadistic males, is considered fair game for the stray hand of an anonymous male making a deft foray into the aisle to grasp a piece of the action that eludes him in ordinary life. Foreign women in particular are frequently subjected to this indignity. So Alpha squeezed into an adjacent car just as the doors were closing.

There is a general pattern foreigners follow in adjusting to a new culture. During the first phase they're enamored with it, appreciating its deep history, the ancient buildings and temples, the language and customs. Then, after a few months, they plateau. The food still tastes good, but occasionally they want to indulge at a local McDonalds, ordering a supersized Big Mac. Then a major holiday comes around, and they feel emotionally depleted due to a lack of supportive social and religious traditions: no family meals with turkey and ham, no pumpkin pie, no Christmas carols, no Christmas Eve service celebrating the birth of the Christ.

A lingering depression sets in, and the host culture is no longer viewed through rosy lenses. Those who thrive in the host culture invariably have to make it through this cycle, ultimately adapting to and coming to appreciate it. Usually two or three years are required—long enough to gain fluency and familiarity—for this transition to occur. Alpha was certainly in this phase: while there was a lot he didn't like about Japan, he was sufficiently comfortable in its culture and fluent in the language, and the idea of spending the rest of his life there didn't carry any negative undertones. At any rate, Japan Air Lines was offering round-trip tickets to America during the off season for around $1,400, so a trip home, with a little disciplined savings, would never be out of reach.

Life is good, Alpha had to acknowledge. Raised as the son of the Vice Counsel of the American Embassy in Japan, he was one of the few Americans students who could speak Japanese fluently. Due to his father's transfer there, Alpha had attended Japanese schools from kindergarten through the second grade and then transferred to the American School in Japan, where he had studied from the third through the twelfth grades.

This reputable school, which was approaching its 100th year of operation, served students from 40 different counties—all potential candidates for becoming future international leaders. For better or worse, almost all of them would be influenced by the subculture and end up becoming TCKs. The Japanese students would no longer be purely Japanese and the Americans no longer purely American.

Several Japanese families who could afford it also enrolled their children at the American School in Japan; they disliked Japan's educational philosophy, with its rote memory, lack of creative thinking, and enforced conformity. In the collectivistic society of Japan, emphasis in education is on how to *do*. In America, an individualistic society, on the contrary, the focus is on how to *learn*. You had better not be left-handed in Japan—if you are, there will be a lot of pressure to become right-handed. As needed, square pegs will be forced into round holes.

Entering the American School in Japan in the third grade meant that Alpha had gravitated toward Japanese students who had also just enrolled, as opposed to the established American cliques that were harder to penetrate. This had carried the unanticipated benefit of helping Alpha develop an almost native level of Japanese speech. He had begun to function almost equally well in Western and Eastern cultures. Most foreigners who arrive in Japan as adults, even with great effort at studying the Japanese language extended over years, never develop to this level. Such a person always remains an outside gaijin. And their language, due in part to atrophy of the muscles of the larynx, will never approach native speaker levels.

Alpha had started college on the American West Coast, focusing on electronics and software programming, found it boring, and switched to a Japanese major, transferring to the University of Hawaii's East West Center, where he had achieved a B.A. in Asian Studies. Given his background, the usually challenging program had not been difficult for him; he had ended up with a respectable 3.4 GPA without having to burn the candle on both ends.

At that point he had enrolled in graduate school and taken one additional semester in international business. During Thanksgiving break he had met a Japanese exchange student who had given him a Japanese newspaper that posted several job opportunities for native English speakers. Feeling burned out from college and eager to try out his wings, Alpha had begun applying, planning to drop out of school after the semester was completed. Once he had decided on a career, he rationalized, he could always return to the books later on to hone his skills.

Preferring to work in the Tokyo area where he had spent many of his younger years, he was overjoyed to receive a response in fairly decent English from Kyowa Shoji, a trading company seeking a native English speaker to teach English at its headquarters in western Tokyo. Alpha had applied immediately, was accepted, and waited until January 16, when airfares to Japan kick into off-season prices. He felt as though he were going home, at least in the limited sense a TCK can experience home. The trading company specialized in electronics and had major customer bases in the United States, China and three other Pacific Rim countries.

It was at this juncture that he had met Rie. Her English was better than that of the others, as she had experienced the benefit of studying in America. It was she who had translated the response to his job application into English. Like Alpha, she was quite at home in both Japanese and American cultures. A true TCK has to be well born, or at least raised in the host culture during their formative years. This Rie was not, although she had absorbed enough of Western culture to emancipate her from the narrow, ethnocentric outlook characteristic of an untraveled person.

Rie's Japanese worldview, like that of most Japanese, was monistic—embracing the perspective that everything is somehow a part of everything else and that harmony serves as the uniting force behind it all. Everything for her was relative, depending on the context. Japanese monism posits that ultimately everything has to come together, to harmonize. Adherents are usually quite tolerant but tend not to become activists. No cause on Earth in their opinion deserves their extreme involvement.

Rie also shared the tolerant cultural chameleon trait that characterizes most TCKs. She could change her color to match her surroundings, choosing to what degree and when to display her opinions and emotions. In addition, she shared traits characteristic of her birth order—she was a firstborn—although in Japan it is really the firstborn *boy*, if a family is fortunate enough to have one, who counts. There were no boys in her family, only two younger sisters. Most families that have three children do so for the very reason of trying a third time for a boy before giving up.

Alpha remembered from his history studies that over half of all US presidents were firstborns. Firstborns tend to be natural leaders, reliable and conscientious. Rie manifested these traits to an extent unusual for females in Japanese society. Her parents had tried to curb this independent streak, to make her more docile. But their efforts were in vain. She remained strong-willed, independent, walking to the beat of her own drum.

Each year on March 3 (the third day of the third month, or the "Double Three"), the Japanese celebrate Girls' Day, or *hinamatsuri*. This holiday, which dates back to the Edo Period, involves the display of dolls that are believed to wield the power to contain bad spirits and thus protect the owner. Originally, paper dolls were put in a boat and sent out to the sea, taking the bad spirits with them. The "spirit" that had resulted in only girls being born into the Nakata family, however, had not gone away. With only girls, Rie's family celebrated Girls' Day with more enthusiasm than most. March 3, however, is not a national holiday in Japan; only May 5 (Boys' Day) enjoys that status. The government tried to appease the displeasure instilled by valuing boys above girls by renaming May 5 as Children's Day. But this token did little to assuage public opinion. Children's Day still remains Boys' Day in the hearts of most Japanese.

Boys' Day on May 5 (the "Double Fifth") also marks the beginning of the rainy season, the time for purification according to the Chinese calendar, which is based on Buddhism and used frequently in Japan. Carp shaped flags (*koinobori*), many of them several meters long, are draped on poles like windsocks at an airport. The largest carp represents the father and the each of the smaller ones his child (commonly understood as limited to each of his sons). But the Nakata family had no koinobori for sons.

As Rie was going through the juvenile transition from girlhood to womanhood, she had experienced her menarche (*shochoo* in Japanese). That very evening, following Japanese custom, her mother had made some special *sekihan* (rice boiled together with red beans and eaten on festive occasions such as New Year's Day and weddings) for dinner to celebrate her entrée into womanhood. When her father, because of the late hours required by the family business, arrived home at 10:00 p.m. and ate the sekihan, he had been able to put two and two together.

It isn't that Japanese fathers are naive; it's just that they're both physically and psychologically absent from the home and marriage due to their long work hours and extensive commuting times. Soon after her menarche Rie witnessed the Japanese version of the movie *True Grit*. This had strengthened her resolve to secure a gaijin husband like Rooster Cogburn—without the eye patch and heavy drinking. If need be, she would go at it with all the resolve of Mattie Ross, with whom she felt a kinship that superseded both time and culture.

So it was that Rie's taste for English and for all things foreign developed. She started going to every American movie that came to town, becoming more and more comfortable and confident with her personality, even though such a high degree of individuality was unusual for a Japanese girl. English became her best subject, and she decided that she would one day study in America, possibly somewhere on the West Coast. In the end she had majored in English at a girls' junior college in her hometown in Niigata City. Most junior colleges in Japan function as finishing schools for girls. Girls study for two years, then work for a few more and eventually marry. Rie had taken the road less traveled by graduating from the junior college and then applying to and being accepted at a small college in Santa Rosa, California, where she had studied tourism and hospitality, anticipating that such studies might open the door to an international career and travel.

After enrolling, she recognized that this had probably not been the best route to take; her lack of confidence in a new environment resulted in her taking the course of least resistance by hanging out with two other female Japanese exchange students and one *ni-sei* (a second-generation Japanese girl, born in the host culture). She was amazed that, in spite of external similarities, her ni-sei girlfriend was much more American than Japanese. She was spontaneous, emotionally expressive, and inquisitive, and her clothes were of bolder colors, in contrast to the customary school uniforms worn in Japan.

Rie's new friends had helped her cope with the stress and unanticipated surprises inherent in the American culture. She wondered whether the Santa Rosa subculture was characteristic of all of America. The pleasure seeking, the rampant individualism, the "live for today and to hell with tomorrow" mentality ran against her Japanese upbringing that insisted "Save for tomorrow" and thus resisted immediate gratification. While she loved the campus environment, with its strong expressions of individuality, the

American guys she met in her program didn't seem to have much macho, didn't come close to resembling the stereotype she'd developed since viewing *True Grit*. She wasn't attracted to any of them and didn't go on a single date during her nine-month tenure.

Still, her independent attitude, outgoing nature, perseverance, and love of things foreign had helped her to fit in with diverse people, and she could unconsciously switch roles between the East and West. This resulted in her being adaptable and outgoing, with the added feature that she developed reasonably adequate English, especially in consideration of her short time abroad.

Many Japanese girls prefer dating gaijin, and even more so if they are American or European. The more polite form of the word is *gaikokujin*—outside country person. Most Oriental women are aware of disproportionally large American houses and sensitive to the fact that the best way to enjoy this lifestyle is to marry an American. Embassy officials, IBM executives and the like often live in private houses in Japan that rent for several thousand dollars per month. Other, non-Japanese Asians, due to the ethnocentric nature of Japanese society, are looked down upon.

For Rie anything was preferable to marrying a Japanese male. She didn't want to spend the rest of her life being a *ka-nai*, the Japanese word for "wife" that literally means "inside the house." Marriage is looked upon in terms of the bride becoming part of the groom's extended family, an arrangement that is often frustrating to a young bride, especially when she has to deal with a demanding mother-in-law and much more if the marriage arrangement is to be a live-in situation.

As spouses, Japanese husbands have close to the worst reputations in the world. To put it mildly, they aren't known for their sensitivity in marriage relationships. Husbands and wives are like trains on two parallel tracks that run next to each other but seldom meet. Consistently working unofficial overtime, having a drink along the way, followed by a long commute, means arriving home after 9:00 p.m. They're typically so exhausted that they find the time only for a meal and a bath before repeating the process the following day. The divorce rate increases in Japan following retirement, when the male starts to be present in the home for long periods of time. Wives often refer to their unaccustomed presence as a *jamamono* (an obstacle or thing in the way). It's hard after so many years to get used to someone for all intents and purposes moving in and imposing on one's personal space.

Rie had long since decided that for her it would be either a good gaijin husband or the single life—a secret she would keep within herself. Already, with her strong independent streak, she had turned down two approaches from her supervisor that could have developed into an *omiai*, an interview with a view to an arranged marriage with an interested male employee. Frequently supervisors perform the *nakodo* function, becoming a go-between for the prospective bride and groom. In a collectivistic culture, dating and other types of individualistic behavior don't develop naturally. So a manager, pastor, or trusted family friend will often take the initiative to help find a suitable mate, one with similar background and education.

Rie had some ideals about marriage, shared with her same-generation friends, that contrasted with those of traditional Japan. She believed that procreation is only a small part of marriage, that love should be present and that both partners should endeavor to keep the embers of love burning. She had noticed that many Japanese mothers were failing to develop intellectually or emotionally after having children, and she wanted nothing of that. She wanted to be loved, to be noticed, to be respected and valued in her own right, for who she was, not just because she was a female and could bear children. Rie still had a desire to please, however, and wanted a relationship based more on love than on convenience or the necessity of carrying on the family line. Her engagement to Alpha so far more than met these expectations.

Considering the challenges involved in an international courtship, their romance was not all that unusual. While the New Year's holiday is the most significant one in the Orient, the holiday during Golden Week, starting on April 29 (the former Emperor Hirohito's birthday) and running through May 5 (Boys' Day), is the longest. Many Japanese firms maintain only skeleton staffs so that the intervening days can also be taken as holidays, resulting for many in seven straight days off. In a normal climatic year this coincides with the peak of the cherry blossoms in the greater Tokyo area. The Japanese personality is characterized by a high degree of melancholy. If unchecked, melancholic people easily become neurotic. The Japanese choose to work so hard in part to derive structure and meaning from their work environment and so to counteract their insecurity, that neurotic tendency latent in the national psyche.

But during cherry blossom time, the most romantic period of the year, even the most melancholic Japanese, unable to resist the exuberant and uplifting influences of spring, emerge from their depressive mentalities, if even for a short time. Still, the analogy of love and cherry blossoms shouldn't be pressed too far. The beauty of the latter is far too transitory. When Buddhists want to make a point about the impermanent nature of life, they inevitably refer to the cherry blossom—so beautiful one day but so quickly gone. Sometimes during a spring rain the blossoms fall so heavily that the effect resembles a winter blizzard.

If nature could be credited for conspiring to nudge two people into love, cherry blossom time would be the period during which one could readily amass the most evidence. Even if transitory, the impact of the full bloom on a romantically inclined couple is irresistible. Personality and physical flaws are overlooked, obstacles melt away and optimism surges unabated.

The Japanese don't believe in a supreme being; belief in nature is as close as they will get to faith in something or someone ultimate. And while it doesn't translate into someone as personable as the Christ of Christianity, cherry blossom time in Japan is the closest one can get to sensing beauty, compassion and love in nature—as though there indeed were someone, a person, behind it all who was loving and kind and had as his nature the altruistic desire to bring two people into a loving relationship.

Thus it was during Golden Week, the time of full bloom of the cherry blossoms, that Alpha and Rie had gone to Ueno Park on the north side of Tokyo where some of the most beautiful cherry trees in the world can be seen—not to mention the beloved Panda bears. There could be no more idyllic place, Alpha had decided, to propose. There had been no mistaking Rie's response when she kissed Alpha as they were sitting under a cherry tree during a pause from eating a prepackaged, boxed lunch, an *obento*. She had been so overjoyed that no words were needed—her nonverbal body language was more than sufficient. Her dream of securing a gaijin husband was about to be realized.

The women of Japan, the housewives, if for no other reason than by default, are the ones who control the purse strings and make more than 90 percent of household-related decisions. Men are just not present, either physically or emotionally. Lengthy work hours, along with a prolonged commute, mitigate against any significant male input in child rearing and in daily affairs in general.

Housewives take the paycheck from their husbands, giving them limited pocket money in return. This *okozukai* often makes headlines, as the amount given is slowly and steadily decreasing—from wives giving their husbands around $800/month in 1990, when it peaked, to less than $300/month today. It has often been said that men work but that Japanese women run the country. Interestingly, the Japanese language has some unique and interesting words for "housewife." "Lightning," for example—*inazuma*—literally means "rice plant wife." The implication: behave, or else. If I can plant rice plants, I can do a lot more. And *oniyome*, literally a devil bride, is one who is strong willed, answers to no one and does as she pleases.

It would be no exaggeration to say that virtually all of Japan's day-to-day affairs are run by women. Rie's home was no different. She knew that the key to securing her parents' approval for her marriage would lie more with her mother than with her father. Her father would sooner or later come around to her mother's viewpoint. Rie had enjoyed seeing *My Big Fat Greek Wedding* and remembered the lines by the bride's mother, Maria: "The father is the head of the house. But the woman is the neck . . . and she can turn the head any way she wants." What's true of Greek society also applies to Japan—women are the neck that turns men's heads in whatever direction they desire.

3

The International Couple

Alpha had his own interpretation as to why male dominated Japanese companies have so many meetings that last so long. It's because the Japanese male is inherently insecure as a solitary or individual being, fearful of making decisions on his own. The weak individual identity of the Japanese male requires significant amounts of social confirmation and feedback. Thus meetings are piled atop meetings until such consensus is derived that no one individual has to take any blame for a possible failure.

This has the effect of producing good cars but poor marriages. Japanese women also have a strong desire to conform but not as much need for the emotional overhead males require—they have the emotional fortitude to make decisions and get on with life with or without input from their male counterparts.

The Japanese place a high value on family and social background. Studies in sociology claim that every culture is to some degree ethnocentric, and Japanese culture is very much so. It's unwelcoming to foreigners, to those of low social status (*burakumin*) and to the indigenous minority (the *Ainu*). The Japanese don't readily appreciate the concept of foreign or mixed blood. Children are generally not adopted out to foreigners, as that is thought to both dilute and pollute the blood line. Since adoption isn't generally accepted, the abortion rate is high.

Rie's parents, not having themselves experienced the mind-stretching benefits of world travel, were no exception. Their initial reaction to the proposed wedding was one of bewilderment, confusion, and opposition. Why marry a foreigner when there were more than enough decent young Japanese males to go around? Why make marriage more complicated than it already is?

But when her mother learned of Alpha's great-grandfather having been the founder of a Japanese university, she knew she would have bragging rights with which no other mother-in-law in her social circle could compete—such a family, such ancestors and such social status! She soon gave her unrestricted permission, and her husband followed suit by the next morning. No other person in the immediate Nakata family line had ever married a Westerner, so there were numerous questions: Did they want to have a family? (yes); Was Rie pregnant? (no); Would they try to have a baby soon? (maybe); Did Alpha have a good job? (Alpha and Rie tried to put this situation in the best possible light); and Would their babies be Japanese? (yes!).

In contrast to America, a society that realizes place of birth as sufficient (if a baby is born to Japanese parents while they are in the States, the baby gets US citizenship), Japan is a *jus sanguinis* country, requiring citizenship by blood, not location. If, however, one parent is Japanese and the couple lives in Japan, the child can receive Japanese citizenship by virtue of having Japanese blood from his mother's side. With this explanation, Rie's parents seem satisfied—their grandchildren could and would be Japanese.

A majority of Japanese people during their lifetime make at least one trip abroad, usually to America and minimally to Hawaii. While Americans may save up for a rainy day, the Japanese are just the opposite—they save up for a sunny day so they can go abroad and stay in three- or four-star hotels in the most desirable destinations. Now Rie's parents could do this, with the confidence and comfort of knowing they could enjoy American travel with their bilingual daughter and son-in-law. When they travel, the Japanese feel a need to know someone in a certain location in order to make their trip worthwhile (since their personal identity is primarily a social identity, they prefer to have a social contact who will serve to justify and validate their trip).

Otherwise, Japanese people need the security of their own culture, which they take with them, typically traveling as part of expensive guided tours in the company of other Japanese. Alpha's parents, to their credit, had both made a serious attempt at learning Japanese while working for the US Embassy. While their accent was quite strong and their grammar fraught with mistakes, their vocabulary was fairly extensive. They might make frequent mistakes during the course of communication, being unable to accurately handle the various politeness levels, but they were respected by the Japanese purely for making the effort, in strong contrast to most other Americans, who didn't bother to study the language.

Still, Rie's parents nursed considerable apprehension regarding the proposed engagement. Living in the relatively isolated prefecture of Niigata meant a considerable degree of xenophobia—more than one would typically encounter in the larger metropolitan areas of Tokyo and Osaka. This, combined with the ubiquitous Japanese ethnocentrism, usually didn't spell out a hearty welcome for foreigners, or for children of mixed blood, especially in rural towns.

The smaller and more isolated the village, the greater the degree of ethnocentrism. Put another way, the less the village is aware of the outside world, the more its people are convinced that their local worldview is correct and the more their suspicion of foreigners is justified in their eyes.

But better infrastructure, including roads and trains, had come to Niigata Prefecture largely through the efforts of one of the most famous people of Niigata, the former Prime Minister Kakuei Tanaka, better known as the "Bulldozer." He is credited with bringing the bullet train to Niigata from Tokyo, a project which at that time wasn't fully justified due to the lack of population. Better communication meant fewer barriers, and foreigners were no longer an unusual sight even in Niigata; they were no longer looked down upon with the degree of fear and suspicion that had been common after WWII and extended at least into the 1980s.

Those of Rie's generation, on the contrary, tend not to appreciate their rich Japanese heritage, in spite of the fact that many textbooks on WWII have been rewritten minimizing Japan's responsibility and atrocious behavior during the conflict. The infamous and inhumane Batan Death March, for example, isn't even mentioned in most of them. Instead, young people in Japan, imitating Gen Xers in the States, are enamored of the high consumerism of the American way of life, complete with the accouterments of a large home, a dog, a boat, and leisure time together as a family that isn't company dominated. The current generation of Japanese is much more hedonistic and materialistic than previous generations.

Marriage in traditional Japan is basically for purposes of producing progeny, of continuing the family name and line. While love isn't necessarily irrelevant, it at the same time isn't a necessary precondition in marriage. It's looked upon as a bonus, not as an expectation. The Japanese often say "You love the one you marry," in contrast to marrying the one you love. But love in the romantic sense isn't often characteristic of traditional Japanese marriages.

Rie had more emancipated ideals about marriage. She wanted her man to be faithful to her, not to be one of the thousands who regularly charter weekend flights to Taipei, Manila or Bangkok. She wanted a husband who wasn't "married" 24/7 to work, as well as some hope that the "best is yet to be."

Alpha accepted Rie at face value, not seeing the necessity or desirability of the extensive background checks usually done by the Japanese marriage bureau on a prospective suitor. To him, background not only wasn't a decisive determinant of character but was largely irrelevant. One doesn't, after all, marry a person's background but the person herself. It didn't matter to Alpha whether Rie was rich or poor, noble or common. He loved her, and other issues simply didn't factor in.

The chemistry of Alpha and Rie's cross-cultural relationship was no different from that of any other couple in love, except that the implications of an international wedding were perhaps further reaching than in a typical same-background marriage. Both Alpha and Rie knew examples of international marriages that had not worked out.

Rie knew of the American wife of a Japanese doctor who just couldn't get used to living in Japan. The husband wouldn't be qualified to practice medicine in America and would have to settle for a menial job if he were to emigrate to the States with his wife. She ended up by relocating herself and their three children back to New York. Both hired divorce lawyers. Were it not for custody of the children, the case might have been resolved for under $10,000. As it was, the total costs exceeded $21,000 for the wife and $11,000 for the husband (attorney fees are not as expensive in Japan).

Rie had a friend who had heard of another case where the couple had met in England. He was from Japan, having gone to London to study English, while she was from East London and had never been either to Japan or to any other part of the Orient. Her international travels had, in fact, been limited to a five-day trip through the Channel to France. And she didn't appreciate the French, whom she characterized as thinking that only French should be spoken. Upon arriving in Japan she had found herself no longer fascinated by or enamored of the Japanese culture. Instead she felt isolated; unable to communicate in Japanese, she had become neurotic, was hospitalized in a mental hospital and was prescribed relaxants and tranquilizers to reduce stress. Frequent subsequent hospitalizations resulted in the inescapable conclusion that she had to return home to London, where she would have more support from family, friends and the social milieu in general.

As a foreigner, the husband had no future in England, which was already crowded with other immigrants from its former colonies, especially India and Pakistan. The couple had filed a mutual-agreement divorce by going to the city hall in a western Tokyo suburb where their marriage had been registered. The whole affair cost less than $20. She had returned to England alone and subsequently became very anti-Japanese. Even though she liked sushi, she would never again eat it because of the negative memories it conjured up.

But Alpha was content to continue living in Japan and had no plans to do otherwise. For her part, Rie wouldn't mind and would even look forward to living in America, should that necessity develop. Both had experienced sufficient periods of living in the other's culture to look back to positive experiences while doing so. Neither of them were overly naïve about what they were getting into. The only naivety they had, in fact, they shared with every other couple in love on the face of the Earth. Forces in the universe would somehow yield to two people in love, they felt assured, and obstacles beyond their ordinary control would somehow give way if only love were present.

After three whirlwind months of engagement they returned to Rie's hometown, Niigata City in Niigata Prefecture, for the wedding ceremony. As in many countries, it is only the civil ceremony in Japan that is legal. All a couple has to do is stamp their names with a name chop (*inkan*) at the city hall and they are married. An additional Christian ceremony was held in one of the numerous wedding chapels affiliated with a large hotel that specialized in weddings. In deference to Rie's parents, a day was chosen, according to the Buddhist calendar, called a *tai-an*, or day of great luck. Although getting married on a tai-an is more expensive than on an ordinary day, her parents considered it well worth the extra cost. They wanted nothing to compromise the future of their firstborn.

Rie, in typical Japanese fashion, didn't mind getting married in a Christian ceremony. If indeed it had been the Christian God who had fulfilled her desire to marry a gaijin, she would not only get married in a Christian ceremony but offer up a prayer of gratitude to him. Another gaijin, a Christian missionary who spoke Japanese, preformed the wedding. He did so in both English and Japanese—an accommodation so that Alpha's friends with a limited Japanese background could understand.

Christian weddings in Japan are actually more affordable than Shinto ones, as the tab for drinks and clothing rentals is far less. And they were popular among Rie's friends, who believed that weddings in the numerous "Christian" chapels gave a good appearance (*kak-ko ii*) and didn't require the expensive rental of elaborate kimonos, make-up and hair styling intrinsic to a traditional Japanese wedding. The extensive preparations for a full-fledged Shinto wedding turned many a cheerful bride into an exhausted, hostile creature by the first day of the honeymoon.

Alpha also preferred a Christian wedding, and his parents, uncomfortable with Shinto weddings, were pleased. Both had been raised in Calvinistic New England and had inherited the Protestant work ethic as a dominant value. Possibly as a result of many years of accumulated stress from working and living in foreign environments, his father had recently suffered a mild heart attack, with the consequence that plane travel for the immediate future was prohibited by his physician. So his parents did not attend. They sent a congratulatory telegram, along with airline vouchers for two round-trip tickets to the States with All Nippon Airways. At some future time Alpha and Rie would travel to Arizona for a second honeymoon and visit them.

Rie, eager to please, wanted to invest time into developing a good marriage and was anxious to foster a relationship based on more than convenience. Alpha more than met her expectations. He enjoyed doing things with her, and she was proud to be seen in public with her gaijin husband. The couple lived in Shakujikoen— the park of the stone god. There is indeed a beautiful park there, and, while the sun sets early in Japan due to there being no Daylight Savings Time, there was usually time after work for Rie to pack an obentoo, and the two would meander down to the park and eat together while watching the turtles in the pond. Their favorite bench was available more often than not. The more they used it, the more other people did not.

Alpha wasn't loud or boisterous like the stereotyped "ugly" American, wasn't overweight, and with his dark chestnut hair didn't particularly stand out in a Japanese crowd. While not being quite handsome, he was decent looking and possessed of above average intelligence and motivation. These qualities gave him a lot of appeal, and Rie's parents soon accepted him as one of the family, at least to the extent that any foreign son-in-law could have been so accepted.

Now married, Alpha—the about-to-be entrepreneur—was feeling a high degree of satisfaction and accomplishment as he began to make the 20-minute walk from his apartment west of Tokyo to the Shakujikoen-eki, literally the "Stone God Well Park Station." Taking his usual route, he passed a small church that called itself the Christian Church of the Stone God Well Park, using the pagan geographic name and blending it seamlessly and without disharmony with traditionally Christian words. The Japanese are good at blending contradictory terms in a seemingly harmonious manner.

Arriving at the station in western Tokyo, he tried unsuccessfully to board the express train in the early morning hours. Too crowded, it was already jammed with commuters who lived further out and had gotten on earlier. The next train began only four stops away. Being a local train that would take more time, it at least offered more standing room. The Well of the Stone God, one of the eight million deities recognized by the indigenous Shinto religion, would keep him waiting for six more minutes.

Today's appointment was with a new client called the New Morning Star Enterprises. It appeared to be some obscure firm not in Shinjuku, which was the hub of many businesses, but in an area called Kabukicho within walking distance to the northeast. About 300 years earlier a Japanese *kabuki* theater—a place where traditional Japanese plays called *noh* were performed. Originally even feminine roles were played by men. The planned kabuki theater was never built, but the name had stuck. Known for its nightlife, massage parlors, and other associated activities, it is called mizushobai, or "water industry," by the euphemism-loving Japanese. The area is also known for being one of the hubs of yakuza activity in Japan. While the new antiviolence law prohibits the public display of signboards and the like related to the yakuza, each major group has its headquarters somewhere in the area.

Kabukicho also has a reputation for being the more dangerous part of greater Tokyo. Even so, by Western standards it is quite safe, as long as one is not speaking in moral terms. As a foreigner one may get an occasional startled look from the Japanese in the area, but otherwise they have nothing to fear in walking its streets and eating at its restaurants. If one is a single male, he will certainly be approached numerous times, perhaps once every three to four hundred yards, by a pimp. There is virtually no danger of being gunned down, as guns are used only very infrequently in criminal activity in Japan, usually within yakuza circles and mainly to show a little muscle.

Still, Kabukicho is the most potentially dangerous spot in Japan for a foreigner, especially a Third World female who is well endowed, although there is very little danger of forced abduction. The approach made is much more subtle, perhaps consisting of an invitation for coffee, followed by the offer of well-paying work. It's at this point that the unwary foreign female may not easily be able to extradite herself from a potentially compromising relationship.

There are three main nationalist mafia groups in Japan, with the indigenous Japanese yakuza being the largest. Much smaller are the Chinese triads and the Korean mafia. Immigrant Koreans and their immediate descendants carved out a highly selective and yet prosperous niche within the *pachinko* pinball machine industry. All three of these groups formed a somewhat strained but nevertheless mostly peaceful coexistence, each monopolizing a different area of turf in the underground economy. And all three groups are headquartered in Kabukicho.

In contradistinction to the Chinese triads, which may use a meat cleaver to sever a limb of an offending member, the unwritten code of the yakuza requires only the severing of the tip of one's pinky finger for an infraction. This practice in Japanese is called *yubizume*. The pinky finger is tightly tied off on the middle joint with a piece of string, the guilty party waits momentarily until it has become numb, and then he himself severs it with a sharp knife. The tip of the finger is gift wrapped and presented to the *oyabun* (yakuza boss, a surrogate parent role) by the *kobun* (surrogate child role; a follower or disciple of the boss), with the promise of renewed loyalty and devotion. Only after this ritual has been completed is medical attention sought. In ancient days losing the tip of one's finger meant that one could no longer grasp his sword with as much strength as before the yubizume. Consequently, he would become more dependent on his oyabun for protection.

"Are you the one from Osaka?" a kobun inquired one day of a mistress who called for his oyabun. "No, I'm the one from Tokyo!" In the aftermath of this exchange the kobun, realizing his mistake of inadvertently leaking the fact that his oyabun had more than one mistress, did a yubizume on his own left pinky finger, wrapped it and presented it to his oyabun by way of apology. A second unintentional but similar infraction two years later cost him the tip of his right pinky. This practice has led to some face-slapping humor. A newspaper reporter was interviewing an incarcerated member of the yakuza. "How long are you sentenced to prison?" the reporter inquired. The prisoner held up his fingers on one hand. "Oh, four-and-a-half years," said the reporter. "No, five years," said the prisoner.

4

New Employment

Married to Rie for four months, Alpha, in characteristic TCK fashion and optimistic about starting his own translation and interpreting firm, had been able to recommend one of his former classmates from the University of Hawaii, a person who also wanted to seek his fame and fortune in Japan, to take over his place teaching English full time. So he had been allowed to quit without complications or repercussions before his contract had expired. In time, as better paying and more interesting interpreting jobs materialized and as his own business grew, he would also taper off all of his other English teaching, which he found to be repetitive and boring.

Today, a Tuesday, he welled up during his commute with the anticipation of a new client. While almost all new business in Japan originates through introductions, Alpha was proud of the fact that this contact had come to him directly, apparently by word of mouth. Or at least through a route of which he was not aware.

One train, one subway, and 50 minutes later he arrived in Shinjuku, the hub for people living in the western suburbs of Tokyo. More than two million people pass through Shinjuku daily, making it the world's busiest subway station. Today Alpha would add his own presence to that number. Finding the eastern exit, he emerged from the vast underground corridors into the daylight. Japan's lack of sequential street addresses (the system uses only lot numbers) typically necessitates a search for an unfamiliar location.

There isn't much rhyme or reason to the numbering, although most municipalities have gone to a grid system that identifies the basic single-block area in terms of north-south (*jo*) and east-west (*cho-me*) coordinates. The system of lot numbers having been in effect, however, since before the Meiji Restoration in the late 1860s rudiments remain to confuse the issue.

Alpha preferred to walk rather than switching to another crowded commuter train, searching all the while for the notorious Kabukicho area where New Morning Star Enterprises was located. After one inquiry at the local police box, he located the building with more than 10 minutes to spare. Some parts of Kabukicho seemed as though they hadn't yet gone to sleep from the previous night, adequately living up to the area's reputation as Japan's largest and wildest red light district—the town that never sleeps.

Japanese men seem to have near miraculous powers of regeneration. Arriving home in a semi-inebriated condition between 9:00 and 10:00 p.m. nightly, they don't appear on the following morning to suffer many ill effects. Lately, however, a new term has been coined: *ka-ro-shi*, from *ka*, excessive; *ro*, labor or work; and *shi*, death (literally, death due to overwork).

This kind of premature death typically affects people in their 40s and 50s, is generally due to a heart attack or stroke, and often occurs with people working more than 3,000 hours a year. Of the 30,000 suicides (*ji-satsu*) in Japan annually, it's estimated that 10,000 are related to overwork (thus *ka-ro-shi ji-sat-tsu*). For those in the Tokyo area, nightlife in Kabukicho—over and above grueling work schedules—is a major contributing factor.

Death from overwork, however, was far from Alpha's mind as he entered the building. He would welcome the opportunity to work for a while, even if it involved some overtime. Anything would be better than to continue on indefinitely without much to do. An interior window providing a reflection, he rechecked his appearance, straightened his necktie and confirmed for the second time the presence in his pocket of some of his newly printed bilingual business cards: "Alfred B. Clark, English-Japanese Interpreter, Translator."

In Japan one is considered highly disadvantaged and ill prepared without business cards. Appropriately Alpha called his new company "Alpha Interpreting and Translating." The level of politeness in an ensuing conversation would be determined largely by the impression provided by one's business card—more academic degrees noted on the card corresponded to a higher status; a greater show of politeness and respect; and, ultimately, significantly higher pay—sometimes as much as double if one had the degrees to reinforce his social status.

The building was older, appearing to date from the post WWII construction boom in the early 1950s. The Japanese, in spite of their reputation for excellent quality control, don't practice preventative maintenance on buildings. This one, while far from being dilapidated, could've used considerable attention. Wondering why the Japanese didn't apply their concept of *kaizen*, or continuous product improvement, to buildings, he took the elevator to the fourth floor. Actually, it was called the fifth floor. Since the word for "four" (*shi*) and that for "death" (*shi*) are homonyms, the Japanese prudently avoid both fourth floors and room numbers using the number four.

Alpha liked the name New Morning Star, also known as Shinkinsei, which could be rendered in two ways: the planet Venus or a splendid victory, in the sense of the appearance of a star that beckons the rising of the sun, the total victory of light over darkness. He entered, presented his business card to the receptionist and was ushered into a mid-sized meeting room that could accommodate eight to ten people. After a wipe down with an *oshibori* (a wet towel, usually hot in the winter and cold in the summer) and a cup of green tea he felt refreshed, although still somewhat nervous and apprehensive.

Punctually at 9:00 a.m. three men walked in the room. Following the usual courtesies and the exchange of business cards, Alpha was motioned to sit at the side of the table facing the window on the outside wall. He knew enough to avoid a seat at either end of the table, as these were reserved for company presidents and visitors of high rank. The receptionist brought out some very black coffee, which Alpha really didn't want but knew enough to accept with evident appreciation. He would slowly sip from the cup.

The man who appeared to be the eldest (and who turned out to be Mr. Kanagawa) took the seat ordinarily reserved for the company president. He was also the shortest of the trio, just a little over five feet tall, and appeared to be in his mid seventies. He was one of those people who, no matter how dressed up they are, still look as though they've recently arrived, fresh, from the country. Nevertheless, it was clear from the deference of the others that he was the one calling the shots. Mr. Kaneda looked the most dignified of the three; he was perhaps about sixty, had graying temples and wore a blue pinstripe suit and a striped gray tie. Mr. Lee was the youngest at about forty. He was clearly the rubber stamp, the "yes" man, the gopher who would act on the wishes, expressed or implied, of his superiors.

All three spoke Japanese as their mother tongue, but Alpha noted with mild interest that one of them, Mr. Kim, was obviously Korean. Alpha took pride in his ability not only to guess with relative accuracy the ages of Orientals but also to quickly figure out the pecking order in a group. Most Americans wouldn't know where to begin.

He soon realized that this was going to be no ordinary interpreting assignment. All three spoke grammatically correct Japanese, and there was no other party present to interpret for—no other gaijin, no Americans, no Caucasians, period. Apparently the work would entail translating documents more than face-to-face interpreting.

The greasing of the wheels that turn conversation always takes longer in Japan, and the introductory topics circling around the real issue varied from the current prime minister to golf (green fees and country club memberships are much higher than in America, often costing in the hundreds of thousands of dollars) to Japan's new bullish economy and Abenomics, (the economic policies of the current prime minister, Abe) to more personal items such as whether Alpha was the oldest son (he was, as his older sister wouldn't have counted in their eyes). Finally, within about 10 minutes the topic turned to business.

"We want to put you on a retainer," announced Mr. Kanagawa. "The work may not demand that you be full time, but you must be available whenever we request your services. We will pay you 350,000 yen per month, on a three-year contract. You will function as an intermediary between ourselves and English-speaking firms abroad, including America. You'll be translating technical specifications, purchase orders, shipping information and other documents. Included is an agreement stipulating that you may not work for a competitor. You must keep all matters fully confidential. And you must be available on short notice."

The directness and even brashness of Kanagawa's approach weren't typical of the Japanese way of doing business. Unlike most Americans, Alpha didn't have to mentally convert this proposed amount into American dollars. Thirty-six months at $3,500 a month at the current exchange rate would go a long way toward settling the fears and objections of Rie's parents to her having married a foreigner who lacked a secure or guaranteed source of income.

Alpha didn't know whether a retainer would make him eligible for the Japanese practice of summer and winter bonuses, which could increase his annual income by the equivalent of three to five months' additional salary. Probably not, since he technically wouldn't work full time. This would be more of an adjunct arrangement, with his employment automatically terminating when the three-year period expired. At any rate, he recognized that this offer was more than reasonable, even bordering on generous, and would put him solidly into a middle class income, providing a lot more financial stability than he had enjoyed to date. Kanagawa was straightforward but not rude, speaking in a manner not representative of the more indirect methods of the Japanese.

Rie would be delighted, as the two were currently covering expenses with some of their savings, composed largely of monetary gifts received at their wedding. While her salary at the trading company had been adequate for a single girl living in the Tokyo area, she hadn't been able to save much. Their apartment, somewhat distant from the train station, was small and modest but still cost the equivalent of $700 a month per person.

Without eating out, and dining on mostly standard Japanese fare, the two of them still needed more than $500 a month for groceries (the price of vegetables and meat had gone up drastically in recent months, even with the lifting of the ban on American beef). When the weather allowed, they ate out—literally. Rie packed a lunch, and they would go to their favorite spot in the nearby park, sit by the pond and watch the turtles, ducks and fish while enjoying each other.

Rie spoke to Alpha: "Do you know what turtles symbolize in Japanese culture?" Alpha reflected that he had seen stone turtles in many temples. Rie continued, "They are one of the four divine animals. We call them *kame*. They are said to live 10,000 years. I hope *we* can enjoy life together for 10,000 years!" Alpha bent over and kissed her. "What about the crane?" he asked. "Cranes only live for a thousand years! That's too short!" Rie replied. "Japanese cranes are monogamous—they mate for life." So that's why, Alpha thought, we received 1,000 origami cranes as a wedding present. Although only 7:30 p.m., it was beginning to get dark. Time to head home.

As Alpha had explained to Rie, the retainer conditions with New Morning Star weren't at all unreasonable. In fact, they were pretty well standard for any interpreting assignment. Since Alpha still had very little other work, he had no competitor to worry about, so that stipulation was a moot point. Being available 24/7 was also acceptable. Alpha and Rie had no children to tie them down, and working late evenings was standard practice for Japanese men. It went without saying that any interpreter who had business sense and commitment to a moral code would jealously guard their client's confidentiality. Not to do so could be suicidal.

There was also a one month's signing bonus, 350,000 yen in cash, inserted in a colorful envelope designed for such cash gifts.

Japan still makes far more payments in cash than most other developed countries, and a lot of this cash never finds its way into the reported income column on income tax returns. Alpha signed two copies of the contract: one for his new client and one for himself.

Having returned home with ¥350,000, the next day Rie and Alpha decided to go out and eat sushi for the first time since moving into their new neighborhood. A family-run sushi shop near the station looked inviting. Some sushi bars were relatively inexpensive, but good, fresh, high quality sushi as standard fare is still off limits for the average salaried employee. Still uncomfortable with spending a lot for meals, they ate slowly and in moderation, and Alpha wasn't surprised when presented with a bill for $70.

The full autumn moon kept pace as they ambled back to their apartment. Sitting low it the sky, it looked unrealistically large and close at hand. This was one of those rare moments when Alpha felt he had *wa*, harmony with the universe—a perfect evening. Alpha felt at peace with life: his prospects were good, Rie was more relaxed than usual, and sex that night was the best they had experienced in their short married life. He didn't use the condom in a small pocket sewn onto the edge of her pillow. They both understood that, if she were to become pregnant, the timing wouldn't be all that bad, even though they had planned to enjoy more of married life together before raising a family.

Tuesday ended and Wednesday came. Nothing from Shinkinsei. Then on Thursday afternoon a short fax arrived, informing Alpha that he was to appear at New Morning Star the following morning at 10:00 . Leaving just after 5:00 that evening to teach English for the last time at the trading company where he had met Rie, he wondered how long he would be kept in the dark about the full nature of his new employer.

It was now Friday, September 10, and nothing had changed at Shinkinsei Enterprises, except for the fact that Mr. Lee, the youngest of the three men, wasn't there; only Kanagawa and Kaneda were present. While waiting in the reception area, Alpha's eyes caught something he had glossed over during his initial visit. On the wall was a framed bronze Olympic metal, dated 1972—the

Sapporo Winter Olympics—with the name Kim inscribed. Kim is a common Korean and Chinese name meaning gold or wealth. In Japanese it is pronounced *kin, or kane*. Friday (*kin-yoo-bi*) is literally wealth-day or gold-day.

The only thing out of place was the country: the metal wasn't for Japan but North Korea. It appeared that Mr. Kanagawa may have been a good Alpine skier who, although living in Japan, may have had Korean citizenship, skied under the Korean flag and surprisingly come in third, earning a bronze medal for a country that evoked only a distant memory to him.

To the right of that was a small collection of four unmatched *sake* cups. This, too, was an anomaly. There should have been three or five cups, for the same reason that four (sounding like death) was not a propitious number in Japan. Maybe they had some symbolic meaning. At any rate they must have been collected on separate occasions and no doubt carried more than purely utilitarian value. They didn't appear to have been placed so strategically on the shelf to be used.

Alpha knew not to inquire too deeply. Japanese is a high context language; the social context, more than the black and white characters on a sheet of paper, determine meanings and interpretations. Somewhat like Arabic, it's a language deliberately developed to conceal accuracy. In stark contrast to English, ambiguity is prized. The best and wisest course of action would be to wait for the proper time and place to learn more details.

Who was Mr. Kim? Where had he come from? How had he learned to ski? Did he possess Japanese citizenship? Could he speak Korean? Alpha wanted to know at least whether he was working for a Korean or a Japanese company, but again he chose to remain in the dark for the time being. Money, in his opinion, is a neutral object—only a means to an end—and their money would buy the same things as anyone else's. It would also bring the same degree of financial stability to his and Rie's new marriage as to anyone else's.

Alpha had known, for example, while he was growing up in Japan that a war criminal named Ryoichi Sasegawa had started a major gambling syndicate, made millions in profit and given at least part of the proceeds to improve Japanese society. In the end, due to numerous well-placed contributions, many—especially older people—had begun to look at him as a saint. Even if the money were in some way dirty, the reasoning went, it could be put to some clean uses.

This time at Shinkinsei there was neither green tea nor oshibori—nothing to wipe oneself off with—but only strong coffee with a small napkin. Already they were starting to treat Alpha like a familiar employee, looking at him as having no special rights. The Japanese tend to assume that all Americans like coffee, like it strong and prefer it with sugar. As their thinking goes, if one spoonful of sugar is good, two must be better. Alpha really didn't care for coffee, either black or sweetened.

Nevertheless, he nursed it slowly as Mr. Kanagawa began the conversation. "We are in the process of purchasing four prototype pachinko machines from an American company. We want exclusivity from them to sell throughout Japan. It will be quite an investment for us, and we do not want this American supplier selling to other companies that would compete with us. They want a confidentiality agreement, which we agree to, and prepayment in full in American dollars by wire transfer. Look this over, translate it and get it back to us by Monday."

Alpha looked over the purchase agreement. In the typical fashion of an American company, everything was in English, with no attempt made to provide a Japanese translation or summary. Four pages long, it specified nondisclosure agreements, confidentiality agreements, and shipment and payment conditions. Perusing it quickly, he satisfied himself that he would have no difficulty rendering an accurate translation. And for the final draft Rie would help with proofreading and other finishing touches. Alpha wanted everything to be perfect, especially during the initial phases of his new employment, so as to make the best impression possible.

Arriving back at the Shakujikoen Station just after noon, Alpha stopped by the photo shop, where a copy machine was available to the public. He made a photocopy of each of the four pages, allowing him to make notes and write down any unfamiliar *kanji* (Chinese characters) on his copy, keep it for future reference and return the original to New Morning Star Enterprises. Rie had prepared a Japanese lunch with soup, rice, fish, and a few vegetables. Alpha enjoyed it and appreciated the fact that he could begin work after eating lunch without that heavy, bloated feeling that followed typical American fare. He had decided some time earlier to forgo hamburgers and lead a healthier life style.

When he had time, Alpha reflected, he would write a book about the connection between Japanese food and corporate success. Diet, he suspected, was the real key to Toyota's greatness in the automotive industry; this had everything to do with the philosophy and habits derived from eating Japanese food. The term *soozai*—*soo* meaning general and *zai* meaning side dish—refers to the practice of beginning each meal with the minimal food basics (rice, *miso* soup and fish) and then embellishing them with a large selection of accessory dishes—as many as five or six—for even an ordinary meal. There could be eggplant, pickled onions and plums, along with four or five other Oriental vegetables, most of which are easy add-ons or takeaways.

In order to become a great company, Alpha mused, you have to begin by having a good eating philosophy—something Toyota, Honda and Nissan, intentionally or otherwise, were good at applying. Besides, this basic lifestyle discipline wouldn't result in obese executives . . . or in obese vehicles. Excellent gas mileage could be more readily engineered into the product following the soozai approach. It typified lean manufacturing at its best—no excess, but always a sufficient variety and amount to go around.

5

Pachinko

Their apartment was a 2LDK, an acronym for two bedrooms with a slightly larger multipurpose living/dining/kitchen room. This allowed one room for cooking, eating and watching TV, a separate bedroom for sleeping, and a second bedroom that could double as a study. It would remain that way until the couple had a child, although Japanese families frequently sleep together with their children until they are several years old. Alpha again sensed wa as he began translating the document. Everything was beginning to come together. Due to the nature of the language, it was best to grasp the entire context, as much as possible, before beginning to translate. For that reason he would read through the entire document before beginning.

Page One: The Gaming Engineering Company (GEM), Inc., 1001 Bay Shore Dr., Palo Alto, California. "Specializing in Merging 21st Century Technology with Adult Entertainment." Alpha concluded that adult entertainment in this context meant gambling, probably with slot machines—not prostitution, as the term could easily be interpreted. And the address, while not denoting a location in Silicon Valley, could possibly have some connection to it. Perhaps the business was a spin-off of one of the aerospace or semiconductor companies. It was quite possible that some of the technology from the Valley's numerous industries spilled over into the entertainment industry. So it appeared that Shinkinsei was planning to import some of GEM's one-armed bandits. Japan—in theory at least—had open markets, so he assumed no trade laws were being broken.

"Summary: Prototypal Machines, to ship by air freight within seven days of the issuance of a formal purchase order, FOB, Los Angeles (LAX). Quantity: four. Price: US$18,300 unit." The total, including shipping, would be about $90,000 for the four machines. Alpha wondered how any gambling establishment could make a profit with such heavy capital investment, especially since the life of gaming machines in Japan is only about 18 months before they succumb to the allure of newer machines with more state of the art technology and better graphics. Something didn't add up, but the groundwork at least seemed to be in place. The offer appeared to be above board.

The rest of the pages contained technical specifications, performance standards and warranty issues—all standard fare and not at all atypical. Alpha had translated some similar documents as part of his undergraduate studies at the East West University, so this was basic work for him.

"Description of Machine: state of the art pinball tracking and geographical positioning devises included." Alpha knew about pachinko, the steel pinball machines, and all Japanese people are familiar with the appearance of pachinko parlors. The word itself is onomatopoeic, coming from the sound of a steel ball rebounding off one of the rubber bumpers. Recently Nicholas Cage had been featured in a series of TV commercials where he had played a pachinko freak. The commercials were up to Super Bowl ad standards and had generated a response over a wide audience.

But pachinko is the bane of many Japanese marriages, producing millions of pachinko widows. Hardly a team sport, it is played in absolute isolation, one man against the machine. It's a form of gambling, with the odds stacked against the human. The Japanese are culturally conditioned to lack a strong individual psyche, instead buying in to the concept of a socially defined identity: I am who you (plural) define me to be, or I am who I think you (plural) think I am. Yet other socially defined conventions—individual insecurity and weak self-identity—determine that I have to remain somewhat socially connected to you. This is the ambience of pachinko. A single, solitary Japanese man, surrounded by hundreds of his countrymen, fulfills his need for social definition. His fellow Japanese are all around him, helping define who he is. And yet his core sense of isolation keeps him comfortably alone.

Pachinko would go bankrupt if it were offered to individual players in private settings. Its lure requires the synergistic effect of the presence of others playing simultaneously and alongside. Although far from ideal, this is the optimum social level attainable for most Japanese men, given their aversion to intimacy.

Alpha had tried his hand at pachinko a couple of times but had found the game not only boring but also pointless. Yet he intuited that there was more to it; on Sunday mornings he would see scores of men, and increasingly more women, waiting in line for the pachinko parlors to open at 10. Most of these aficionados didn't leave for hours, and a few serious devotees (called *pachi-pro*, short for pachinko professionals or frequent players) remained until closing time a full 14 hours later. These enthusiasts take pride in their identity, distinguishing themselves by the 100 yen coins forgetfully left wedged in their ears, or by the cups of 100 yen tokens placed on the horizontal counter on the front of the machines.

Pachinko was invented in the late fifties, and two companies dominate the manufacture of machines in Japan. The larger of these, Heiwa, was founded by Korean-born Kenkichi. The present day pachinko industry has strong ties to the North Korean mafia (*Jopok*), which is known to do anything necessary to protect its turf—warning, threatening, bullying, intimidation—even abduction and murder if nothing else works.

Possibly, Alpha conjectured, GEM as an American manufacturer was trying to break into the lucrative pachinko industry by using New Morning Star Enterprises as its springboard. Or vice versa—New Morning Star might be attempting to gain a foothold in the marketplace using GEM's machines. Still another scenario was a combination of the two, a synergistic arrangement. At any rate, at this point competitors and market conditions weren't Alpha's concerns.

In the sixties and seventies pachinko pinball machines had included a spring-loaded lever the operator flicked with his finger, shooting near vertically a spherical piece of polished steel, indistinguishable from a ball bearing. With just the right force, after bouncing around a bit, instead of falling to the bottom this projectile would enter a high scoring hole, and the operator would be rewarded with more balls than he had lost.

Pachinko parlors are not legally allowed to pay out cash, and the Japanese media discreetly refrains from pointing out the obvious: that every parlor has a cash payout window. This unspoken arrangement exemplifies the typical Japanese approach, which tolerates flagrant inconsistencies and a high degree of ambiguity between *de jure* and *de facto*. An alternative to dealing in cash is to trade in accumulated balls for tokens at a nearby hole-in-the-wall for cigarettes, washing powder and brand goods. These establishments then sell the tokens back to the parlor, after taking their cut.

The Japanese practice of *kaizen*, or continuous product improvement, is adequately illustrated in the pachinko industry. The latest kaizen was to include in existing machines a slot machine function, complete with a lever—turning them into *pachi-slo*, pachinko slot machines. Some newer types eliminate steel balls, relying instead on electron random number generators and LCD screens. This advanced feature, Alpha thought, might have attracted New Morning Star Enterprises. If GEM Industries manufactured slot machines for Las Vegas, its prototypes might be expected to merge this state of the art technology with more traditional pachinko machines—an example of kaizen at its best.

Twenty-first century machines are completely automated, with sophisticated acoustics and graphics requiring elaborate electronic processors. The operator can sit by almost passively, occasionally adjusting the lever—which functions like a throttle—to a preset location and simply watching hundreds of steel balls bouncing off pegs and bumpers, producing cacophonic sounds to the uninitiated. But to the devotees, the din is like the sirens of ancient Greece. These sirens' songs have a way of completely captivating those unfortunate enough to wander too close, ensnaring them into an opiate-like state of bondage. Very few, once addicted, ever escape the clutches of pachinko. The fast-changing visual graphics, the intense audio effects and the random reinforcement of winning is for most enthusiasts extremely habit forming. Pachinko players experience altered states of consciousness, with high levels of adrenalin flowing.

In Japan the yakuza enjoys a policy of peaceful coexistence with the police, who know the names and addresses of all prominent yakuza members. The Yamaguchi-gumi (group) is the best-known yakuza gang, but corresponding groups exist in other trades, an example being in the Sagawa Kyubin, the equivalent in Japan of the American UPS. A visitor could enter any local police station (kooban) and inquire without raising any eyebrows about the location of the local yakuza. While the officers may choose not to divulge this information, they know exactly where the local yakuza live and operate.

Less prominent yakuza members are identified by their extensive tattoos, and in some cases by the absence of the tip of their pinky finger, usually on the left hand but sometimes on both. Since these individuals stand out from the crowd, there is typically no need for the interested party to ask about addresses and locations. In addition to these not-so-subtle distinctions, members usually sport permed hair, pointed black shoes, and a flamboyant suit. As is often the case with self-proclaimed nonconformists, they are almost amusingly conforming.

While prostitution in Japan is technically illegal, the yakuza controls the industry, with the police turning an accommodative blind eye. Many barbershops offer magazines featuring photographs of prostitutes, complete with detailed specifications (measurements). The yakuza, for its part, regulates itself and has some inviolate rules—no overt violence, no guns, no shootings, no public disturbances, and absolute loyalty between the oyabun and the kobun. Nothing is tolerated that would overtly create a negative public image.

On the face of a Japanese hanafuta card no blemish is allowed. Comparably, in exchange for keeping law and order (disallowing social blemishes), no one—neither prostitute nor patron—worries about being arrested for the act. There is also extensive self-regulation with regard to the drug trade. The yakuza allow no hard drugs—crack, heroin or powerful hallucinogens. They do allow methamphetamines. Not quite as addictive as crack, methadone, or speed (as is known so well in the United States), it is easy to manufacture domestically, and its intrinsic appeal creates repeat users—people more psychologically than physically dependent.

As many as 2,300,000 Koreans were in Japan by the outset of WWII. Some had migrated to escape the famine that had followed Japan's annexation of Korea in 1910, and some females had been forced to come as comfort women for the Japanese troops during the expansionist era culminating in WWII. Still today Japan doesn't typically grant citizenship to even third-generation Koreans, many of whom have intermarried and undergone name changes in a process called *soshikaimei*.

The common Korean names, like Park, Lee, and Kim, are changed for equivalent but expanded Japanese counterparts. The name Kim, for example, meaning gold or wealth in both Korean and Chinese, would be rendered *ka-ne* in Japanese. A second character is added, such as one denoting a paddy field, resulting in *ka-ne-da* (field of gold), *ka-ne-ya-ma* (gold mountain) or *ka-ne-ga-wa* (river of gold or wealth). A further euphonic change sometimes occurs when, for example, *ka-ne* is changed to *ka-na* for easier pronunciation; this results in Kaneyama becoming Kanayama and Kanegawa becoming Kanagawa.

While the origin of pachinko is somewhat unclear, it is believed that people of Korean descent living in the Kansai-Nagoya area developed the first machines shortly after WWII. From its inception the pachinko industry in Japan was dominated by permanent foreign residents, most originally from North Korea. Pachinko's links to organized crime—the Korean yakuza—are well documented.

The Korean-affiliated yakuza in Japan funnels back a high percentage of the pachinko earnings to Pyongyang, where relatives and other recipients use the money to escape poverty, achieving a standard of living and a degree of security otherwise impossible under Kim Jong Il's disastrous dictatorship. Most of this repatriated money, much of it laundered, gets through only because bribes have paved the way.

Alpha, beginning to translate the portion of the document regarding the global positioning system function, wondered why a pachinko machine would require such expensive options; they appeared to be as unnecessary as they were non-cost-effective. Why would a manager want to know where his machine was located, when he could confirm its location by a quick visual inspection? Granted, installing pachinko machines with physical (as opposed to electronic) metal balls requires precision leveling; the smallest degree of a tilt can skew results. It wouldn't be feasible, once a machine has been installed, to move it so much as a fraction of an inch. There would be no reason that Alpha could determine, even without physical steel balls, for a GPS function. Since his further research on the Internet indicated that there were in fact no metal balls—only electronic ones—the leveling function seemed completely pointless.

Yet the redundant tracking feature was specified by New Morning Star Enterprises. With it, all information could be stored, compiled, and forwarded through satellite transmission to any location around the world. Like an absentee landlord, an absentee manager could download the information and know at a glance how any given machine was performing. Included also was an 800 gigabyte storage USB that provided more than 30 days of memory, doubling for data backup. A lot more storage than could possibly be needed, Alpha noted skeptically, but such digital storage no longer added significantly to the cost of the product.

Another specification was a series of four programmable chips in each machine, model IC 681141. These chips could be programmed with several layers of ladder logic, meaning that they could operate on several levels simultaneously and yet independently of each other. Each level was accessible by an electronic ladder, a narrow and specific electronic digital passageway that could be programmed with a special code via remote coded access. It was even possible to program and store data on one level and preserve it, completely isolated from all other data and calculations that would occur on other levels.

Only a person knowing the special secure code to those levels could access them or even detect their presence. Although one could never say never with access codes, no hacker had yet found a way into the deeper levels of an IC 681141. Even if security were to be compromised by a sophisticated hacker, the codes could be instantaneously altered from a remote location, and the hacker would have to start over with hundreds of hours of trial and error coding to make any headway. For additional security, the codes were changed monthly.

The Japanese language, importing Chinese kanji from around the eighth century a.d., is unfit for technical translation. But the Japanese routinely "Japanize" foreign words. Most of the technical words in the document could be easily translated into *katakana*, one of the two phonetic alphabets. Thus *chippu* is chip; *kondensa* condenser, and the like.

By Friday evening the translation was nearly complete, and the weekend weather forecast called for lovely conditions. Excluding the brief season of cherry blossoms, early autumn is the optimal time of year in Japan, offering frequent sunny days with afternoon temperatures often peaking in the upper 70s and crisp, exhilarating evenings. On some mornings the tip of Mt. Fuji is visible before the smog rolls in, and numerous maple trees showcase their red and golden hues. Alpha and Rie decided to go to the Ueno Zoo on Saturday to enjoy the fall colors and the baby pandas. They would also visit the spot under the cherry tree where Alpha had proposed in order to relive the moment.

Saturday arrived, and true to forecast the autumn sky showed only small traces of clouds. Since the translation wasn't due until Monday morning, Alpha felt no stress.

Nevertheless, something troubled him about these pachinko

machines. Was it the high purchase price? Or the unnecessary, excessive hardware and software, and the exorbitant memory? Eager to make a good impression on his new client, Alpha would try to learn more about these specialized chips. On the way to the zoo, he and Rie would walk through Akihabara, the electronics center of Japan, located in eastern Tokyo. From there they could enjoy a ramble north to Uneo Park. Perhaps they could discretely gain some knowledge about the brains that would run the new machines.

The zoo via train was only two stops away; on foot it would take about 20 minutes from Akihabara. Either way there was plenty to see. Hundreds of shopkeepers peddled their wares, and brightly-lit household electronics stores displayed the latest in household appliances. Within about a 10-block radius, about a mile long and a quarter of a mile wide, were to be found faster CPUs, motherboards, individual components—in fact, just about anything in the electronics industry, from parts to completed products. There Alpha could inquire anonymously and inconspicuously about the IC 681141 chips.

The first shop wasn't helpful, catering as it did to lower-end stuff, much of it surplus and already out of date. And the owner was disrespectful, obviously displeased that he was being bothered about something that wouldn't immediately profit him. They walked deeper into the arcade area, where shops competed more fiercely for space. Every eight to ten feet, different tiny electronics shops specialized in connectors, PC boards, or cables. Finally Alpha spotted one carrying large chips that looked like the CPU chips found in most computers.

Alpha asked whether they had any IC 681141 chips in stock. The clerk, a young man in his early twenties, asked him to repeat the number. "Just a moment, please," he responded before disappearing behind the wall. They could hear him making a cell phone call but could make out nothing else. In less than a minute he reappeared, hollered over to the vendor in the adjacent stall (it appeared he would cover for the clerk during a brief absence), and stated that he would show them where they could get assistance.

Instead of guiding them to another electronics shop, their self-appointed guide ushered them into a small restaurant about a block to the north that offered a limited number of set menus on the sozai principle. Upon entering, the clerk-turned-guide bowed and excused himself, and two Japanese men, one elderly—perhaps 70—and the other middle-aged—perhaps 40—offered to purchase coffee. They didn't look too different from Mr. Kanagawa and Mr. Kanayama, though perhaps a little more sophisticated, and they were considerate enough to inquire, so that both Alpha and the clerk, introduced as Makiko, ordered black tea instead.

While courtesy dictated the exchange of business cards, the impromptu nature of this meeting, plus the enigmatic matter of the setting, suggested that this would be forcing the issue. Exchanging business cards wasn't something ordinarily done thoughtlessly or with complete strangers. To do so would imply a connection, and with every connection came responsibility and even obligation. The Japanese do not incur *giri*—obligation—easily or happily. Letters of introduction (*shokaijo*) are normally necessary. Knowing these conventions, Alpha didn't feel completely comfortable.

The older of the two men introduced himself as Suzuki. The younger remained Mr. *Mukuchi*—as the Japanese say, Mr. No-Mouth. At any rate, there was nothing distinctive about him. Taciturn, he was that person seen on a hundred subways, the type who could blend into any woodwork. Mr. Suzuki complimented Alpha on his Japanese and on his attractive wife and then asked how he might be of assistance.

Alpha knew that Suzuki was one of the 10 most common names in Japan, and, while it could be and probably was the man's real name, it would be virtually untraceable: this Suzuki would be one in as many as two million. "I only want some information on a chip, an IC 681141." In the typical Japanese noncommittal manner, Suzuki inquired further: "What connection do you have with such chips?"

Alpha thought of his retainer with New Morning Star Enterprises, with its nondisclosure and confidentiality conditions. Ambiguity is valued in high-context languages like Japanese. In instances like this, Alpha was thankful for the opportunity to converse in Japanese rather than in English. Better to offer an indefinite response than a blunt refusal. In Arabic people often say "If God wills" to avoid a committed response. The Japanese, who don't put much stake in any of their eight million gods, prefer to use the word *chotto*—"a little," "not much" or "nothing important." The response carries the implication that no additional information will be volunteered and that none additional should be sought. To avoid offense, Suzuki wisely deferred from pressing for information, stating instead that he would be glad to assist them in the future.

The Japanese frequently refer to this approach as the tatamae, the façade or outward appearance that may or may not represent one's true inner feelings—one's hone. Alpha understood that all initial relationships begin on this level, and he also knew that most Americans read into it far more than is actually intended. There was enough strangeness in the context already, with two complete strangers drinking tea and coffee with a couple they had just met—enough unusual behavior for one occasion. Suzuki offered his business card without appearing to expect one in return.

"Suzuki of Akihabara—Electronics," Alpha noted. He accepted the card, finished his tea and excused himself, walking outside with Rie. Mr. Mukuchi had already taken care of the bill. Alpha's head raced, baffled at why a simple inquiry about a chip would have evoked such an uncharacteristically enthusiastic response.

Taking advantage of the good weather, they decided to walk northward to Ueno Zoo, after which they were obliged to wait for more than two hours in a long line to see the baby pandas. It would have been better, Alpha acknowledged to himself ruefully, to come on a weekday. As it was slightly chilly for an autumn day, they stopped in a *soba* (Japanese buck wheat noodle) restaurant and enjoyed a bowl of hot noodles. One thing the Japanese take very seriously is their food. You could buy soba noodles at a soba shop and ramen noodles at a ramen shop, but no ramen at a soba shop or vice versa. The sun was beginning to set, and they decided to head back to their apartment. Rie thought she had seen Mr. Mukuchi at the zoo but acknowledged that a lot of other visitors might look like him.

They were back home by 6:30 p.m., as it was already getting dark. Alpha decided to finish the translation that evening. Nothing unanticipated emerged—only company introduction and history, list of products and accessories, model numbers, name of the insurance carrier, conditions of payment, bank transfer account number, and the like. By 10:00 he was finished. Rie would type it on Sunday morning, using the Japanese word processor they had purchased in Shinjuku.

The old Japanese typewriters were heavy, bulky and inefficient. It was a daunting task, both mentally and physically, to type with thousands of characters that resembled printer's type. With the new word processor, phonetic script would be entered, and the software automatically suggested which combinations of kanji (Japanese characters that had originally been Chinese) were most likely to be used, in the order of probability.

6

Pachinko Experiences

Sunday is one of the busiest days for pachinko in Japan. With more than 30 million regular devotees, the industry employs 330,000 people—three times that of the steel industry in Japan. A ubiquitous presence throughout Japan, the parlors' flamboyant neon architecture is seen in front of nearly every major train or subway station. As Alpha had not been in such an establishment in more than three years, he and Rie decided to visit the one near the Shakujikoen station to see whether they could glean more information. Outside the sign read pachi-slo. The parlor fortunately offered updated machines. Fads come and go in Japan with great speed, and if a business doesn't keep up with the latest they'll soon find themselves out of business.

Each purchased tokens for 1,000 yen, equivalent to 250 balls, and they found adjacent seats. pachi-pros, pachinko professionals, have their favorite machines, and an area of five machines in a single row was vacant. These machines apparently did not earn the trust and respect of the frequent patrons, who apparently thought they were programmed too much in favor of the establishment. But Rie and Alpha were not there so much to win as to learn, to try to put together some pieces from the New Morning Star Enterprises puzzle. They were glad to have some localized privacy.

Not being used to playing, Alpha was out 1,000 yen (about $10) in less than 15 minutes. Rie was more fortunate. Before her supply of balls was exhausted, she hit a jackpot and was awarded 250 more balls, probably enough for another 15 to 20 minutes of play. These new and popular machines were called *deji-pachi*—digital pachinko machines. Colorful *anime* (animations) appeared on the LCD screen, accompanied by sound effects. The LCD indicated her jackpot, or "fever."

But what appeared next caused even Rie, an emancipated, newly married woman, to be embarrassed, totally unprepared as she was for the *hentai* (erotic) content. She could hardly have anticipated the raw, sensuous pornography that appeared on the screen. Apparently this was the proprietor's preference, as not all pachinko shops are like this. Before her startled eyes gleamed unadulterated perversion—genital, masochistic, erotic and sadistic, all at once. Surprised by the degree of revulsion she felt, she sat back, subdued and passive, as the final round came. Feeling somewhat violated, the couple left together after she failed to win another fever—not that she wanted to.

The fact that her father ran a pachinko parlor in Niigata City did not influence her thoughts. She had only a vague idea of the family business and knew that, while the family machines might have the capability of such programming, this kind of perversion wouldn't happen in their establishment. In Japan, except for a few enterprises like farming or small family business establishments, a father's vocation is entirely separate from his family life. Colleagues from work don't visit the homes of coworkers, and corporate and family life doesn't mix. The wife of one colleague would probably never meet the wife of a coworker. And children ordinarily would have nothing to do with the family business. All of the emphasis would be on education, with particular focus on passing the college entrance exam.

Deciding to stop for lunch, they entered an *okonomiyaki* (Japanese pancake) shop. Into the dough went squid, shrimp, cabbage and other vegetables. As the concoction slowly cooked in front of them, they cut it up into wedge-shaped segments, topped it off with sauce, and began to eat slowly as they discussed their experience at the pachinko parlor with the deji-pachi. They realized that the newer machines provided more than a gambling experience, delivering as they did hard-core porn, so that any player could indulge in erotic and perverted fantasies. Another feature allowed for remote tracking, as well as the possibility of remote programming and sending images.

For a female patron unaccustomed to hard porn, the anime could be toned down and tailored more to feminine tastes, while for the pachi-pro it could be turned up. Add to this a customization catering to each customer's preference, and you have a tailored pornography industry that will both supplement and enhance the pachinko experience.

But one should not be too hard, Alpha mused, on either the deji-pachi or people who patronized these establishments. Native Japanese religions don't include any concept of sin, original or acquired. In the thinking of a typical Japanese, sin is limited to the extremes—to murder and bank robbery, to the men who forcefully molest minor virgins. To provide a few erotic pictures to over-worked and under-stimulated men would not, by any stretch of the imagination, qualify as wrongdoing under any definitions from Shinto or Buddhism. Nature is ultimate in Japan, and the concept includes natural urges. This was one of the problems behind Christianity's cool reception in the country—it was too unnatural, holding out too high a standard, one to which Japanese men simply couldn't measure up.

But Alpha, uncharacteristically, had some non-Japanese thoughts, possibly prompted by the revulsion he noted on his wife's face. Dirty machines for dirty men. Customized porn, tailored to each man's degree of depravity and degradation. Making money off people's depravity was as old as time, only now the process could be customized, upgraded and "improved" without the individual even having to go on site. But still one piece of the puzzle didn't fit. Why the sophisticated geographical tracking device? Why the need, or desire for, remote tracking?

The pair headed home, Alpha anxious to look again at the specs for the machines from the GEM Company in California. As Rie made some Japanese tea, Alpha asked, "Where is the copy of the documents with all my notations?" "It's in your study," Rie replied. "Where in my study?" "Just look for yourself."

Try as he could, however, Alpha couldn't locate the documents, and he became frustrated with Rie. They didn't argue often, but now he found her for the first time in their short married life genuinely uncooperative, bordering on defiant. They had been married long enough for the initial infatuation to wear off—but not long enough to make sufficient adjustments for long-term compatibility.

Japanese wives are not the docile, obedient spouses they're made out to be in overseas stereotypes. They have to be tough, if for no other reason than to survive their husbands' excesses and neglect. With husbands often absent, both physically and psychologically, they have to develop a degree of mental toughness not ordinarily manifest in patriarchal societies.

Rie simply didn't know where the documents were, nor was she able to locate them. Fortunately, the original English copy was filed away in a small cardboard file cabinet, and the Japanese translation was stored in Alpha's laptop.

There is a theory in the study of linguistics called the Worf-Sapir hypothesis. This states that the language you learn when growing up determines in large part how you will view reality. If you learn, for example, the Inuit ("Eskimo") language, which contains more than 50 words for snow, you will tend to look at snow in a much more precise manner than if you initially learn English, with only a few words for snow.

The Japanese language, reflecting the domestic security its homogeneous society experienced for centuries, didn't until modern times make a distinction between lock and key. Maybe this was the reason neither Alpha nor Rie, having been raised in Japan, considered that these papers could've been stolen, that someone could've entered their apartment and taken them.

Due to recent and drastic increases in the number of home break-ins, new construction in Japan entails a much higher focus on security. Most older Japanese houses are notably insecure; they can be broken into with little effort, often with a plastic credit card inserted behind the sliding lock. But there was no evidence of a break-in, and nothing of evident value was missing.

On Monday morning Alpha was off again to New Morning Star Enterprises with the translated documents. Expecting only to hand them over to the receptionist, he was caught off guard by the presence of the original three, Mr. Kanagawa, Mr. Kaneda and Mr. Lee. He was ushered as before into the meeting room, where coffee was served.

This time the president, Mr. Kanagawa, took a more paternalistic approach to his new employee: "Mr. Clark, thank you for this translation. We will soon have much more work for you. You must be careful to maintain a high level of confidentiality with these documents. We do not want any of our competitors to become aware of this transaction."

Alpha replied, using the polite and honorific word *Kashikom-airimashita* (meaning "I heard your request and will comply with it"). Typically in Japanese the longer the word, the more polite it is, and this was no exception.

Mr. Kanagawa presented Alpha with what looked to be 20 or so pages in Japanese, for translation into English. "Let me know when you have them finished." This time such polite deference wasn't needed, so Alpha responded with a simple "Yes, I understand." The word "yes" in Japanese can't, or at least shouldn't, be used alone. It has too broad a meaning and can be construed inaccurately. A simple "yes" in this instance would have meant too little, something like "I heard your request." The addition of "I understand" implied that he would comply.

7

The Order

Eye strain and physical and mental fatigue set in when you translate either into or from Japanese. Mistakes begin to multiply if you attempt to translate for more than two hours running without a sufficient break; five to ten minutes for every hour is in order. Eager to remain on his employer's good side, however, Alpha burned the candle on both ends, completing the translation in a little over two days. Then he slept on it for a night, reviewed it again, and made some minor corrections.

After this work started to flow in steadily from New Morning Star Enterprises, typically requiring between one to four hours daily. Most of the documents arrived by fax and could also be faxed back. There were no unreasonable deadlines, no surprises and nothing out of the ordinary: usual fare included exchange rates; a stipulation of which company would bear the risk for which currency; whether or not to purchase futures on the dollar, which carried a 5 percent overhead; when the Letter of Credit would be redeemed for a bank transfer of funds; bills of lading; customs clearances; and the like.

English is the language of international trade, and Alpha was quickly helping New Morning Star get up to speed as a twenty-first-century international company. A little more than a week into his relationship with his new client, Alpha felt secure and satisfied. Most of the work he could do at home, and the somewhat steady, though varying volume meant job security.

It was now Tuesday, September 24, and New Morning Star faxed over the airfreight bill from GEM. With this the conditions to redeem the Letter of Credit were met, and GEM was in the final stages of getting a wire transfer from the Japan Development Bank branch office in California. Alpha wanted to confirm that everything was legitimate, so he looked on the Internet and did locate a branch on S. Figuerola Street in Los Angeles. The amount of the wire transfer also seemed to be in order: US$85,067.29—four machines at $18,300 each, plus shipping, handling and insurance.

Satisfied, he faxed over the documents, with a translation, to New Morning Star and awaited a response. With the time change the goods would ship via JAL Air Cargo, leaving the Los Angeles airport on Friday, September 24. A customs freight forwarder would clear the shipment through customs at Narita on the following Monday, and they would be ready to ship within Japan by Tuesday, September 28. Clearing Japanese customs is ordinarily a quick procedure, but now and then it can be uncharacteristically slow.

A Chinese manufacturer, Leshan Radio Co., Ltd., had begun to produce pachinko machines for the Japanese market but had been unable to penetrate it, in spite of manufacturing machines virtually indistinguishable from Japanese-made models. There were too many hidden trade barriers within the Japanese market. So the Chinese vendor had tied up with New Morning Star as its exclusive agent and was offering low cost machines at ¥ 1,772,000 each, or about US$17,000—less than the cost of GEM's and with much lower shipping and handling costs involved. Quality control shouldn't have been an issue, as such machines have predictably short product life spans, nearly always less than two years. Nevertheless, the vertical structure of Japanese society and business meant that owners of pachinko businesses couldn't easily cut themselves loose and go independent by purchasing machines on their own. The repercussions were too great and the implications too dangerous. It was easier and safer just to pay the higher price. Until there appeared one day an innocuous-looking advertisement in the Japanese *Yomiuri*, the largest daily newspaper in the world, with a circulation of more than 10 million. The Far East Branch of the US Department of Defense (DOD), in deference to Japanese employees and spouses on bases, and wanting to accommodate the growing popularity of pachinko among American servicemen, planned on installing pachinko machines on its four major bases, including Okinawa, Yokosuka (Navy), Yokota (Air Force) and Camp Zama (Army). Part of the profits, if any, would go to local charities; the remainder would be in the form of coupons given directly to the players and redeemable through the Army & Air Force Exchange Services (AAFES) at each base's BX or PX.

The pachinko machine contract was open for sealed bids, and its being offered by the US DOD meant that the bidding process was relatively clean and unrigged, virtually independent of the intricate relationships of Japanese society. It also meant dealing in dollars, thereby absorbing all the risk of currency fluctuations. There were to be 43 machines initially, with 12 going to bases on Okinawa and the remaining 31 divided up among the other three on the main island of Honshu. New Morning Star won the bid at $18,300 per machine.

More of the puzzle was beginning to come together for Alpha. One of the reasons New Morning Star had put him on a retainer was probably that of credibility: being the son of a respected embassy diplomat created spill-over credibility. The company wanted not only to use his translation skills but also possibly to leverage his standing. In dealing with DOD, having an American on board would certainly not be construed as a negative. But what didn't make sense was the pricing: New Morning Star had submitted a bid considerably lower than their actual costs.

The Japanese have a reputation of taking a long-term approach abroad; American firms, in contrast, have a reputation for shortsightedness. To gain market share, Japanese firms have been known to undercut the competition until it goes out of business and then to raise prices to compensate.

For New Morning Star Enterprises the competition was too big and too nebulous. It could be suicidal to try to compete with the two major domestic manufacturers of pachinko machines. Their pockets were too deep and their connections too extensive for any start-up company to have a fighting chance.

Why would a small firm willingly lose a considerable amount of money on this order? Alpha wondered. Just to gain a very tenuous foothold? For 43 machines: if 4 came from GEM in America and 39 from Leshan Radio in China, New Morning Star could be in the red for as much as $200,000. This seemed like a big hit on a small firm. And why would they feature two different models, one costing 20–30 percent more than the other?

The DOD bidding documents didn't specify that American-made machines were required, only that they would be serviced free of charge for 12 months and then have a service contract for 24 more. If New Morning Star were to sell only the Chinese machines, they could eke out a small profit. There was something inherent in the GEM machines that seemed to require their usage, even though such usage wasn't specified by DOD in the bidding documents.

A further complication had to do with the power supplied to the machines. GEM, in typical American fashion, produced machines only with American supply voltage, 110–120 VAC at 60 Hertz. Japan in those areas uses mainly 100 volts, with the area east of the Fuji River using only 50 Hertz. The Chinese machines were plug-and-play ready, with simple voltage/Hertz switches on the back near the power supply cord. The four American machines, on the other hand, would have to be altered after their arrival in Japan.

Papers to be translated arrived almost daily. On Tuesday, September 28, while the machines were still in transit, Alpha received a set from GEM specifying in detail the modifications to be made to convert the machines to Japanese voltage. As he had expected, this would be done by a firm in Akihabara specializing in such modifications. What he didn't expect was the name of the firm: Suzuki Electronics. He wondered whether this was the same Suzuki he had met during the visit to Akihibara on the way Ueno Park.

Just to be on the safe side, Alpha made sure not to leave any fingerprints, physical or electronic, on his translation. And Rie would use their word processor, printing it on plain paper without any company logo. To prevent his fax number from appearing, he chose to hand deliver the document to New Morning Star Enterprises. He would hand it personally to the receptionist under the pretext of having other business nearby.

Familiar now with much of the specialized vocabulary New Morning Star used, he could do most of the translation without resorting to dictionaries. As a precaution, he went to Akiharbara and purchased one of the new programmable electronic portable dictionaries for ¥13,200 (about $130) that was just a little larger than an iPod. For ¥ 6–9,000 (about $90 more), he could have inputted the latest specialized vocabulary—medical, electronics and chemistry terminology, for example. But for the time being, the generic dictionary would suffice.

On Wednesday, September 29, in order to avoid the most crowded commute time, Alpha left Shakujikoen Station after 9:00 a.m. and arrived unannounced at New Morning Star shortly after 10:30. Four men were in the conference room, in addition to President Kanagawa and his assistant, Mr. Kaneda. Two of the four wore black pointed shoes, and one sported extensive tattoos, visible above the neckline on his shirt. He also was missing the tip of his pinky on his left hand. They didn't quite look Japanese, and Alpha took them to be Korean. It would be evident even to a relative novice, though, that the men weren't ordinary Koreans but part of the yakuza, most likely the North Korean yakuza. The receptionist took the translation without fanfare, and Alpha excused himself and left.

After returning to his apartment, he did some Internet research on the yakuza in Japan. He already knew about the practice of severing the tip of one's pinky to make atonement to one's oyabun, and he was familiar with the tattoos and pointed shoes.

Once, soon after arriving in Japan with his parents and enrolling in the American School, the family had made a trip to Kobe on consulate business and had extended their stay by one additional day for a family trip. Not far from Kobe, on the far side of a small mountain range, was a historic *onsen*, a Japanese hot springs mineral bath resort, dating back six or seven centuries. Not keeping the late schedule required by his parents, Alpha retired early, woke up early and decided to try wandering in the large onsen area on his own.

If no one else were there, he could get away with a short swim, although that was not a culturally accepted practice. At least it would avoid the embarrassment of being naked in front of other people, a humiliation an eight-year-old wasn't ready to endure. But instead of having the onsen to himself, he was chagrined to see seven or eight men already bathing. All had tattoos on their torsos, arms and legs. Oddly, they looked as though they had clothing painted on.

Alpha had not been frightened by their appearance, only curious to know why grown men would go around with colorful dragons, flowers and landscapes all over their bodies. His first response was one of amusement, thinking maybe they had fallen into some paint. They looked kind of dressed up, even though they were "dressed" down to stark nudity. All also sported curly hair, the result of expensive permanents.

While he was wondering how to respond, vacillating between curiosity and a disinclination to make a fool of himself, one of the men asked his name in English. "Alfred B. Clark." "What kind of soda do you like?" "Orange." Within moments four of the men were drinking orange soda, and one additional bottle was presented to Alpha. While his mother didn't approve of him drinking soda, especially prior to breakfast, this made him feel like a man making it in a man's world. Putting his initial apprehension to rest, these men in their decorative tattoos for the moment became Alpha's pro tem surrogate uncles. They seemed delighted to have a gaijin nephew, and Alpha felt both a sense of bonding and one of accomplishment as he returned to his room in time to join his parents for breakfast. He didn't tell them about the encounter.

His other experiences with the yakaza hadn't been so direct. In fact, one of them hadn't even involved him. When he was a junior at the American School in Japan, three senior girls, two Americans and one Canadian, were asked whether they wanted a ride in a *gaisha*, a foreign-made car, which turned out to be a large, black Mercedes Benz 540. Two Japanese men with curly hair and tattoos took them out to a coffee shop, where they were treated to coffee and cheesecake. The men remained polite, and the girls were dropped off without incident at ASJ in time for their basketball game that evening. They hadn't told their parents.

During his studies at the University of Hawaii, Alpha had used the yakuza's influence to his advantage. Sumo is popular both in Japan and in heavily Japanese-influenced areas such as Hawaii. While he was at the American School in Japan, he learned of yakuza influence in sumo, in the form of rigging matches. There are 6 main sumo tournaments a year, with 15 bouts per tournament. While there are hundreds of sumo wrestlers, the top 36 make up the *juryo* and *makuuchi* divisions. There is a large discrepancy between the top 40 (who may earn more than $200,000/year) and those ranked 70 or below (who may earn less than $20,000/year). Along with low rank goes lowly service: they must tend to their superiors, performing everything from housekeeping to back washing.

If a sumo wrestler maintains a winning record—winning at least 8 of the 15 bouts in the major tournaments—his ranking will rise. So a wrestler entering the fifteenth day of a tournament with a 7–7 record has a lot more at stake than another with, say, an 8–6 or a 9–5 record. Both of the latter could lose the final bout and still maintain a winning record.

To the uninitiated, this would appear to be a decent bet: putting your money on the wrestler with the best record and wagering even money that the wrestler with the better record will win the final bout, reducing the sumo wrestler with an even 7–7 record to a losing record of 7–8. If pure odds dictated the outcome, that would be the case: the odds of the 7–7 sumo wrestler winning would be less than 50–50 when facing an opponent with a better record. In reality, however, the 7–7 wrestler wins nearly 80 percent of the time, followed by less than half this number (40 percent) in the next rematch against the same wrestler in the subsequent tournament. The hand of the yakuza is involved. Being aware of its influence allows you to cash in, using the rigged odds in your favor. Alpha had a lot of fun winning bets that superficially appeared to be against him, and he had obtained a little extra spending money from his fraternity friends.

Alpha also knew, however, not to mess with the yakuza. Several years ago, while he was still in high school in Japan, two former sumo wrestlers had started to come out with allegations of match rigging, drug use, sex, bribes and tax evasion among the wrestlers. After having arranged a conference with the Foreign Correspondents Club in Tokyo, both died shortly before the conference, on the same day in the same hospital of the same mysterious respiratory ailment. There were no further inquiries into the matter, at least none with substance.

Further Internet research confirmed what Alpha had already come to know in part: that Kabuikicho was the center of much yakuza activity; that the Japanese yakuza was the largest organized crime group in Japan, but that the Korean and China yakuza were also thriving; and that the Korean yakuza had a virtual monopoly on the pachinko industry. He could find no specific information about New Morning Star Enterprises, although some of the companies mentioned included the Yamaguchi-gumi in the construction industry and Sagawa-gumi in the parcel delivery business.

Another discovery became a source of considerable apprehension. He read of oyabuns collecting sake cups from the kobuns— each kobun presenting a sake cup to his oyabun as a token of this relationship.

Alpha recalled the set of four unmatched sake cups he had seen during his visit to New Morning Star Enterprises. Did that mean that President Kanagawa had enlisted four kobuns? Were Mr. Kaneda and Mr. Kim bone fide company employees, or were they yakuza members? Or both? Similarities with Christian Holy Communion crossed his mind—the cup as a symbol of devotion, and even of sacrifice. The wine in the cup imbibed to express identity with and bonding to an all-powerful and eternal God. However, in the case of the yakuza the bonding is to one who carries considerable clout within a limited context.

A great deal of harm, the Japanese believe, is done by trying to eliminate the ambiguity that inadvertently accompanies daily life. The Japanese language was engineered to protect this inherent vagueness. How convenient to deal with a language where "yes" doesn't necessarily mean yes and "no" rarely means no, at least not in comparison to how it is used in the West. Alpha had earlier found himself in interpreting situations in which he had even realized that the Japanese response of *hai* (for "yes") in reality meant "no."

With regard to his new employer, Alpha wondered whether or not to seek further details. Discretion being the better part of valor, he decided to bide his time for a while. It was hard to imagine the situation getting more uncertain than it currently was. He could live with this degree of ambiguity, providing as it did a certain amount of intrigue. And who was he to complain? New Morning Star was paying him adequately and on time.

Part of the answer came from an unexpected source. The Japanese celebrate Labor Day in late November, around the time when Americans commemorate Thanksgiving. Since he was self-employed, he and Rie could take a long weekend vacation before the Labor Day scramble. Most Japanese do things in unison, and this includes taking holidays. Getting a head start on the crowds often meant the difference between arriving predictably on time and getting caught in traffic making a four-hour trip may take three or four times that long.

Rie and Alpha decided to take the bullet train to Niigata to visit Rie's parents for the weekend. Other than having met them in conjunction with the wedding, Alpha hardly knew them. Her parents had, following Japanese custom, paid for their wedding. Even a Western style wedding in a wedding chapel attached to a hotel could easily cost upwards of $20,000, and Alpha was quite sure their bill had come to considerably more than that. He both respected and liked his parents-in-law, believing the feeling to be mutual.

Now they were on their way back to Niigata City. They could line up on the non-reserved platform to save more than one-third of the fare. If they stood in line long enough, allowing one or two trains to depart without boarding, they could board the next train prior to other passengers in line. It would take them about an hour to get to Ueno Station, where they had recently visited the famous zoo and where bullet trains depart for the northern areas of Japan. A two-hour trip on the Joetsu Bullet Train, and they would be in Niigata. Along the way Rie began to tell Alpha more about her family background to orient him for his second exposure to her parents.

Being a TCK, Alpha wasn't Japanese in his thinking, and Rie started to explain typical Japanese perspectives with regard to marriage. She began by explaining that, in some ways, the Japanese take one's bloodline a lot more seriously than do Westerners. More often than not the bride's parents hire a marriage agency to check into the prospective groom—a practice the groom's parents also pursue from their side.

If these background investigations show any substantial deviation from the norm—such as burakumin (outcast) blood—the marriage is usually called off. The burakumin used to deal in leather (handling hides and tanning), perform executions and serve as undertakers, handling dead bodies. Historically, they were the perennial victims of discrimination, and as such they had proved to be fertile ground for yakuza recruits, about 60–70 percent of whom are estimated to come from this class.

Other reasons for family members to call off an engagement might be possible exposure to radiation from an atomic bomb or being the offspring of a person who was exposed (it is ironic that Niigata, where Rie was from, escaped having an a-bomb dropped on it because of the weather); possible mixed blood (although the Japanese islands were probably originally settled by immigrants from east Asia passing through the Korean peninsula); descending from a family with mental illness; or having a handicapped sibling or other near relative who is considered less than normal.

Alpha wondered why Rie was deviating so far from the conversation he had anticipated. Yet she seemed intent in getting this out in the open and off her mind. Alpha knew enough by now to not try to correct or stop her. At any rate, Rie's background wasn't a factor for him. He believed that nurture, not nature or bloodline, is prominent in child development.

8

Niigata

Niigata Prefecture is famous for its harbor, rice, sake, and koi (expensive, colorful Japanese carp). It produces nearly 70 percent of Japan's rice crop, and it is of such quality that much of it is used to make sake, or rice wine. Niigata Prefecture faces the Japan Sea to the west, and traveling there had in the past been quite inconvenient. It had, however, one thing in its favor. It was the home of former Japanese Prime Minister Kakuei Tanaka, nicknamed the Bulldozer. With his support, despite its relative smaller population, Niigata Prefecture had been able to get its own bullet train, a pork barrel project called the Joetsu Shinkansen. A toll road, called the Kanetsu Expressway, had also been built. Both run northwest from Tokyo to Niigata City. These two projects opened up considerable development in the area but also displaced numerous rice farmers whose families had owned the land for centuries, raised only rice, and knew no other means of livelihood.

One of the displaced farmers had been Rie's grandfather, Nakata. He had lived far enough out in the country that the harbor pollution had been no problem. There were no factories nearby, so the air and water were clear, and the rice, with any cooperation at all from nature, was excellent. In 1971 he was forcibly relocated but did receive slightly more than fair market value for his land. However, no amount of money could repay him for his loss of self-esteem.

The Japanese lack a metaphysical sense of identity, an identity keyed to who they are and that continues to exist unchanged, regardless of what they do or what occupation they pursue. Rather, Japanese people in their own minds *are* what they do. To take away one's land and work is to rob him of his identity, in effect stripping him naked in the eyes of his peers. Nakata had been a rice farmer, but not the run of the mill type. The family for several generations had cultivated the famous rice that is used to make sake, the Japanese rice wine that contains about a 10–15 percent alcohol content.

The area around Niigata had perfected a strain of rice that on one hand contains high starch levels in the kernel and on the other low oils and proteins in the shell. High oil levels in the shell tend to produce strange or unpleasant flavors. The Nakata rice farm was only one of 14 in Japan with the Imperial Seal, authorized to grow rice to make sake for the Imperial family. The only thing that had prevented the family from becoming wealthy had been the size of the farm—at less than ten acres it couldn't support large capital investment in the implements required to automate.

All the Nakatas had owned was an Iseki farm tractor to work the rice fields and a rice seedling planter manufactured by Kubota—no capital-intensive machinery. Just the desirable rice fields which were amongst the highest in value of farmland in all of Japan. And raising rice is a labor intense endeavor; Japanese rice farmers try to get the entire family to help with transplanting the seedlings. Two local Niigata breweries each specialized in one variety of sake that had the same Imperial stamp of approval—listed as approved fare for the emperor's table, where foreign dignitaries would drink of it and be satisfied.

The Nakatas were quite certain, though lacking absolute proof, that their sake was drunk by the kamikaze pilots in WWII prior to their fateful missions, thus sealing their suicidal vows. Until recently Nakata rice had found its way in the form of sake to numerous Shinto ceremonies and weddings, where sacred vows are still sealed by drinking a cup. The use of sake for ceremonial occasions isn't all that dissimilar to Christians' participation in communion. Christians drink wine to remember that Christ gave his life for his people, while the Japanese drink sake to express devotion and willingness to offer up their lives for their emperor and the empire. Sake is the symbol for life—for one's very blood.

Nakata's livelihood as a rice farmer having been wrenched from him, the family relocated to a new home some 12 miles away. This did little to assuage his feelings of having been personally violated. The Japanese have only an active identity: they are what they do. If they cannot *do*, it goes without saying that they cannot *be*. They're existential to the core, explaining why Japan has been called a nation of 120 million overachievers. This is by far the lesser of two possible evils—certainly preferable to being a nation of that many paranoiacs. Paranoia would become pandemic if overwork didn't inhibit it.

Thus Nakata-san, Rie's grandfather, feeling vulnerable and helpless, found a voice, along with a new sense of belonging, in the newly formed *Seishi-kai*, the Youth Ideology Study Association. Despite its innocent sounding name, it had as its organizer Tomeo Sagoya, who was implicated in the 1930 assassination of then Prime Minister Hamaguchi.

The Seishi-kai took up anti-governmental causes, providing a voice to victims who otherwise had none. One of these causes had to do with the second recorded outbreak of organic mercury poisoning in Japan. The first outbreak had occurred in Minamata, Kyushu, in southern Japan, when during the 1950s the Chisso Corporation dumped 80 tons of mercury, mixed with 600,000 tons of industrial sludge, into the shallow Minamata Harbor. Some concentrations were so heavy (about two kilograms per ton) that the company later found it profitable to set up a subsidiary to re-mine the sludge from the harbor floor.

The second outbreak had occurred along the banks of the Agano River in the Niigata countryside during the mid-1960s. This one was caused by a Showa Denko Corporation factory, which employed an industrial process nearly identical to that of Chisso's plant in Minamata. Victims of the disease develop a sponge-like brain, crippling and rendering them incoherent and bedridden.

The Japanese lack effective cultural or religious patterns to process disabilities. In answer to the question posed to Jesus, "Why was this man born blind?" the Japanese can't respond as Christ did—that this misfortune was neither the man's own fault nor that of his parents. They can only surmise that such adversity must be due either to one's own shortcomings or to those of his parents. Consequently, parents with disabled children face a double burden, one physical and the other social. They must care for a child who won't get better, and they're obliged to bear shame— guilt defined in a social context—since Japanese society looks at such challenged people as having less value than a wage earner.

With all litigation in Japan, the admission of guilt is anathema. Chisso, although being aware of the deadly effects of the lethal by-products dumped into Minamata Bay, reluctantly admitted only minimal responsibility, and then only after the outcry could no longer be ignored. The Seishi-kai was largely responsible for this protest coming to the fore and did achieve some justice for the families affected.

While the immediate Nakata family, being rice farmers near Niigata City, wasn't directly affected by the mercury poisoning, some of their extended family, first and second cousins to Rie, were farmers who had lived in the Kanase village area irrigated by the Agano River. Consequently they had eaten from the food chain contaminated by the factory owned by Showa Denko.

During the latter half of the 1960s, catches of fish from the river had dwindled without apparent reason. And cats that ate the discarded entrails from the fish went crazy, running in circles and foaming at the mouth. Pregnant mothers experienced a much-increased rate of spontaneous abortion, while others gave birth to children who were both mentally challenged and physically deformed. Misshapen extremities suddenly became more than a hundred times more common. The medical community believed at the time that the placenta would help protect the fetus from toxins in the bloodstream. While that is the case with most chemicals, it was exactly opposite of the situation with the methyl mercury that contaminated the countryside—tragically, the placenta removed it from the mother's bloodstream and concentrated it in the fetus.

Handicapped children in Japan, especially those with severe disabilities such as the Minamata sickness produces, are treated as pariahs. In a society that knows only you-get-what-you-deserve karma and not the Christian concept of a good God with righteous providence, such ill fortune can only be interpreted in negative, shameful, and embarrassing ways. So instead of attempting to mainstream any such children, isolated facilities in small towns, away from the spotlight, are developed.

Rie explained to Alpha that her second cousin had been born with the dreaded Minamata disease. He had been well fed and clothed, but always by others; his mental state rendered him as dependent as a newborn. He had never developed bowel control and had been placed in an institution near a small village 22 miles northeast of Niigata City, where he had died three years earlier, one month short of his twelfth birthday.

Alpha was glad Rie had opened her heart to him, and the only difference the information made was to make him appreciate her more. People intimately associated with the disabled usually develop humble, tender hearts, and he noticed in Rie a kind of sensitivity that hadn't come from academic pursuits. With their honeymoon already history, he knew that a long-term relationship between the two of them would have to transition to and be based upon mutual respect.

The political situation in Niigata Prefecture was much like that of the rest of Japan. Donations to the right politician at the right time resulted in elected government officials looking the other way for infringements of all kinds. Politics join hands with industry in Japan in a manner that would be considered scandalous in most Western developed countries. Thus it was that organic mercury pollution could continue unabated, in spite of some localized opposition, until its effects were so devastating that it could no longer be ignored. Through all of this Nakata-san, working with the Sei-shi-kai, had developed a sense of belonging and purpose, even though the group's actions could sometimes be considered a bit unethical and they at times resorted to strong-arm tactics.

The Seisihi-kai provided fertile recruiting grounds for the yakuza, and Nakata-san had soon found himself gainfully employed, owning and managing a new pachinko parlor in Niigata City. As pachinko rapidly gained popularity in the mid-sixties, the family found themselves projected on a path to prosperity that would've been unthinkable during the farming days. All of this would've been unaffordable and unattainable without assistance from a group that loaned the Nakata family the equivalent of 2.1 million dollars to go into the pachinko business.

Pachinko is in no way a family affair like rice farming. In spite of the flamboyant architecture and neon signs, all pachinko players prefer to sit by themselves, surrounded by but in social isolation from all other Japanese. As such, only one supervisor and one or two assistants are required for each shift. One could run an entire pachinko parlor with as few as two full-time, along with eight to ten part-time employees. The assistance of the owner's wife, children, and other relatives is not only not required but undesirable. The heavy smoking and numerous special sound effects in the parlor aren't conducive to the development of mental health and concentration.

For the Nakata clan, formal membership in the Niigata Seishi-kai meant that transition to membership in the Niigata yakuza could be an almost seamless and natural next step. While there was a lot of potential profit to be made, however, it was almost impossible to navigate the rocky road to profitability as long as payoffs were in place. Tattoos, especially outside large metropolitan areas, were no longer required or expected of those engaged in legitimate businesses with the public, although it was still common for lower ranking members to display them. Such outward exhibitions of self-identity assured them of better service at hotels and restaurants but at the same time identified them as outcasts. Even the common practice of severing the tip of the pinky finger (yubizume) was falling into disfavor, being allowed by only a handful of older oyabuns.

Rather, the local yakuza desired to move more into legitimate businesses in an attempt to develop a more positive public image. Operating popular pachinko parlors was one method of doing this. For the proprietor this primarily involved a monthly payment, a "fee" offered in gratitude for services rendered. The first generation of Nakatas, those involved in opening the pachinko parlor, looked at this as a way to discharge some of the obligation (giri) they had incurred by borrowing the money. The second and now third generations, including Rie's peers, saw it more as protection money. Either way, this was a cost of doing business in Japan. And it was considered far better than the alternative.

9

At a Japanese Onsen

Arriving in Niigata at 1:30 p.m., the couple was met at the bullet train exit by Rie's mother. The Japanese generally age gracefully, and at 54 she still looked fit. The diet of seaweed, with all the trace minerals needed for healthy skin and body; green tea with its antioxidants; and fish, along with low meat consumption, all had their positive effect. Only a few gray hairs were starting to emerge, but like most Oriental people she carried her age well. And she had a surprise. They would stop at home briefly, freshen up for a few moments, pick up Rie's father and go by car immediately to the Yuzawa Onsen, an old and well established hot mineral spring located in a more remote area of Niigata Prefecture.

It was one day before the Japanese Labor Day holiday, but there were still vacancies for this one night. Rie's two younger sisters were excessively proud of their gaijin uncle. In their girlish ways they both had a crush on him, and each had asked at the time of the wedding whether he had any younger brothers. No one else at school had a gaijin in-law. But this time both were gone for the extended holiday. One had a three-day school trip; the other was staying at her cousin's for the weekend.

The two couples would have to share the same suite in the on-sen hotel, but separate *tatami* (straw mats, each measuring three by six feet) rooms were divided by *fusuma* (light-duty, decorative sliding paper doors). There would at least be visual privacy, and, provided snoring wasn't too loud, sleep on the futons was generally sound—usually better than on most Western beds. Bathing in the hot mineral spring was, if not therapeutic in the strict medical sense, certainly relaxing, providing a more pleasing effect than a total body massage.

Alpha appreciated the gesture. He was aware that the cost of staying overnight at an onsen would be in the range of $200 per night per person. While the sozai philosophy of eating still applied, the food at an onsen was generally like a 12- to 14-course meal, including crab, shrimp, oyster, steak, and eight or nine other selections of vegetables and relishes, followed by fresh fruit for dessert. Green tea would be included with the meal, followed by coffee and then sake, along with Japanese beer, unless something like Budweiser was specifically ordered. He thought back to his first experience at an onsen with his own parents—drinking orange soda with the tattooed Japanese—and wondered with a touch of humor whether this experience would be anything like that.

Dinner was scheduled for 7:00 p.m., and the kimono-clad attendant would prepare it for them in their tatami room. Each suite had two bedrooms and a common larger room with a TV, ashtrays and a small refrigerator. There would be sufficient time for a bath prior to supper. While coed bathing could still be found in some of the more remote country inns, the bathing here was gender separate, as it is in all the more prominent modern onsen. There were three different types of mineral water baths, each with distinctive characteristics: one clear, looking like hot water; one a muddy color that appeared to have iron oxide in it and smelled a little rusty; and the last a silver color with a faint but distinct sulfur smell.

Alpha would go in with his father-in-law, Rie with her mother. A usual course meant that you would soak in all three, minimally five to ten minutes in each. You were expected to wash adequately outside the bath before going in the first time and to scrub thoroughly before entering the second time; the third time required just a cursory rinse under the shower to wash away one's sweat. But tonight there would be time only for the first course, probably soaking a few minutes in one bath before going to dinner. The full course of three baths would have to wait for the next day.

There is a certain philosophy about onsen, and Alpha had a pretty clear inclination about what to expect. Swimming suits aren't allowed. You wash your entire body outside the bath, place your washing towel into a nearby basin and then soak naked with other guests, squatting in the hot water up to your neck. Thus onsen have became the great leveling ground in Japanese culture, the places where the hierarchical nature of the society is temporarily flattened as people, young and old, rich and poor, talk to each other as equals. This makes the experience conducive to intimate conversation, with many of the cultural barriers to heart-to-heart talks removed.

Most Japanese companies know that, if they want to find out what a client is really thinking—what their honne is—an overnight stay at an onsen is a good investment. So they budget accordingly. Rie's parents may have had this as their ulterior motive, but Alpha wasn't offended by that possibility. They wanted not only to draw Alpha closer into the family circle but also to gently introduce him to the real family. He could also get to know them on a deeper level.

Scores of books have been written about the Japanese psyche. Alpha had known from childhood that it is more difficult to become friends with the Japanese—they have inherently thicker social barriers to friendship and intimacy. Ironically, though, once one penetrates that barrier there is far less resistance to being open than what an American will have. There just isn't that strong of an individual ego to protect. The barriers to friendship with Americans are much more permeable, but once permeated there are far more psychological obstacles to personal intimacy.

The end result, Alpha decided, isn't all that different. Once the Japanese develop *amaeru*—literally "to be mothered" but implying that the relationship has developed to the point of mutually indulging each other without fear of retribution—one is in. The noun form *amae* (literally "sweetness") means that the other party won't take advantage of you, that you can unload your excess psychological baggage on someone else without fear of reprisal.

Nakata was now relating to Alpha in this complicated context of amae, and Alpha felt accepted and comfortable in that role. He realized, based on his studies in international business, that there are no synonyms across cultures. Friendship doesn't mean quite the same thing, nor does family, the company, or corporate culture. Whatever the cultural definition of friendship being manifested here, it felt good to Alpha.

Compared to Western countries, and especially America, in Japan a lot more lubrication is required to oil the gears of conversation before they can run smoothly, especially when the conversation encompasses two cultures. A cup of sake and two bottles of Asahi Super Dry later, Nakata began talking.

He started with his childhood. He had been born as the second son and third child into a rice growing family that traced its ancestry back seven generations, from the Tokugawa period, well before the Meiji Restoration in 1868. During this time imperial power was restored, Tokyo became the new capital, the royal household ordered Niigata sake for state functions, and the Nakata family was one of only two approved households that could grow rice specified for the Niigata production of imperial sake. Among rice farmers there could be no greater honor. If the weather promoted a good harvest, a correspondingly good income could be realized—comparable to that of a factory worker.

Alpha reciprocated Nakata's openness. Due to his father's employment for the Department of State, he had as a child moved around every five or six years, but he had lived in Japan the longest. He explained how he had come to speak Japanese almost like a native, as well as the fact that Japanese blood flowed in his American body. The onsen, with its magic powers to relax, to dissolve stress, to emancipate, was beginning to work its magic. Already Alpha felt that Nakata was treating him as the son he'd never had.

Back in the room, both men remained dressed in their *yukata* (a casual summer Japanese kimono or robe), appropriate dress for an onsen. In Japan it doesn't take much of an occasion for a photo, and this was one such time. But by the time a couple of frames had been taken, a female voice at the door announced that she was about to commit a rudeness—and dinner was served.

Alpha again realized why Japanese food is considered by connoisseurs to be among the best. Esthetically beautiful, with pine needles and chrysanthemum pedals for accent, it has the perfect combination of artistic presentation, flavor, variety, and volume. One isn't overwhelmed by excess; everything comes in a natural order; and the person is comfortably full, but not overstuffed, by the conclusion to the meal. Such an elaborate meal at a good onsen is a manifestation of *shibui*, a type of beauty that's in perfect harmony with nature. *Musubi* also came to mind: that undifferentiated coexistence between man with nature. While "mother nature" is probably the most inconsistent pair of words that exists, the Japanese have at least captured her good side. And the onsen experience is especially synergistic, with body and mind gently massaged by nature's delicate and subtle beauty.

Serious business matters are ordinarily off limits for conversation during such an elaborate meal, giving way to rather pleasant if not superficial topics. The compounding effect of the sake means that the conversation gets mellower in proportion to the amount drunk. At least in this case, however, it didn't become more meaningful. The only negative comment Nakata made the entire evening was that this sake from the onsen was very inferior to that which had been made from the family rice; he quipped that "he should have smuggled some in," to which everyone laughed.

Rie, for her part, ate very little—so little that, had she not been her father's daughter, this would have presented a rude impression, one of not being appreciative. She also drank only one cup of green tea and no alcohol. For no apparent reason, she explained, she didn't feel very well. The meal took nearly three hours, and she was glad to retire to the futon shortly after 10. Possibly her churning stomach was due to the stress and unpredictability of her gaijin husband relating in depth for the first time to her parents. Yet so far there appeared to be no cause for apprehension.

As Alpha lay on a separate futon next to Rie's, before the food and drink lulled him into a deep sleep, he thought about the Nakata family. Decent, upright, polite, generous, treating him more as a son than as a son-in-law—he wondered what the next development might be. Aware that marriage in Japan isn't just the union of husband and wife but also that of the wife to the extended family, he felt as though the tables had been turned. It was he, Alfred B. Clark, who was being adopted, accepted into the extended family. Again he felt the mysterious sensation of wa, of being in harmony with the world around him, as that world is in harmony with the universe.

As they awoke the next morning, Alpha recalled again the time when he was eight years old, staying at another onsen and drinking orange soda. Deciding to go for a morning bath, he noticed a vending machine that sold a hot coffee for 120 yen. After buying and finishing a cup, he entered the men's bathing area. This time there were no surprises, only three other men, all of whom appeared to be at least in their seventies, taking a bath. These three, Alpha guessed, were from a small village nearby. Unaccustomed to seeing a gaijin, they bordered on being overly inquisitive and even intrusive.

Alpha wasn't in a mood that morning for opening up with strangers, preferring to avoid anything that might disrupt his newfound tranquility. He entered one of the three baths the men weren't using, the one with silver colored water that smelled of sulphur. He wanted some time to think before breakfast but found this difficult, as bathing in an onsen is a rather overwhelming experience and only the most overwrought of individuals can prevent himself from relaxing. Whatever serious thinking he had to do would have to wait until they were back in Tokyo.

Breakfast was provided in a large common dining room. It was on a par with dinner the previous evening—sozai at its best, except that no sake was served. One could have plenty of drink after mid-morning, before entering the second and third baths.

Probably out of consideration to Alpha, a full pot of freshly brewed coffee was brought. Rie's parents were proving to be the perfect host and hostess, anticipating his every need. The coffee went well with the grapes and cantaloupe that completed the final course. Everyone but Rie drank some, she preferring the mellowing effect of green tea.

The foursome opted for a morning walk before entering the bath. Now everyone being dressed in yukata and using *geta*, traditional wooden shoes about four inches high, became the occasion for more photographs. They returned to the onsen in time for the full course—bathing in all three baths, with Asahi Super Dry beer being chased down by sake between the courses.

Nakata wasted no time in getting to the bath prior to the majority of patrons, who had more time to spare. Since they were relatively clean from having bathed the previous evening, only cursory scrubbing was necessary prior to entering the first bath. Nakata seemed eager to continue his story, picking up where he had left off not much more than 10 hours earlier.

The Nakata rice farm hadn't been large, nor did it have to be. What the rice lacked in quantity it more than made up for in quality. But traditions forged by generations changed quickly when the Nakata family, and more specifically Rie's grandfather, lost his land, and with it his very reason for existence. *Raison d'etre.* In the mental and social confusion that followed, decisions were made that had far-reaching implications. The Nakata family, looking for a new livelihood, again discovered that the Seishi-kai could be helpful with its extensive contacts. The Seishi-kai would provide the necessary shokaijo, letters of introduction that would open the right doors at the right time to the right people.

Pachinko was just becoming popular, and already the extensive contacts of the Seishi-kai had infiltrated the pachinko industry, opening up an extended network of relationships, many, if not most of which were fully legitimate. Rie's father, being a rice farmer, lacked the business acumen for complicated entrepreneurial endeavors and was content to have something to do, some means for making a livelihood; one pachinko parlor would be more than adequate.

Nakata had contacted a local English teacher, a former classmate from elementary school, for his suggestions for a trendy name.

Thus the new pachinko parlor in Niigata City came to be called *Zaa Happi Aua*—Japanized English that meant in the Good Hour. In the sixties Japanese businesses began using foreign names to give the impression of being international—and thus carrying some mystique or spillover credibility. So rather than choosing a name derived from a combination of one to three of the thirty thousand Chinese characters available, they wrote it using characters from the katakana alphabet, used mainly for writing foreign words.

Katakana has 51 characters. Another alphabet, with the same number of characters, *hiragana*, is used to add sounds, declensions, particles, etc., to the numerous Chinese characters. These three—the Chinese characters, hiragana, and katakana—blended together to form the Japanese language. It isn't at all surprising that one of the first missionaries to Japan in the sixteenth century, a brilliant Catholic named Sir Francis Xavier, is credited with saying that "the Japanese language was invented by the devil." If one isn't born Japanese or raised in Japan, they'll face a formidable struggle in mastering the language, especially the writing part.

The Good Hour thrived, riding the wave of the increased popularity of pachinko in Japan. And the Nakata family, despite some below-the-surface drawbacks of operating such a business, enjoyed the benefits of the post-war wealth boom in Japan.

Ironically, it has been said that the best way for a nation to become wealthy is to lose a war with America. The Marshall Plan had worked beyond expectation. But something else was needed to make its benefactors successful—*hoshonin*—guarantors who would help entrepreneurs establish credit and take responsibility for their behavior and character. Of course for Nakata, as others, this came at a price, but the potential profits outweighed the periodic payments required. Years later it wouldn't be too heavy a financial burden for Rie to study abroad at a private college, despite of the high cost of nonresident tuition.

The extended and peripheral relationships incurred with membership in the Niigata yakuza were generally irrelevant to the Nakata family. Perhaps two or three times a year special donations were solicited for a kingpin's funeral, or for the celebration of a kobun's release from prison or for other expensive events that required an infusion of significant amounts of cash. Otherwise, there was just the monthly gratuity, paid in cash. Mr. Nakata interpreted this as giri—as a perpetual obligation, a monthly repayment in gratitude for the monetary loan and other assistance from the Organization that had made his new endeavor possible.

With membership came some positive benefits, not the least being job security and surrogate family membership. And one's immediate family was secure, both socially and financially.

Mr. Nakata began explaining the subculture of the Organization to Alpha, at first substituting "Organization" for "yakuza." Nakata-san apologized for having kept Alpha in the dark, but no outsider was to know the internal working of the Organization. He himself didn't know a great deal, choosing not in any way to challenge the powers that were and preferring to remain blissfully ignorant.

Now Nakata was letting Alpha inside, eager to share this burden with his son-in-law. But, he warned, becoming an insider could almost inevitably turn into a one-way trip for Alpha. The heavy responsibility, he explained, of maintaining confidentiality and secrecy wasn't ordinarily entrusted to anyone outside the yakuza (Nakata at this point dropped the pretense of referring to "Organization"). This applied especially to one who had once been inside but who had been excommunicated, or given a *hamon*. There were basically two varieties, a red hamon and a black one. The red is the more serious of the two, usually involving some grave or unforgiveable infraction.

Sometimes a person desiring to leave the yakuza will have to go into hiding to avoid its "hounding out of existence" tactics. The Japanese take group membership seriously, and when a member desires to disassociate from the group serious repercussions can develop. Such a breaking of ties would result in *ronin*—a situation of having no master to serve, no duties to perform and no group to belong to.

Japanese television networks often go so far as to broadcast a yakuza member's release from jail. Kobuns keep the secrets of the Organization even to the point of having to serve time for several years. The oyabun sends his chauffeur with his black Mercedes 540 to meet the kobun upon his release from jail, and he is escorted in style to the headquarters; given a lavish party with all the accoutrements, including the accompaniment and cooperation of the opposite sex; and presented with a lump sum in cash to cover his prison time. "Donations" from other members of the Organization pay for this.

Second, Nakata-san continued, a member must never violate the wife or children of another member. They're sacred, off limits to friend or foe, including anyone within the same or another kumi or gumi (group, gang or band). Because of this code, children and spouses of yakuza members are generally more secure than those of nonmembers. Anybody touching them could be subject to double jeopardy—of Japanese law and of the unwritten law of the yakuza. Rie, who had indirectly benefited from this, had never faced a dangerous moment while she was growing up, although her naïveté had been considerably tempered by her year of studies in California.

"We hate hard drugs," Nakata went on. "Nobody in our organization may be involved with narcotics. Any member who attempts to use or sell will be subject to severe discipline." The yakuza shows considerable restraint in keeping its hands off hard drugs—no cocaine, crack, heroin or morphine. "As a matter of fact," Nakata narrated with an ironic smile, "they've done a far better job than those Americans in regulating narcotics traffic—and at no cost to the government." It was obvious Nakata wasn't including Alpha in his generalization, and for the first time Alpha felt as though he belonged to a Japanese family.

Nakata, evidently well versed in history, referred to the famous sinking of the Normandie in New York Harbor at the onset of WWII, in 1942: "This is why we think America might be better off to have a covert association with the mafia, like Japan has with the yakuza. Among the yakuza, the story of the sinking of the Normandie is well known. One of the New York mafia kingpins, Luciano, was in jail, and sabotage by the New York longshoremen on the docks was rampant. To show their muscle the Normandie, a French ship, rechristened as the Lafayette, was sunk by the mafia. Luciano was then released, and all incidents immediately ceased. The docks of New York immediately became safe to use for the war effort and the longshoremen became cooperative, due largely because it was now being policed by one of its own." Whether or not this was an appropriate analogy Alpha wasn't sure. He did know that the yakuza was far larger in Japan than the mafia in the States, and yet there was much less violence in Japan.

Alpha remembered reading an annual "White Paper" on Japanese crime statistics during his sociology studies at the East West University. Deaths due to narcotics in Japan constitute less than one-tenth of one percent of the total. Due to rampant drug abuse, America has over one thousand times as many drug-related deaths per capita. "If we could go to America we could save tens of thousands of lives every year," Nakata-san boasted, a wry smile on his lips. Alpha didn't know whether to construe this as a tongue-in-cheek remark or a serious statement. Probably both. Humor doesn't tend to translate well, and Alpha thought it best not to interrupt or challenge his father-in-law while he was on a roll. Nakata continued, "The example of covert cooperation between the yakuza and the legal forces—police or government—isn't without precedent. Do you remember in WWII when General Paton invaded Sicily?"

"No," Alpha conceded. He was aware of Paton's successes in the European theater but had no specific recollection of what had happened on Sicily. Nakata forged on, "After securing a beachhead in southwestern Sicily, the Seventh Army launched an offensive into Italy's mafia land, heading directly toward Palermo. There were more than sixty thousand Italian troops in his way, along with thousands of road and land mines. Do you know how Paton marched his army over these unfamiliar and dangerous roads, arriving in Palermo in only four days?"

Although such was clearly not Nakata's intent, Alpha felt intimidated and again answered with a meek "No." He wanted to counter some of Nakata's statements but lacked the information to do so.

He would never have expected to be verbally outgunned by a former rice farmer from Niigata.

Again Nakata took up his virtual monologue: "It was all due to the courtesy of the Sicilian mafia, La Costa Nostra. They made a truce with the American Mafia don Lucky Luciano, who in turn communicated with Zu Calo, the local unchallenged leader of the area mountain region through which the American army would be passing. They not only had a safe journey but were also provided with guides, kept safe from snipers, and enjoyed enthusiastic welcomes. Soon the Americans appointed Zu Calo mayor. Similar to the Japanese yakuza identifying with right wing causes, the Sicilian Mafia became a natural anti-communist ally."

While growing up in Japan, Alpha hadn't once heard of hard drugs being peddled. Nor was he aware of a single student at the American School in Japan who had access to them. In terms of narcotics, Japan was probably the safest country in the world. And he began to appreciate that this was due largely to the Organization—the 893, the yakuza.

The Japanese seem to tolerate temperature extremes better than Americans, and a hot bath is no exception. While Nakata didn't seem fazed by it, Alpha was beginning to feel the heat—probably due, he thought tangentially, to some ethnic metabolic differences. Nevertheless the two exited together and enjoyed a cold Asahi Super Dry before entering the second bath. There was no particular order protocol for entering the baths, but entering all three was recommended for those who had the time, in order for them to enjoy the fullest therapeutic benefit.

Alpha was intrigued by Nakata's unexpected openness. Very few foreigners, he was sure, were privy to knowledge of the inner workings of the Organization. Once the two were alone again in the second bath, Nakata-san continued, "Furthermore, we pay interest every month. The Fourth Commandment is not to withhold money from whom it is due. We Japanese have a deep sense of obligation, of giri. That's why we're always giving presents, to either pay off our giri or avoid incurring it to begin with. Sometimes, though, our giri is lifelong. That's what we don't like about American society. They have no sense of giri, of duty or obligation. They don't feel the need to reciprocate favors or discharge their obligation adequately. That doesn't make any sense to us Japanese."

"So, how do the Japanese incur giri?" Alpha asked. He knew the technical definition of the word but wanted to find out what it meant specifically for the Nakata family—without asking in an overt manner. Again Nakata-san was forthcoming. When the family was displaced on account of eminent domain laws for a coming expressway, they had received enough money to replace their house, but not enough to begin anew in a new place with a new vocation.

Only a small fraction of rice farmers can grow the rice required for good sake, and there were no other suitable rice fields available. The Japanese don't sell the land they've owned for generations. And it takes years of preparation, using the right water, compost and fertilizers, as well as years of learning, to properly cultivate rice for sake. "So, contrary to our wishes, we were forced to move, and forced to find a new means of living. It was at this point that the Organization provided assistance to our family, setting us up with our own pachinko parlor. That was before the real estate bubble burst. Commercial land prices were high, and the huge capital investment was something we could never have afforded on our own. Having incurred this giri from the Organization, we now continue to honor it by making a monthly donation."

Alpha took this as a euphemistic way of talking about protection money but knew better than to inject his thoughts into his father-in-law's narration. Protection money isn't quite the same as extortion; with the latter, no value is, or ever had been, added in the relationship. Yet he knew in his heart that these monthly payments, while being the cost of doing business in Japan, were probably not made spontaneously or with particular alacrity. The concept didn't resemble the Christian idea of giving with a joyful heart. He knew the Japanese, in contrast to Americans, to be tightfisted when it comes to bone fide donations. The United Fund in Japan receives less than one-tenth the amount of donations per capita—a figure that includes those from the underworld.

Japanese religions have no stories similar to that of the Good Samaritan. If something like that scenario were to have happened in Japan, the man robbed by the thieves would've had to seek out his benefactor to figure out a way to repay the giri he had incurred—quite possibly for the rest of his life. Whatever happens, the Japanese believe that one is responsible for their own deliverance, while not obligated to alleviate someone else's misfortune, especially if that someone has no connection to the individual. Japanese giri thus is not universal but limited to those who have provided material or other assistance to the one now obligated in time of need.

Alpha was quite surprised by the degree of elocution of this former rice farmer. He didn't consider himself to be a Christian in the strict sense of the term. Having been raised in the politically-charged context of the American Embassy, he understood that talk about religion was off limits except in conversations with one's closest friends. He thought, as did most Japanese, that the teachings of Christ were rather exclusivist; his own thinking was much broader than that. Christianity's overall lack of appeal in Japan, he thought, was due in part to it's not being very accommodating. The pragmatic Japanese just can't comprehend the concept of "One Way."

The Japanese also shrink from the notion of sin, relegating that to the lives and hearts of serious felons. While Alpha knew Japanese faith to be highly inclusive, the trade-off is that it doesn't produce serious devotees. He couldn't think of a single Japanese Shinto or Buddhist martyr, even though there had been numerous Japanese Christian martyrs, both at home and abroad. A true Buddhist would be detached from the material world, and he knew the Japanese to be, if anything, more materialistic than Americans. If they weren't, it was because they couldn't afford it—not because they were committed to Buddhism.

In Alpha's experience all who claimed to be Buddhist (thereby professing belief in detachment from this material world) were as much in pursuit of the almighty yen as the next guy. If the allure wasn't money, it was power; and if not power, it was sex—or, more often than not, some combination of the three.

There were many Buddhist temples around with less than honorable reputations. And Shinto was hard for Alpha to put a handle on. More than a teaching or a way of life, it seemed to constitute a vague way of expressing a certain politeness toward some of the eight million local deities believed to exist—that may or may not have some degree of control over local events.

There have been martyrs to a way of life, like those chronicled in the movie *The Last Samurai*, but very few religious martyrs in Japanese history. Neither Buddhism nor Shintoism has a book that in any way resembles *Fox's Book of Martyrs*. There will never be a Mother Teresa coming out of Japanese Buddhism or Shintoism.

At any rate, "mandatory donations" to the Organization were predictable, required and upwardly adjustable; with more profit, more donations were expected. Alpha was curious how this equated to actual yen but knew enough not to ask. He guessed it to be at least equivalent to more than a couple thousand US dollars monthly.

Nakata-san's narration continued. "Another rule is that one must not fail in obedience to one's superiors [one's oyabun]." He went on to explain that loyalty to superiors is the main manifestation of Confucianism (*jukyou*) in Japanese society. Children are loyal to their parents, an employee to his employer and a kobun to his oyabun. Employees tighten their belts when necessary and benefit in return from life-long employment and security from the company.

Nakata-san told Alpha about an electronics firm in the Kansai area that made internal parts for cell phones. During one particular period everyone needed to work overtime, but the company, in difficult financial straits, couldn't afford overtime pay. So all employees punched out promptly at 5:00 p.m. before returning to work without pay until 9:00 p.m. After more than two years of this unpaid overtime, the firm was back on its feet. All employees kept their jobs and again received summer and winter bonuses and overtime pay. As this degree of commitment is required, failure—for the individual or for the business—isn't an option. Nakata put in another jab: "That's why those Americans can't manufacture a good automobile. They're more committed to themselves than to the company."

Alpha, anxious not to fail the loyalty test, was again glad Na-kata-san hadn't said "you Americans." Yubizume, he knew, is one of the lesser but well-known punishments for failure. Ostracism from and rejection by the Organization can also occur, and there are very few alternatives available for ex-yakuza members. The general practice is to hound them out of existence. There was one he knew of, a Suzuki-sensei, who had converted to Christianity and now pastored a parish in Funabashi City in Chiba Prefecture. More than once the man had been forced to go into hiding to escape the threats that had developed as a result of his leaving the organization.

As a rule is often proven by its few exceptions, not many ever leave the Organization. Without an oyabun they would be like the masterless samurai, the 47 ronin of Japan's feudal period who, observing the *bushido* code—the code of honor of the samurai warrior—had collectively committed suicide (*harakiri*). The Sen-gaku-ji temple in western Tokyo, where the 47 are buried, still preserves their gravestones and offers up incense daily to their spirits. While not an outstanding temple in the architectural sense, it remains a popular tourist attraction. Alpha and Rie had gone there once while they were dating. The site remains a testimony to the Japanese concept of giri, which must be observed, even at the cost of one's life.

After two thermal baths and the bonding that had ensued, the two men exited and walked to the small lobby of the bath, where their clothes awaited in a large plastic box. Lockers, though nearby, were unused. No one took valuables down to the bath. The most common item was a pack of cigarettes and a disposable lighter. The father-in-law ordered two more Asahi Super Dries. Very likely the heat from the baths was accelerating the beers' effect. Nakata-san showed no psychological effects from drinking, only sweating more than usual. But Alpha, even with a significantly larger body mass, was beginning to feel the effects and was glad they had to this point drunk only one bottle each. They were off to the third bath.

Nakata-san continued his one-sided narration. Another invio-late rule was that members could never appeal to the police, the law, or any other third party. The Organization quickly and efficiently takes care of everything that comes its way. The yakuza is a law unto itself, settling all internal matters without outside interference. Alpha remembered hearing a sermon, while he was growing up, at an English service at an Episcopal church in Tokyo about Christians not going to court. He wondered briefly now whether the Sixth Commandment of the yakuza organization was something like that.

The seventh and final commandment is to never make any public disturbance. Whatever business has to be done should be handled in private, away from public eyes and ears.

Alpha was beginning to suffer from sensory overload, and the hot spring bath was starting to overheat him. He excused himself, took a *tenugui* (Japanese bath towel), covered his private anatomy and exited the bath for the third and final time.

The foursome would check out of the onsen and drive back to Niigata City, enjoying a light lunch of *udon* (Japanese noodles) along the way. Together as a group in the family car, Nakata-san seemed a little more restrained; the topics of conversation became more superficial in the presence of the mother-daughter combination.

As Alpha visited his in-laws' home for the second time, Nakata-san stressed the positive benefits of membership in the Organization. He had committed to memory the writing on a scroll on the wall of his small office at the pachinko parlor. It was a copy of part of a speech by Shotaru Hayashi, one of the richest men in the Sumiyoshi-kai, a Tokyo based yakuza second in size and influence only to the Yamaguchi-gumi. He quoted to Alpha: "The *yakuza* is a necessary vice for Japanese society. But in the future our biggest task is to become entrepreneurs, to become clean, and pay taxes. The age of the *tekiya* (street stall operators) is over; you have to do it aboveboard now. Business will be our main way to survive. As long as you pay taxes you're okay."

Coincidentally, Shotaro Hayashi's daughter had been the only known child of a prominent yakuza to marry an American. And given this connection, Hayashi frequently opened up his schedule and his heart to foreign—and especially American—journalists.

Alpha laid no particular significance on the realization that he wasn't the first to marry into a family with yakuza connections. He was blessed with excellent in-laws, and it felt good to have their home opened to him and a family to belong to.

As a TCK, Alpha had never experienced the security of having a long-term physical place to call home. While Japanese houses generally don't last for more than 40 years, there's something about Japanese architecture that seems integrated to the eternity of time, something that helps makes a person feel unhurried and relaxed. Alpha appreciated the combination of the Japanese architecture and a Japanese family. This was shibui at its best.

Many Japanese people, on the other hand, view themselves as being cursed by ties to home; if they moved away they'd be condemned as perpetual strangers, isolated in the new neighborhood and always looked upon with distrust. One can never take their home with them when they relocate in Japan. This phenomenon has had the effect of creating a great many job-transfer widows. The family can't move and the husband can't commute. So they lead separate lives for months and even years. There's a phrase for the situation—*tanshin funin*: taking up a new post and leaving one's family behind.

Alpha and Rie would stay one additional night at the Nakatas' home and try to head back to Tokyo by noon on Sunday, hopefully just ahead of the holiday crowd. Rie still felt unwell, in spite of having spent the night in her childhood home. Japanese homes aren't very soundproof, so she and Alpha didn't talk much during their stay. Unknown to them, her concerned mother had made a separate trip to the station, switched their tickets on the *Shinkansen* (high speed train, or "Bullet Train") to reserved seats and paid the extra fare as a gift.

10

Unexpected News

An additional night's rest in their apartment still didn't do much for Rie. Still having no appetite, she decided to visit the doctor. Most medical care in Japan is provided by privately owned clinics, and a longtime friend of the family had a son who ran a clinic less than an hour from Shakujikoen. They were able to get an appointment for the following Monday.

Alpha, contrary to Japanese custom, accompanied Rie to the clinic. On the way there they passed the Shibuya station, and Rie began to narrate the story of Hachiko: "There was an Ainu dog that went to the west entrance of the Shibuya station daily to send his master, a college professor by the name of Ueno, off on his train. Hachiko then went again to meet his master on his return on the 6:00 train. When his master suddenly died of a stroke, Hachiko still went daily to the west entrance to meet him. Eventually becoming emaciated and full of parasites, he was rescued by a dog lover. Hachiko still insisted on his daily trek, however, in a vain attempt to meet his master. After the dog failed to bond with his new benefactor, she gave him to their gardener, who lived near the station, making Hachiko's twice daily commute a lot easier. For nearly 10 years, until his own death, Hachiko kept this vigil. There is now a bronze statue of him at the west entrance to Shibuya station."

Alpha didn't fully appreciate the import of the story, even though it was true. It was tragic and melancholic and without a happy ending—a tale of blind loyalty when the facts dictated otherwise. Alpha understood, though, why such a story would appeal to the Japanese. It reminded him of the kamikaze pilots in WWII who remained loyal even after the war was finished.

Alpha was uncertain whether the stares from the other Japanese wives were motivated by envy or by the fact that his presence with Rie constituted a deviation from the norm. It was probably a mixture of both. Such departures are usually considered to be wrong. The Japanese consider that what *is* is precisely what ought to be—that a woman is able to fend for herself and thus shouldn't be accompanied by a man. The fact was that he wanted to be with his wife, and at moment like this she was especially thankful for her gaijin husband.

Family connections resulted in her being seen promptly, without having to endure the customary one- to two-hour waiting period. And the doctor instructed her to wait for some of the results of her urine and blood tests. Certain results they could process in their small lab; others would require a week and probably an additional visit to the hospital in order to rule out any viral or bacteriological infections. Alpha remembered a conversation between his parents when he had been a teenager about a private clinic in the west Tokyo suburbs that purposely misdiagnosed female disorders in order to make additional profit. He was aware that treatment in Japan is overall of high quality, the only question being whether or not they are treating the person for the right disorder. If the diagnosis is correct, the patient will receive pretty good treatment. He was thankful for the family connections that had led to an introduction to a clinic and a physician they could trust.

After only about 40 minutes Rie was again summoned to the consulting room. Alpha asked whether he could go with her, and the doctor, evidently too astonished to refuse, agreed. "I have some news for you," he opened. "You are six weeks pregnant." Rie looked to Alpha for initial feedback, anxious to see whether it would be forthcoming and, if so, whether the response would be positive or negative. She wasn't disappointed. Again Alpha made her proud. She bonded, then and there, on an even deeper lever with her gaijin husband—bonded in the way that only the news of a baby, her baby, their baby—could have produced. Still too early to determine the gender of the fetus, the doctor assured her that her nausea and loss of appetite were indeed symptoms of her pregnancy.

Expected children in Japan aren't always looked upon as blessings. Alpha wondered how the Nakatas would respond to the prospect of having the first mixed-blood baby born into the family since as far back as anyone could remember. The high Japanese abortion rate is disguised by deflated statistics; this is the main reason the Japanese population peaked in the first half of the first decade of the twenty-first century and then began to decline after 2006.

At a Japanese OBGYN clinic it isn't unusual for the same doctor to administer fertility treatments to one patient, extending all of his technical expertise in an attempt to get her pregnant, and then go on to perform an abortion on another patient in an adjacent examining room. Japan has very lenient abortion policies, corresponding with minimal respect for fetal life.

In both Niigata and Tokyo, Alpha and Rie had visited Buddhist temples with *mizuko jizo*—a combination of *mizuko*, literally "child of water," the word used for an aborted fetus, and *jizo*, the Buddhist figure for stillborn, miscarried and aborted fetuses. *Mizuko kuyo*, memorial services, are conducted for them, and *ema*—wooden plaques—are displayed by the thousands at Buddhist temples. They are signed by heartsick mothers, and sometimes by the entire family, and are erected to signify a pregnancy not seen through to completion. Typical messages to the spirit of the unborn state include *gomen ne* ("Please forgive me") and *yasuraka ni nemutte kudasai* ("Please sleep peacefully").

Many Buddhist temples have been brought back from the brink of bankruptcy and transformed into profitable endeavors due to profits from the *mizuko* business (miscarriage, stillbirth, or abortion). Rie was thankful that their child, if they had anything to do with it, would not become a mizuko. They would take whatever precautions were necessary, and Rie would immediately begin a specialized diet for pregnant mothers to help ensure healthy development and a safe birth.

"How ironic," Alpha thought. As a couple they hadn't yet made any plans for a family, though neither had they planned for *not* having one. Men who marry in their late twenties and attempt to begin a family after their peak reproductive years have already passed often face insurmountable difficulties. Pollution in Japan reduces the sperm count by that time, with the result that the number of children per married couple is at an all time low. Coupled with a high abortion rate, the result is that the Japanese are as a people declining in population.

On the way back from the clinic Alpha thought he noticed Rie walking a little differently, with a little more swaying motion, not completely unlike a duck walking. He didn't know whether he should bring this to her attention. Maybe it was a psychological adjustment to her new condition, although the thought occurred to him that the reason might actually be physiological. Either way, he thought it best not to comment. She didn't appear to be in an emotional state where teasing might be an option.

There are times when couples have a lot to talk about, when the shared excitement of pleasant experiences, perhaps over a bottle of wine during a quiet evening together, is as good as it gets. But the Japanese have at the core of their personality a strong degree of despondency perhaps not found in any other people group. Even great occasions for celebration are frequently tempered by the harsher realities of life.

Nature cannot ultimately be relied upon to be kind and gentle, and belief in nature is as close to believing in a god as most Japanese would ever get. Rie was no different, being pulled in two simultaneous directions. She felt the joy of anticipating their own baby, of being a mother, a wife with a child; yet she was overwhelmed by fear of the unknown, apprehensive that nature might throw a curve ball at her. She felt like crying, intimidated by her upcoming new responsibilities. Not desiring to make a public display of her conflicted feelings, she remained mostly silent on the return trip.

Japanese society is, on the whole, still not friendly or open toward foreigners or people of mixed blood, and this prejudice is manifest in inverse proportion to the population, with smaller towns and villages exhibiting more prejudice. This ethnocentrism would certainly be worse in Niigata, where her parents lived, compared to their location just northwest of Tokyo. As for her own parents, she was not too apprehensive. Surprisingly, they had expressed only minimal objections to her marrying a foreigner.

The Nakatas' main objections were not against her marrying a gaijin but related to their future plans: where they would live and how they would make a living. They didn't want their daughter living in some dangerous part of some foreign country, like Chicago or New York. Once Alpha had convinced them that he had no plans of leaving Japan, a fortuitous (as in "lucky") day was chosen, the wedding plans commenced, and her parents paid for a wedding lavish even by Japanese standards. Surely they would be happy to have a grandchild, even if the child were not pure Japanese. Especially if it were a boy. The eldest boy has a special status in Japanese society; he is expected to carry on with the family Buddhist altar and worship of the deceased relatives, as well as to provide an offering to the Shinto altar in order to maintain daily peace and prosperity. This Alpha himself could not conscientiously do. Japanese use Buddhism for death and funerals, and Shintoism for success in daily life, but don't really adhere to either.

The route home took them through Ikebukuro, a major train station with numerous stores. Rie, feeling better in spite of the train ride, wanted to look at some baby clothes. Alpha was hungry, and Rie thought she could eat some Japanese food, as long as it wasn't deep fried and had no greasy smell. They decided to eat dinner out. Alpha selected broiled fish, rice, soup and vegetables, while Rie, wanting something spicy, chose a bowl of soba, which she could season as she liked. She asked for low sodium soy sauce and flavored it with a safe amount of spices.

Tired from their visit to the clinic, they decided to retire early. Announcements of the pregnancy could wait until the following day; this brief delay would give Rie time to think about how best to tell her parents. The phone rang, though. Rie's mother, not having heard from them on Sunday, wanted to know whether they had arrived home safely from Niigata. In her typical way, Rie blurted out the fact of her pregnancy. The Japanese don't usually express emotion; if they get excited they tend to express it by increased activity, becoming not unlike an ADHD child, with their excess energy converted into action and increased planning. Was it a boy or girl? Too early to tell. When was the due date? July 12. Possibly just before Sea Day, the annual holiday when Japanese people go to the sea, which is celebrated on the third Monday in July.

Japanese doctors, not wanting to be inconvenienced, encourage delivery exactly on the calculated due date, using, if necessary, a hormone that induces contractions and forces deliveries right on time—as in during office hours. Either Rie's mother would come prior to the due date to help out or Rie would spend the last days of her pregnancy in her childhood home in Niigata, under her watchful care.

A night's rest seemed to clear up any reservations Rie had experienced regarding motherhood. Alpha had never seen her so contented, except possibly on their honeymoon. Her time had come to experience her own *wa* (harmony).

11

Surprise Relatives

The reality of having to get back to work tempered the excitement of the upcoming birth. During their absence more than 10 pages of faxes had come in from New Morning Star, all of which needed Alpha's immediate attention. The company was sending out inquiries all over the English-speaking world, including Australia, New Zealand, Singapore, Canada, and America, offering their services and expertise as a trading company seeking both to export Japanese products and import foreign products into Japan. While a trading company adds costs, generally around three to six percent, to a transaction, they also add value. Being on the inside, they help foreign firms overcome many of the invisible trade barriers. And for smaller Japanese companies seeking to export, they could offer introductions abroad, provide trust, and guarantee timely payment. Alpha himself was being relied upon as one of the company's main bridges—if not its only bridge—to the international community.

Word had come regarding the arrival of the American-made pachinko machines from GEM Enterprises. After a customs broker paid the import duty for Shinkinsei, the machines cleared customs at Narita and would soon be transported by enclosed truck to a warehouse less than a half hour away, with only about one additional hour to Tokyo. The town of Sakura had followed other towns in taking advantage of a bowling boom of the sixties and seventies. Then most had gone out of business as the fad had faded. Former bowling alleys had been converted for other commercial uses, and the one in Sakura was being used primarily as a warehouse.

The rent and other overhead were much less for this area, which was still largely rural, although it served as a bedroom town for those commuting to the Tokyo metropolitan area. The company in Sakura also provided a small service area where boxed goods could be unpacked, containers too large for the narrow Japanese roads could be broken down into smaller units, and the GEM machines could be converted to Japanese voltage. The converted machines would remain there for a few weeks until the American bases requested their installation.

The influx of faxes proved to be just a foretaste of things to come. More and more documents were arriving daily, and the deadlines were getting shorter. Nevertheless, the income from Shinkinsei was steady, predictable, and more than adequate. And almost all of the translating could be done from home. Alpha was glad to avoid the typical hour-and-forty-minute commute each way that Japanese workers on average have to endure.

With the system of socialized medicine in Japan, if the correct diagnoses are made, treatment, while tedious, is usually of high quality. A pregnancy typically requires check-ups at two-week intervals. Japan boasts about half the infant mortality rate of America and is ranked as one of the top five countries in the world in this regard. In most areas of Japan foreigners are allowed and even required to enter the National Citizens Medical Plan. Compared to soaring medical costs in America, quality care can be accessed by the average citizen at a very affordable rate. Higher salaried earners pay more into the health system, in effect subsidizing the lower wage earners.

Babies were now very affordable in Japan, and financial incentives were being discussed in the Japanese Diet to encourage a higher birth rate. Maybe, in the very near future, the Japanese government would even pay women to have babies. Colleges have closed because of the serious decline in students.

Generally customer confidentiality is maintained by all quality companies. However, this doesn't preclude putting out on the table a list of one's customers, as long as private and confidential information about them isn't shared. One day a fax arrived from the company providing the historical background of Shinkinsei— New Morning Star Enterprises—including a list of its customers and a timeline.

Translating this into English would demonstrate to foreign firms that this was no upstart company but an established firm that had done significant business with numerous firms for more than 40 years. Since names of people and companies in Japanese often have more than one pronunciation possibility, Alpha would need Rie's assistance to confirm the correct reading on the Internet.

In deference to her health he decided to begin by doing as much as possible by himself while she napped. The list wasn't lengthy, including around 200 firms. Alpha didn't get far into it, however, before he was caught off guard. About the tenth or twelfth firm listed was called the Good Hour, located in Niigata City. New Morning Star Enterprises appeared to be the firm scheduled to supply pachinko machines to Alpha's father-in-law's parlor. There was evidently some association, some esoteric connection, between Kanagawa-san and his colleagues at New Morning Star Enterprises and the Nakata family. Maybe it was only business, and maybe this was just coincidental. Alpha didn't know whether his discovery of this fact had been intentional.

Rie slept for over an hour, felt a bit better and was able to assist Alpha with some of the more difficult company names, especially in finding the correct usage for those names that had alternative readings. She didn't think much about the association between her father's business and New Morning Star Enterprises. "In Japan, you are very limited as to who you can make major purchases from," she told Alpha. And in Niigata there probably weren't any other possibilities. "What difference does it make, at any rate, who my father bought his pachinko machines from?" Her voice, usually pleasant, manifested an irritated undertone.

For the first time in their married life, Alpha had doubts about what his wife was telling him. He had the impression she was addressing him on the tatamae (external) level, the "What do you want to hear?—and that's what I'll tell you" type of response typical of the high-context nature of the language. While this would have blown right by most foreigners, Alpha, the wary TCK, was tuned in. Had Rie known previously about her father's association with New Morning Star? Or had she been raised in typical Japanese fashion: extremely naïve, with no knowledge or awareness of the family business? For the time being he decided on the latter interpretation. But he would store this lingering doubt in his memory to consider at a later and more convenient time.

Alpha had the option of faxing the translated documents or bringing them in person to New Morning Star Enterprises. The main factor was getting them there on or before the agreed upon deadline. The last time he had gone unannounced, in person, he had learned a lot. And he had in no way been reprimanded. On the contrary, he felt welcomed, almost expected. The company president, Kanagawa-san, never seemed overworked or overstressed and was always ready for visitors. Alpha respected him for this, knowing that company presidents who find the time for reflection and entertaining visitors are more likely in the long run to succeed than those who constantly overwork.

Rie was a bit cranky, and since all pending work had been completed he decided to pay another personal visit, under the pretext of bringing the translated documents. Personal delivery minimally implied greater commitment. Since he was now married into the Nakata family, and since the family had received "assistance" or osewa from New Morning Star, Alpha could use the enigmatic phrase in Japanese Osewa ni narimashita—"You have been a help to us, to our family." Then, having baited the hook, he would wait and see what type of bite he would get. He wanted to get Kanagawa-san's perspective on the relationship, if indeed there was one to talk about. That alone would be worth the train fare.

Monday morning came, and Alpha purposely waited until after 9:00 to board the train for Kabukicho. That way he could avoid the worst of the rush hour commute and arrive at New Morning Star after the initial business of the day had been conducted. Now a known and frequent visitor, he was ushered by the receptionist into the reception room where he had first met Kanagawa-san and his two cohorts, Kaneda-san and Lee-san. Today the president was alone; he appeared not only more tired and unkempt than usual but genuinely glad for Alpha's visit. While he appeared to be 15 or 20 years beyond the normal retirement age of 55, people who have held high positions in Japanese companies generally do not retire well. They have nothing to do—no hobbies and only narrow interests. So many of them, having no appealing alternatives, keep going well past their prime.

To avoid the strong black coffee, Alpha told the receptionist that Japanese green tea would be fine. After the initial formalities (which thankfully were getting shorter as Alpha was becoming better known), Alpha led off with his prepared opening line: "I see in translating these documents that you have been a help to our family in the past." The Japanese language being deliberately ambiguous made it easier to approach the subject. Kanagawa-san could choose not to respond or could provide the information Alpha was eager to learn. Either way, he wouldn't be put in a difficult position.

The president's response was forthcoming, and unexpectedly on the honne level. Probably less than 10 percent of communication in Japan occurs at this level. Nevertheless, he began: "Nearly 50 years ago Nakata-san, Rie's grandfather, was a rice farmer. Just at the time when Japan started to experience the post WWII boom, everyone was moving to the towns and cities where the factories were located. It was hard to find wives for rice farmers. They make only half the salary of what factory workers make, and the wives are required to help with the hard work during planting and harvest, and sometimes all through the growing season. It got so bad that some Japanese villages went so far to advertise, to offer monetary rewards for prospective brides who would offer to become a rice farmer's wife."

He continued, "There were not enough brides available to meet the demand, so the search went far and wide. Finally a possible spouse for Nakata-san was located, but it came from an unusual source. I was asked to be the go-between [nakodo], since she was a relative of mine—my younger sister. Although there was non-Japanese blood in her veins she was a beautiful lady, and the engagement went ahead. Photographs were exchanged, and both sides gave the green light, so the omiai [marriage interview] was set up. After that, both sides decided to proceed with the wedding, so the *omiai kekkon*, or arranged marriage, was approved. Since it was immediately after the war, Japan was still very poor. The American occupation troops were still here, and no one could afford an elaborate wedding. "We," Kanagawa-san continued pointedly, "decide to love the one we marry. That works better than marrying the one you love."

Alpha knew that in traditional Japanese marriages there is seldom much in the way of deep feeling for one another. He wondered how he and Rie would feel in five or ten more years. Marriages in most parts of the Orient are based on necessity, and love, if present at all, is an added benefit but not a requirement. He immediately wondered how the situation had been between Rie's grandparents—had they loved each other, or was theirs merely a relationship based on convenience and necessity?

This was a lot for Alpha to process in a moment's time. A person who is truly bilingual doesn't need to translate back and forth in his brain. If spoken to in Japanese, he can think and respond in Japanese without defaulting to his mother tongue. Nevertheless, in this instance Alpha found himself translating into and out of English, probably due to the emotional overload he was experiencing. There were too many far-reaching implications to sort through in one sitting. Yet Kanagawa was neither reluctant nor hesitant in his response. He was straightforward and cooperative, speaking to Alpha as directly as a father would to a son.

The first implication impacting Alpha was the fact that his own wife, Rie, wasn't pure Japanese. Not that it mattered to him. Most Americans have mixed blood; almost no one is pure anything, unless they have recently emigrated. He thought that people of mixed blood, especially females, are generally better looking, combining the best features of each race. And he was aware that intelligence studies confirm that mixed-blood people generally test out higher than average—although this may be due to upbringing and environment, the more stimulating exposure multi-cultural families enjoy, rather than genetics.

In Alpha's thinking Rie was a good example of this. At least to him, she was much more attractive than the average Japanese woman, and also more intelligent. Yet he felt somewhat betrayed. Not that it would affect his relationship with her, but this would have been nice to know prior to the engagement. He could have found out by going to the Niigata Prefecture Office Department of Records and gotten a family register for only about three dollars. But he had seen no need to do this prior to the wedding, nor would it have affected the outcome. He was in love with her, and her background had nothing to do with it.

Alpha continued thinking about the mixed blood. This almost certainly meant that Rie's grandmother was at least part Korean. He knew why many Korean women had been brought to Japan during WWII. That too was history and irrelevant. It is also something the Japanese government is understandably reluctant to talk about, nor is it quick to offer compensation for the indignities forced on the comfort women.

Finally, a thought occurred to Alpha that should have been more readily obvious. The company president, Kanagawa, wasn't only in some manner in the past a benefactor to the Nakata family but was also some type of a relative, possibly a great-uncle or even a great-great-uncle.

There are two phrases every student of the Japanese language should initially memorize. Using either or both of them, one can reply appropriately to perhaps as many as two-thirds of all questions. The first one is *"So desu ne,"* loosely translated as "Yes, I agree" or "Yes, I was aware of that" or "Yes, I already knew that." The second, resembling the first, is *"So desu ka,"* meaning "Oh, this is new information to me," "Is that so?" or "Now I get it."

Alpha, aware that the haziness of the Japanese language requires frequent feedback, found himself repeating "So desu ka"
over and over again. This was all new knowledge to him. Perhaps
even Rie knew nothing about it. But then again, maybe she did.
Determined to maintain a marriage in which shouting or arguing
would be neither desirable nor necessary nor allowed, he decided
they would discuss the matter calmly.

Trains leaving greater area Tokyo prior to 3:00 p.m. are generally not crowded. On this morning there were numerous empty
seats, and Alpha thought better when seated. A few things were
coming together, but it seemed as though for every piece of the puzzle that did fit, there were two or three additional ones that didn't.

One of the big pieces that didn't fit was the company, Shinkinsei Enterprises. With all that was going on, Alpha wasn't actively
seeking additional clients despite knowing that it's never wise to
have all one's eggs in a single basket. While he had thought the
opportunity at Shinkinsei had coincidentally fallen into his lap,
it now looked as though that might not have been the case. To
end up working for a relative, albeit it a distant one, had to be
more than coincidence. If someone had orchestrated the relationship, then who? And why? And were there ulterior motives? Alpha
wasn't aware of any deception. He had gotten accurate information whenever he'd requested it. But sometimes the real truth may
be found in that which remains unsaid.

Rie was in a better mood when he returned and had a Japanese lunch prepared. It seemed like a good time to talk, so he
asked more about her background. Yes, she admitted that her
grandmother was one hundred percent Korean. That made her
one-quarter Korean—a fact one didn't wear on her shirtsleeve in
Japan. Although anthropological evidence is scarce, along with
DNA research it points in the direction of the Japanese islands
having been originally settled by immigrants from the Korean peninsula. While the Japanese won't admit it, they all may have Korean DNA far up their ancestral ladder.

Rie's grandmother spoke good Japanese, having been both
blessed with a good language aptitude and forced to learn the lan-

guage during the Japanese occupation. She had acquired a reasonably good command of the language prior to marrying into the Nakata family and was a good wife to Rie's grandfather. Yes, Rie knew some relative ran a trading company near Shinjuku, but that was as far as it went. Rie evidently had no idea that relative and the president of Shinkeisei Enterprises were one and the same person. The Japanese aren't enthusiastic in searching out blood ties, knowing they might encounter just this kind of embarrassment. Yet Rie saw no problem with the arrangement—what difference did it make? Wasn't it even better to work for someone in the extended family than for a total stranger? And wasn't marriage with her a matter of the present, involving two people alone, separate from the previous generations? She accused Alpha of thinking too much like the Japanese. Noting her negative nonverbal feedback, he wisely opted not to pursue the subject.

Alpha again was forced to make a choice: to believe what his wife was telling him or to conclude that Rie was lying to him, that she had known at least some of the facts ahead of time and had deliberately concealed them from him. There are times, albeit rarely, even in Japanese society when the truth should be told, even at the expense of harmony. But Rie demonstrated that she was still in her innermost being Japanese, a person who would go to extremes in order to maintain harmony.

Alpha chose to side with his wife. But even in doing this he had to acknowledge that more than mere chance had brought him to New Morning Star Enterprises. Kanagawa, he reasoned, must have some long-term purpose for which Alpha might prove useful or desirable. While respecting the man's age and superior status, he determined to try to ferret out what that was.

12

A Meaningful Visit

With faxes arriving daily, Alpha didn't have to wait long to seek an occasion for another audience with Kanagawa. As the volume expanded due to some inquiries from the States, five to six hours daily were now required to keep up with the work. Some days there was very little to do, while others required eight to ten hours. Alpha became better acquainted with the range of products Shinkinsei Enterprises was handling: they included Chinese-made household appliances, pachinko machines, and arcade games made by South Korean manufacturers.

Initially resisted by the Japanese market due to quality issues, improved quality and some lingering effects of the recession meant that housewives were beginning to purchase cheaper foreign-made products. Even if they lasted only half as long as similar products manufactured in Japan, at half the price these goods appealed to the Japanese mindset of always wanting the latest model. And GATT, the General Agreement on Trade and Tariffs, was having some effect in opening up the Japanese domestic market to foreign goods. At any rate, household domestic products were usually discarded long before they had broken down, becoming victims to newer technology in the hyper-consumer Japanese economy. Japanese products, including their automobiles, are discarded long before necessary. Older though functional products have no place in Japanese society.

With the increased volume of work, responsibility demanded that Alpha keep in touch with the company home base. As usual, he would use the ambiguity of the Japanese language to try to get Kanagawa to express more of his thinking, as well of more of where he—and hence Alpha—was going, a question with sufficient vagueness that Kanagawa could take it and run in any direction he pleased.

Arriving again one morning a little after 10:00, Alpha was ushered in with the usual courtesies, although both he and the receptionist knew there was no real meaning attached to them. They were just part of the tatemae, the lubrication that keeps Japanese society well oiled. Kanagawa appeared to have everything in control, with the exception of his appearance. He looked even a bit more tired and disheveled than the last time Alpha had seen him. And Alpha's initial impressions remained intact: Kanagawa simply lacked an appearance that could be significantly improved by a nice suit.

There were two other visitors, so Alpha was instructed to wait. They looked like normal Japanese businessmen, both middle aged. The younger of the two, Alpha noted almost immediately, was missing the tip of his pinky finger on his left hand. In less than 10 minutes they left, and Kanagawa motioned for Alpha to join him in his office rather than in the reception room, allowing for greater privacy and intimacy. Alpha was ready to use his baited question, but this didn't prove necessary. Kanagawa wanted to talk.

He started off shooting straight: "I am actually not a Japanese citizen. My older brother, my younger sister, and I came to Japan together, as there was no work and nothing to eat at the time in Korea. I got to know your grandfather [by this he meant Rie's grandfather] when the arranged marriage with my younger sister was decided. To present a better appearance we went through soshi kaimei and changed our name from Kim [kane, gold or wealth] to Kanagawa, adding the second character *gawa* [river]. Soon after my younger sister married into the Nakata family they fell on hard times when their land was taken from them because of the expressway coming in, and they had no means of livelihood. I contacted some of my friends, and with their help they opened the first pachinko parlor in Niigata City. Now his son, your father-in-law, continues on with the business. He takes care of his obligations each month, and there is enough left over for them to live in comfort."

Alpha wondered what Kanagawa meant by "taking care of his obligations each month." Somehow he sensed that this implied more than paying off his bills; it probably had something to do with giri, some obligation incurred that required periodic financial payments. Alpha, wanting desperately to ask to whom these payments were made, restrained himself.

Kanagawa continued in a somber tone. "For more than a month I have not been feeling well, and the doctor tells me I have pancreatic cancer. I didn't have any symptoms until recently, and now I am told that it cannot be treated. I do not look forward to going to my ancestors, but I know I must make this trip. In fact, it won't even help me at this stage to give up smoking. It is too late for that now. I will have to have a seat in the smoking section in the afterlife. Next time I change my name it will be a *kaimyoo*" (according to Japanese Buddhism, a posthumous name a temple gives to a deceased person, who becomes a Buddha upon his death).

Alpha appreciated this deft attempt at humor, but the graveness of the situation precluded a humorous response. Japanese temples, inconsistent with pure Buddhism but fully consistent with capitalism, award better names to those who make bigger contributions. Originally, this was similar to a new Christian baptismal name given to those who formally embrace the faith. Consisting of two characters, it denotes the deceased person's rank.

But people who contribute substantially to the temple are often rewarded with additional characters and the higher rank that accompanies them. Recent price gouging by some temples have shocked families of the deceased by charging bills of several million yen (in the range of $50,000). The average cost of a funeral in

Japan is roughly four times that of the US, around $30,000. And some Buddhist temples, especially those in California, have begun awarding (or more literally selling) kaimyoo prior to one's death, in a manner similar to last rites performed in the Catholic tradition, before the person expires.

Kanagawa smiled while he told Alpha he had found a loophole. Since he had a tarnished record, he had found an entrepreneurial temple that started selling *seizen-kaimyo* a lot more cheaply, for under a thousand dollars. *Seizen* means "before one's death," so a seizen-kaimyo amounts to a kaimyoo given while one is still alive. These come with the guarantee and assurance that they've been properly prayed over and are thus legitimate insofar as Japanese Buddhism is concerned.

However, there are five conditions, having to do with not killing, stealing, committing adultery, lying, or committing certain other crimes. Alpha wondered why the Japanese would be completely unobservant of these infringements while alive and make a serious effort only during their final days of life. "So I need to wait a little longer, to take care of some unfinished business. The people of Japan cannot afford to die—that is why they have the longest life spans in the world." Nakagawa chuckled as he showed Alpha a white piece of paper with some brush writing. The combination of rare Chinese characters and the artistic nature of the brush writing meant that Alpha could make out only what one of them meant. Here was Kanagawa's seizen-kaimyo. Alpha noticed that it had three characters.

The bane of every translator is the need that sometimes arises to translate humor across two different cultures. Nevertheless, Alpha thought Kanagawa's quip would make sense in both cultures. He came to respect him more than he had before—this dying man who in some way could make a joke about his journey to *ohigan*, the other shore. The Japanese in reality lack any concrete conceptions about life after death. All other things being equal, they would just as soon jettison the whole idea of an afterlife. For one thing, the prospect sounds both expensive and time consuming, with no tangible benefits on this side. The Buddhist *hooji*, memorial masses for the dead, are to be conducted periodically—7 and 49 days after one's death, respectively—then yearly and at 49 years. Sake is drunk at these services, and a typical Buddhist priest may conduct several of these daily. If they're held without much time in between, inebriation sets in after the third or fourth service.

Kanagawa continued, "We would like you to think about taking a more active role. For two generations the Nakata family has not been blessed with any male children; your wife's siblings are both girls. And we don't have any living children. My wife had a very difficult pregnancy and gave premature birth to a baby boy. He weighed less than two kilograms [4.4 pounds], was very weak, and succumbed to pneumonia four days after he was born. Three years after that my wife contracted tuberculosis. During the war there was a shortage of medication, and she died during the Occupation. Now my closest living heirs are those of the Nakata family. And I'm running out of time."

Alpha felt a surge of simultaneous emotions covering a wide range. Chief among them was pity for this man whose days were numbered, who, in spite of the material success he'd carved out, was strangely empty and alone. The Japanese call this feeling *kodoku*. If they were to describe hell they wouldn't refer to fire and brimstone. Rather, kodoku would top the list, signifying solitude and isolation—a person all alone. The concept is that of being deprived of the key ingredient of one's self-image, the collectiveness that holds together Japanese society.

Kanagawa's only attempt to alleviate these feelings of anxiety and monophobia had to do with waiting for the proper time—the last possible moment—to buy a kaimyoo. Whatever the people of Japan think about the afterlife, it isn't something they look forward to in the positive sense that Christians anticipate heaven. The national trait of self-reliance, or *ji-riki* ("self strength," as opposed to grace, or *ta-riki*), doesn't seem to have much relevance as one's body weakens. Only negatives apply—one is robbed of his own strength, relieved of his ability to work, and devoid of any productive existence in the economic sense.

The Japanese can't imagine an afterlife in which anything, including *being*, is more important than *doing*. Death is viewed in a stoical, passive way. At best it's an unwelcome intruder, no matter how old one is. Alpha continued to feel a range of contradictory emotions; on one side he felt used by this sick man who had very limited alternatives. But he also felt pride and gratitude, knowing that Kanagawa hadn't come to these conclusions easily. And Kanagawa had opted for Alpha.

Concerned about his own legal status in Japan, Alpha asked, "What about my visa?" No sooner were the words out of his mouth than he knew the question needn't have been asked. "Visas are no problem for us," Kanagawa replied. Koreans raised in Japan and denied full citizenship status by the Japanese government know every aspect about obtaining visas.

Ordinarily in Japanese, when one responds with "I will think about it," the implication is a polite refusal. Alpha had encountered other situations in translating when Americans had mistakenly construed this as a positive response. He had to think for a moment about how to respond in Japanese in a manner that implied he would really, honestly, seriously think about it. Sometimes, especially when clarity is desired, the ambiguous nature of the language is a drawback.

Theoretically a foreign son-in-law, according to Japanese law, could be adopted into his wife's family as a son, assume the wife's family name and carry on from there. Sons-in-law, in fact, when there were no male heirs, were not infrequently adopted into the wife's family, assuming her family name. Referred to as *mukooyoshi*, the man selected to be married and adopted into the family is chosen for his ability to run the family business.

Mukooyoshi is practiced when there is no suitable male heir to preserve the family business and name. Numerous Japanese companies with common household names like Suzuki, Canon, Kikkoman (soy sauce), and Toyota have all adopted this practice. It's usually considered an honor to be selected for this role. But all of that maneuvering might not favorably posture a person for Japanese citizenship. Alpha didn't think that issue was on the table. At any rate, citizenship was probably unnecessary on account of his Japanese wife.

If Alpha's take on the situation were correct, Kanagawa wanted him to take over the business, was in fact offering him the leading role in Shinkinsei Enterprises, that of the *shacho* or company head. He was familiar with a book written by a second- or third-generation Japanese author in Hawaii on being an entrepreneur, as opposed to working for the other guy all of one's life. It had been required reading for one his courses in international business. Alpha had found this book, titled *Rich Dad, Poor Dad*, credible and had developed a personal dream of eventually becoming an international businessman. His interpreting was a steppingstone to that goal, and now this offer might be another road to the same end. At any rate, Alpha felt honored that Kanagawa would go to such lengths, with such clarity and directness, to groom him for this position.

It's a valid stereotype that Japanese companies dominate the lives of their employees.

But there's a trade-off: the company often becomes something like a surrogate father to them, at the expense of the employee being able to fulfill his role in his own family. The intimacy craved but never experienced between father and son is later sublimated by the "son's" giving his all to the company. The company in turn takes care of him, finding him a wife if necessary and handling a whole array of other personal affairs. This complicated relationship—becoming highly dependent on the company with the company in turn meeting all the personal needs of the employee—typifies amae.

While no one fully understands the dynamics of amae, it goes something like this. When a baby is born it separates from its mother, becoming independent, both physically and psychologically. In the West mothers encourage this new human to become less and less dependent, to stand on its own two legs. In the East, and particularly in Japan, mothers' child rearing practices are aimed at making the child re-dependent. So the child is indulged, coddled, protected from pain and provided with every creature comfort imaginable. The mother sends out a clear message: "I'll give you everything you need; the only thing I ask in exchange is your total devotion." Stated otherwise, in exchange for me, your mother, providing for your needs, I need you to always be there for me."

As the male child grows and becomes a man, he transfers this maternalistic dependency to his company. True, the company will look after him pretty much as his mother did, but it will also demand the same degree of devotion and commitment in return. Alpha, in true TCK fashion, would never quite be able to think in these terms. A company, no matter how much appeal it has, is, he reasoned, in the final analysis just a company. Alpha considered that, over time, at least 99.9 percent of any company's products end up in the junkyard. He found it hard to be so devoted to something that produced products destined for the scrap heap.

Yet Alpha was overwhelmed by his ambivalent and complicated feelings for Kanagawa. On the one hand he saw an old man, deteriorating and depreciating rapidly, with nothing to show for his life other than some wealth and a small company. Obviously he was a highly disciplined and self-sacrificing person who had not come by his limited wealth easily. While death seemed to him at this point of life like a distant visitor, Alpha wondered how someone with so much business and planning ability could come to the end of his life without planning for the inevitable. But the most prominent emotion Alpha was sensing was that of compassion, verging on pity. It was as though Kanagawa were saying to him, "Won't you be my son? Even at this late date, in the sunset years of my life, will you become to me the son I never had?"

Kanagawa continued to reveal more of his heart. "In the past I've committed a few indiscretions." Again the ambiguity of the language made it difficult to know exactly what he meant. Usually such talk would have sexual connotations. But it was clear he didn't mean some two-hour visit to a nearby hot sheet hotel. Kanagawa's office was in the red light district, and such places he was no doubt more than accustomed to. Rather, he seemed to be implying some business decisions he had made in the past that were still bothering him. "I will clean all of this up before my *ohigan* [visit to the opposite shore]." Alpha's reticence, his ambivalent feelings toward Kanagawa, melted away before the humble appeal of this desperate man.

On the train back to Shakujikoen, Alpha thought of the Japanese maxim "Don't be afraid of a blind snake." As long as he could become the eyes, the new vision for the company, he reasoned that he would have nothing to fear. The wishes of a dying man are held in high esteem in Japan; some people even believe bad luck will ensue if they aren't carried out.

Rie had more reservations. She didn't want an absentee husband, and working with a Japanese company on that level usually entailed long hours on the job. On the other hand, the days of receiving a monthly retainer from Shinkinsei Enterprises now appeared to be numbered and would probably cease with the death, or even the incapacity, of her distant uncle Kanagawa.

Better income would enable Alpha and Rie to eventually purchase a house. Even where they now lived a starter home could cost around half a million dollars; anything with more substance might be double that. Most younger Japanese people have given up the thought of owning their own house. If they don't inherit it, they can't reasonably anticipate saving enough for a purchase. Instead they spend their discretionary funds on travel, new automobiles, and other toys. The only other alternative for Alpha would be moving further away from Tokyo, forcing a one-way commute approaching two hours—a recipe for burnout and karoshi (death from overwork).

So with trepidation, but nevertheless with the optimism only youth can muster—untempered by the personal experience of hardship or adversity—they decided to go along with Kanagawa's wishes. No capital investment was required. That was a moot point anyway, as Alpha and Rie had no capital to invest. So now, instead of working out of his apartment, Alpha would have a one-hour commute—well less than average for the Japanese. The first day of this new arrangement would be Monday of the following week—October 10, beginning at 10:00 a.m.

Alpha, while not superstitious, half believed that good things come in threes; the three tens that make up October 10 at 10, he mused, might be more than coincidental. He took this so far as to conjecture that God might be blessing his endeavors. Rie certainly thought so, especially since she was enamored with the idea of her husband carrying on a relative's business. Certainly Providence was smiling down on them.

The weekend came, the weather was decent and the maples were beginning to don their fall colors. They decided to buy a couple of *obentoos* and eat out. This was their private joke—for most people eating out meant an expensive meal; for Alpha and Rie, it meant eating a cheap meal outside. They would walk down to the park, sit on the bench by the pond, watch the turtles, eat their packaged lunches and return before dark. Most of the time Rie felt pretty well, especially by the late morning.

"Alpha," Rie asked without preamble, "Do you want a boy or a girl?"

Alpha replied without hesitation: "Both!" "Twins?" asked Rie, somewhat incredulous. "No, triplets!" Whatever the gender, the joy of greeting a new life they had created together made them feel as though nothing could go wrong.

Monday came. Alpha knew the train schedule by heart and could time his arrival at Shinkinsei Enterprises pretty closely. Nevertheless, impatience took over, and he arrived nearly 15 minutes early (too early to go in). So he decided to walk around the Kabukichoo neighborhood. It became obvious that much of the activity was devoted to mizushobai, the entertainment industry, including numerous bars and not a few hot sheet hotels. He felt revulsion at the appearance of men in their sixties walking around with short-skirted girls in their twenties and thirties. To be sure, these young women were gold diggers, but Alpha felt they earned every bit of their compensation. This was Japan, and in Japan money is about the only thing that speaks loudly. Many wealthier businessmen retain the same companions for years, keeping them in tow with an apartment, spending money and gifts. But this was still early morning in Kabukicho, and the neighborhood was still waking up from whatever sleep had been afforded it the previous evening.

Just before 10 Alpha walked into Shinkinsei. Kanagawa ushered him into the meeting room. Again the receptionist brought out a hot oshibori, followed by coffee for both. Kanagawa looked, if anything, more tired and unkempt than previously. He began by stating directly, "Soon I will be gathered to my ancestors. I am getting all of my affairs in order so I can depart this world in peace. So I have already purchased a pretty good kaimyoo. Your coming to Japan was not as accidental as you may think. The Japanese student who planted in your mind the seed to come to Japan is the son of a colleague of mine. We paid him 100,000 yen to persuade you to come here. We were looking for a person with good Japanese and good entrepreneurial skills. So we set it up for you to come here. We arranged all the events so you could work first at Kyowa Shoji Company, meet Rie, and then work for us. You made it much easier by marrying her, which we had hoped might happen. Now you are a part of our family."

Alpha listened intently. He had the uncanny sensation that Kanagawa was reading his mind, anticipating every thought, question, and concern. Kanayama-san continued: "Being in the family now means that everyone will accept you as the natural successor in my company. We put you on the payroll a few months ago, not so much for the fact that we needed you then but because we wanted to confirm that you are a hard worker. And we wanted you to get accustomed to working for us. We wanted to keep it that way for a couple of years, but my health no longer affords me the luxury of proceeding slowly. I may have as little as six months left. Even less if I don't quit smoking. Your role as the new president will be to transition the company from being a *kigyo shatei* [literally, a "little brother" company, a front company for the yakuza] into a bona fide business. We now have enough sales and established accounts to be a completely clean company. Can we count you in?"

There was enough of the TCK in Alpha that he knew not to answer directly. All he could come up with was "I deeply appreciate your offer, and I will talk it over with Rie." This, Alpha recognized somewhat after the fact, was a decidedly non-Japanese response. Even though all Japanese men would have to talk over such important matters with their wives, they would be extremely reluctant to admit so in front of other men.

To the uninitiated Westerner such responses come across as dishonest, deceiving and misleading. In a cohesive, group-oriented society, however, harmony is always valued above truth. A person skilled in interpersonal relationships will have to use these dynamics to his advantage.

Alpha wanted to find out how much Rie knew about her great-uncle, as well as how much incentive, if any, had been offered her to go along with the entire arrangement. He wondered whether Rie was just a pawn in the hands of her parents and uncle. Or was she naïve, unaware of the family background or of her family's yakuza connections? But he wondered most pointedly about his marriage. Was Rie really in love with him, or was their marriage based not on true love but on convenience, something to promote the family business?

One secret to a successful marriage is for the couple to know how to fight, how to do so fairly, and then when to bury the axe. Early that evening, shortly after dinner, the confrontation began. Alpha asked Rie, "Why didn't you tell me about your background, your great-uncle, his past, and all the background of Kyowa Shoji?"

Rie's answer was short and pointed: "I didn't know." Filled with the skepticism that is invariably a part of the TCK personality, Alpha found it hard to believe that his otherwise street-smart wife could be so naïve regarding her family affairs.

Her response continued: "I thought you loved me for myself, for who I am, apart from my family connections. Whatever kind of relatives I have or don't have doesn't matter." Alpha was taken aback to hear such an untypical Japanese response. But in his heart he knew she was right. As least insofar as his thinking was concerned—DNA, pure Japanese or otherwise, didn't really matter.

"Did you go along with the setup?" Alpha asked. "What setup?" "When you were conveniently set up as the receptionist, with the additional responsibility of looking after my welfare and orienting me to the company?"

Marriage counselors will tell you that one of the rules for arguing is that you don't use loaded terms that push the interpretation of the situation further than it should go. Rie didn't appreciate Alpha's use of the term "setup." It made her feel used, degraded, conniving.

Rie's reply was a suitable tit for tat: "Did you go along with the setup when you were in Hawaii and they told you about the 'job' teaching English? Or when you first went to Shinkinsei Enterprises and came home with 350,000 yen?" "I had nothing to do with that."

Before the situation got too emotional, reason began to prevail. Both came to the realization that the circumstances weren't pitting one against the other, husband against wife or vice versa, but that both had to some extent made free choices that appeared in retrospect to have been orchestrated by others. Alpha had willingly returned to Japan, had freely made the transition interpreting for Rie's relative at Shinkinsei Enterprises, and had freely married Rie. He regretted none of these choices. The same was true for her.

Alpha thought back to his first college philosophy class and discussions there regarding free will. If there is a god, or a higher intelligence ordering our affairs thorough providence, can we make genuinely free choices? While not wanting to press the analogy too far, he realized that both sides of the equation could be true. He had fallen in love and married Rie based on his own free choice—no one had coerced him in any way. And if other people, or a providential higher power, were responsible for orchestrating this, he should neither harbor any regret nor conclude that his free will had been diminished.

After these confrontational moments the two, spurred by the love that had brought them together as husband and wife, kissed and made up. They were now on the same page, trying together to determine why someone had gone to such lengths to bring them together and then to arrange Alpha's employment with Kyowa Shoji.

Armed with fresh insight and the backing of his wife, Alpha decided it best to grab the bull by the horns. All indications pointed to the president of Shinkinsei Enterprises, Rie's great-uncle Kanagawa, as being the instigator. So far Kanagawa had been surprisingly candid with Alpha, who believed that he, as a terminally ill man, most likely wanted to clear his name and die with a clear conscience. Perhaps the lure of money, along with other earthly desires, was fading; at any rate, Kanagawa according to his own words didn't have long—probably six months maximum and maybe a lot less.

13

Death

The Japanese, in spite of being melancholic, are resilient. Centuries of facing "the four disasters" (earthquake, fire, flood and typhoon) have forged them into a people who don't give up easily and aren't easily deterred. Even though there are strong elements of fatalism, despondency, and stoicism in their national character, when faced with a major catastrophe like the great Kobe earthquake in 1995, or the Tohoku Earthquake, tsunamai and nuclear disaster of 2011, an inner resolve awakens within them. Consequently, progress is made many times faster than in most other countries suffering similar catastrophes.

Alpha thought to himself once when translating the phrase "acts of God," "How do you put this into Japanese?" The English documents from GEM specified exemptions from responsibility for "acts of God" such as an earthquake or tsunami or the outbreak of hostilities. The Japanese, not believing in a single supreme being, use the word *fu-ka-koo-ryoku* as "a not possible to resist force."

This same temperament carries over into one's personal life as the Japanese face other irresistible forces, outcomes as inevitable as old age and death. Nevertheless, Alpha realized that all

Japanese believe in the immortality of one's being, that their degree of self-orientation precludes the thought that one day they will not be.

Second, Alpha realized that, put very simply, the Japanese believe that they are right; this basic assumption has given birth to the phrase "We Japanese," in distinction from all other classes of humanity. Correspondingly, they believe in the omnipotence of one's thoughts and feelings, that somehow an all-powerful influence is exerted over one's world. And, consistent with the Japanese mindset, the assumption is that, if we believe it, it must be true.

The Japanese have no fear of hell; they don't believe in it. Yet they continue to believe in spillover credibility regarding the afterlife. Good money will be or has already been paid for a kaimyoo (that posthumous Buddhist name), and the credibility inherent in this they believe will transfer over into their next life. The power and connections enjoyed in this life possess some continuity, implying that there will be more of the same in the life to come. Everything depends on ji-riki—one's own strength. The concept of grace—ta-riki, or someone else's strength—is foreign to them. So it was that Kanagawa, while not looking forward to death, was at the same time not overly pessimistic about the prospect. He had faced numerous obstacles in his 73 years; death was just one more to be dealt with.

Alpha's daily presence at New Morning Star Enterprises seemed to bring new life to Kanagawa. Alpha didn't know whether the progression of pancreatic cancer could be slowed down or even reversed by a positive attitude, but Kanagawa seemed at least to be holding his own. Alpha did know from the results of numerous research studies that both faith and an otherwise positive attitude reduce recovery time and improve healing.

Alpha did know that he had come to appreciate this aging country bumpkin; Kanagawa and he were bonding in a manner uncommon to most same-blood father-son relationships in Japan. Kanagawa in all but the legal sense had taken on Alpha as a son. Soon the fact that Alpha was a gaijin seemed to have been forgotten. The negative aspect was that he no longer received preferential treatment but was looked upon and treated the same as other company employees.

Politeness in the Japanese society carries with it social distance; you are polite to those who are socially superior to or distant from you, to those not in your immediate circle of friends. Soon Alpha's conversation with his fellow employees was on the informal level. It felt good to belong to a group again. While the Japanese sacrifice a lot of personal liberty for the sake of belonging, the return, the belongingness, is worth more than the payment. Alpha was beginning to feel some roots set down in a place. And he was enjoying every moment of it.

One morning came with Alpha arriving punctually. His colleagues appreciated his not pulling rank. Kanagawa, however, didn't appear in the office. Being a company president means, of course, that one needn't answer to anyone; on a few other occasions Kanagawa had been late without advance notice or any excuse after his arrival. But ordinarily in Japan even personal matters are taken care of at work and during work hours. Perhaps he'd had a doctor's appointment or picked up some medication en route to the office.

Then, just before 10:30, two policemen arrived unannounced. There had been a death several hours earlier, at around 2:00 a.m. Someone had committed suicide by jumping off a nearby love hotel in Kabukicho. Alpha immediately sensed the irony, as "four" and "death" are homonyms in Japanese. While positive identification was still pending, the police were quite sure it was Kanagawa. There was no suicide note; all that was found on the body were some business cards with his name, his wallet with 32,000 yen, some small change in his pocket, three credit cards and a partially used pack of Japanese cigarettes.

The Japanese look at suicide quite differently from Americans; in many instances they view it as a means of providing an honorable exit from this life. Rather than waiting for an illness to progress so far as to take an individual on its own terms, suicide is looked upon as honorable to accept, and even embrace death on one's own terms.

An autopsy was still mandated due to the circumstances; the man's stomach was found to contain a large amount of sedatives. While his appearance was badly distorted from the fall, there was no mistaking the fact. It was Kanagawa.

Cremation is mandated in Japan. The company secretary handled the details; a pine coffin was to be burned with the body inside. The process takes less than an hour, during which time the gathered mourners share a drink and reminisce. While beer is generally the drink of choice, in memory of Kanagawa everyone ordered sake, his favorite drink. Usually some nails in the coffin lid are not pounded down until just before the cremation. Close relatives and friends are invited to hammer in those final nails, thus sealing the coffin and symbolically acknowledging the end of the life of the loved one. Rather than attempting to make a dead body look alive, the Japanese allow themselves to be more heavily impacted by death. This approach makes the grieving process more intense, though not as long in duration.

In contrast to Christian funerals, there is no clear message of hope, or of resurrection, at a Japanese funeral. Japanese religions are often described as politeness toward possibilities. Virtually everyone in Japan is born Shinto (standing for health, wealth and happiness) but dies Buddhist (the funeral religion in Japan). No clear message is ever presented, just esoteric ritual, including Buddhist priests reciting Buddhist chants. The local temple uses the occasion to make a maximum profit.

For those who have sung a Christian hymn at a Christian funeral, the contrasts are strong and numerous. Alpha felt that much of Japanese life is summed up in the person's despondent and discouraging funeral: the cry of a departed soul forced to make a journey for which he hasn't prepared.

While pure Buddhism is supposed to guide it adherents into *muga*, or self-renunciation—the annihilation of self with the extinction of all desire—Buddhist priests ironically seize the occasion of funerals to make as much earthly profit as possible, often gouging the families of the deceased during their vulnerable moments of tens of thousands of dollars. As Kanagawa had already purchased his own kaimyoo, part of the claim of the local temple was preempted. While the cost of the funeral per se wasn't as significant, the bill still came to nearly $6,000 for a 40-minute service. Ordinarily a Buddhist temple can count on more than $12,000 from a single funeral, including the cost of a low ranking kaimyoo.

In honor of Kanagawa's passing Shinkinsei was closed for the rest of the week. During this time Alpha and Rie tried to sort things out. Her parents made the trip from Niigata to attend the funeral. At both Alpha's and Rie's insistence, they would stay one night in their daughter and son-in-law's apartment in Shakujikoen. In the Orient it is customary to refuse twice before accepting an invitation. If asked a third time, it's acceptable to accept. Alpha asked three times, insisting that his in-laws wouldn't be a burden. One night stretched into two as her parents began to feel a genuine welcome; they obviously enjoyed the break from their daily routine. The Japanese, with their work-alcoholic mentality, need some excuse to take a few days off. Kanagawa's funeral provided just such an occasion.

The foursome went out to eat sushi at the same place Alpha and Rie had gone to celebrate Alpha's new employment with Shinkinsei. While this would ordinarily have been in bad taste, the dinner conversation kept drifting back to Kanagawa's death. While it hadn't exactly been unexpected due to his terminal illness, none of the specifics seemed to fall into place. As far as any of them could determine, he hadn't been the type to frequent love hotels or keep a mistress. And he hadn't seemed to be depressed. On the contrary, his association with Alpha seemed to have afforded him a new lease on life, even if it had been short term. He wasn't the type to leave loose ends untied, and his departure had certainly left a lot of them.

While the overall suicide rate in Japan is less than that of the Scandinavian countries, it's still high for an industrialized nation. Committing suicide by jumping from a building or in front of a train isn't uncommon (there's even a special word for it—*tobiori jisatsu*, a death leap). But Kanagawa's particular suicide was out of character for him, and its timing made no sense. The sedatives found in his stomach during the autopsy presented another anomaly. A

Japanese person would want to face death on his own terms, with a clear, lucid mind.

Finally Rie voiced what probably shouldn't have been brought up: "Perhaps it wasn't suicide." At first her parents were reluctant to comment. Feeling that Alpha could now be entrusted with family secrets, however, Rie's father launched into a narrative, starting with some history of Kanagawa's trading company, which dealt with pachinko machines. He began: "The pachinko industry is almost completely controlled by the North Korean yakuza. If you want to play in that league you have to play by their rules. Kanagawa was a Korean, though born and raised in Japan. With no immediate successors or sons, he requested me to seek out someone to become his successor. We were getting tired of making our monthly payments and getting nothing in return. By our calculation we have long ago made more than sufficient payments to discharge the giri we incurred when we first tied up with them. We are no longer obligated, so we developed a plan for Rie to marry a foreigner.

"We believed that any foreigner from a significant country would be too prominent, if for no other reason than their foreignness for the yakuza, for them to come after them. So we assumed you would be safe. If anything happened to an American in Japan, even the FBI and Interpol could get involved. And with your father's previous employment at the embassy, you make even a more ideal successor. You would have a degree of safety and security that no Japanese would have. So our mutual plan—Kanagawa's and mine—was to come completely clean. Both his business and mine would become independent from the yakuza and no longer pay protection money. We now use part of the money for your retainer; with the rest we had planned to hire guards to keep the yakuza at bay. And very shortly extensive surveillance systems would have been installed at both companies. But then the unfortunate and untimely death of Kanagawa occurred."

Alpha immediately noticed that, although his father-in-law stopped short of using the word "murder," he didn't say "suicide" either. Feeling comfortable by this point in his role as son-in-law,

Alpha asked Nakata, "Do you thing the yakuza had something to do with *ojisan's* ["uncle's"] death?" Alpha didn't know much about the symptoms associated with progressing pancreatic cancer. He guessed, minimally, that they wouldn't enhance the sex drive. Nakata replied, "I just don't know. It wasn't like Kanagawa to leave something unfinished. He was a thorough and persistent person. My heart tells me he would not have committed suicide, at least not at this point. Maybe later, as death drew nearer, but not now. And he had been frugal all his life. With no children, he had few expenses. He could afford to have his own mistress if he wanted one. He would not have had to visit a love hotel. Maybe long ago, just after his wife died, but not now. He never took any drugs, but they found drugs in his stomach during the autopsy. And there was no suicide note. We just do not have any information other than the fact that his death was caused by a fall from a fifth story window."

Alpha noticed his father-in-law's change to the passive tense: not "jumped" but "fell," perhaps even suggesting "was thrown." He suggested that, as a place to begin, they obtain a full police report. Maybe they could find something in it that would indicate suicide on the one hand, or homicide on the other—and, if the latter, whether the yakuza or some other party had been involved.

After dining the two ladies decided to do some shopping together. The men would meanwhile take the Marunouchi Subway Line eight stops to the Tokyo Metropolitan Police Headquarters in Kasumigaseki, the main location of government services. They would meet back at the apartment for dinner.

Arriving at the large, wedge-shaped building in Kasumigaseki, Alpha and his father-in-law were directed by a helpful receptionist to the Record of Deaths section. Locating Kanagawa's record took less than a minute; everything was computerized, and a print from a digital record, costing 500 yen, would be available within the minute. Upon receiving it Nakata and Alpha decided to take a break and have some iced coffee (government buildings in Japan frequently feature cafeterias and sell drinks). Soon they were sipping five-dollar, six-ounce cups of coffee while looking over the material.

There was nothing new in the report, nothing beyond the time, location, and cause of death (fractured neck and internal injuries). Very likely out of respect for the family, nothing in the report overtly indicated that the death had been a suicide. Just a fall from a window from Room 5219 of a building call the Ichiban—Number One. No other person—no accomplice or companion—was mentioned. The two took the report and retraced their steps back to Kabukicho, where they had no trouble locating the Ichiban. It was one of the more prominent love hotels in the area, just four blocks from where Kanagawa had established the Shinkinsei Company.

The love hotel industry generates an estimated 30 billion dollars in income per year in Japan. While love hotels have been around since the Edo Period (1603–1867, when Japan was under the rule of the shogunate), versions have become larger and more lavish, and they have recently begun to offer food and play station types of entertainment. So a sexual encounter can lead to, or be preceded by, pleasure in other areas.

The appearance of an elderly Japanese man and a younger, taller American man going together to a love hotel might lend itself to some misleading interpretations. But Japan is a land of noninterference, a land where I indeed am *not* my brother's keeper. Check-in to such an establishment is almost totally anonymous. Photos of rooms are lit up, and if the room the patron desires is available, he merely presses the button next to it. At this point a faceless person behind a dark glass takes his money (or swipes his credit card) and hands him a key through the small hole. Nakata seemed to know what he was doing—there was no indication of surprise or discomfort on his face as he had paid the 6,000 yen and secured the key. Alpha, already trying to process a degree of shock, remained in the shadows. In all likelihood they would stay in the room for only a few minutes. Nevertheless, Alpha had the discomfiting sensation that he was somehow complicit in a crime.

Room 5219 was available. It was likely the staff had purposely avoided renting it out, as the Japanese believe that a departed person's spirit lingers around the place of death. Room 5219 was similar to Shinkinsei's office—actually on the fourth floor but designated to be on the fifth due to the similarity between the words for "four" and "death" in Japanese. As they entered the room, the garish layout was at first overpowering for Alpha. Nakata looked around with an unreadable, stoic expression.

Alpha took in a large round bed that slowly rotated, numerous mirrors on the walls and ceiling, and the ambience of an ancient Roman temple. Everything seemed to shout "Go for it. You are the master of your fate." Japanese people, including their Buddhist and Shinto priests, like the Greeks and Romans of old, see no disparity between sex and the sacred. On the contrary, sex is often looked upon as a well-deserved respite from a pilgrim's meditations. At any rate, some of the Shinto gods leave a lot to be desired; putting it mildly, most wouldn't serve as models for the celibate life.

The whole scene was repugnant to Alpha. He didn't for a moment believe these hot sheet hotels, no matter how elaborate the décor or seductive the ambience, could offer a quality substitute for the true love and dedicated sex between a husband and wife. While not having been married for long, he at least felt that the real was better than the contrived. He felt a tinge of sadness for the male population of Japan, these misguided men who were not content within the sacred bounds or bonds of marriage.

There was large plasma screen TV on the wall with a Play Station Four hooked up to it. The bathroom was perhaps the most opulent and decadent accouterment, featuring a large, circular and transparent bathtub large enough for two, as well as the inevitable mirrors on the walls.

They proceeded to the casement style window with a crank at the bottom. There was a screen fixed on the inside, with six hand tabs, three down each side that could easily be removed. Looking out the window, the pair could all too readily visualize the unobstructed path of a falling body hurtling toward the concrete. The room had no other view than that of an alley that would almost certainly be deserted in the early morning hours. Alpha realized with a slight intake of breath that the distance was more than 40 feet to the concrete below. There was no sign of the impact of a body, and it appeared that they had nothing additional to learn from their visit. The pair had established the fact that a person could easily have removed the screen and leapt to their death. They also noted how easy it would have been for someone else to take a body of the diminutive stature of Kanagawa, throw it out the window and disappear within a moment's time.

Less than 15 minutes had passed since they had entered the room. Both understood that there was no point in lingering. They would go from Kabukicho back to the apartment in Shakujikoen. It being after 3:30 and the beginning of rush hour, this would mean that both of them would have to stand all the way. Most Japanese males don't give up their subway seats easily, believing that as men they have priority, often to the point of stubbornly occupying their seat with a pregnant woman or elderly person standing nearby. Alpha was feeling exhausted from the stress of the day; his father-in-law, on the other hand, if he was tired betrayed no sign.

14

The In-Laws Visit

Disembarking from the train, Nakata expressed a desire to purchase a drink for the evening. He and Alpha stopped at the *sakaya*, a local liquor store on the south side of the train station, and walked the rest of the way to Alpha's apartment with two six packs of Asahi Lite, a large bottle of sake, and a smaller bottle of Johnnie Walker Double Black. Alpha was painfully aware that the evening promised to be a long one. While he didn't dislike the taste of sake, he preferred genuine wines made from grapes: a good white Zinfandel or Riesling or even a red—possibly a Merlot, which was about the only affordable red in Japan. Rice wine to an oenophile isn't really wine. Instead of fruit, rice starch has been fermented, converting it to sugars that in turn ferment into alcohol. Alpha hoped Rie had some genuine wine on hand; otherwise he'd have to be very careful. He knew he stood no chance drinking one on one with Nakata. But tonight it looked as though it would be the Japanese way. Sake typically contains about 20 percent alcohol, and sometimes even more, which means that it's about twice as potent as table wine made from grapes.

Rie washed the rice for dinner, let it soak for 20 minutes and turned on the rice maker. Her mother broiled some fish, purchased fresh from the supermarket. Miso soup took only minutes to make from the concentrate. Seven or eight other small dishes were set out, including pickled plums and egg plant, some seaweed paste and some dried seaweed and sesame seeds to sprinkle over the rice. Another sozai meal, with all the basics and extensive variety, yet not labor intensive to prepare.

While Rie's mother drank only green tea with the meal, her father began with the Asahi. In Japan the custom is to fill each other's glasses—in fact, not only to fill them but also to keep them full, replenishing them each time they're half drained. This custom is a sign of mutual trust and acceptance. Alpha purposely kept his father-in-law's glass full. By the end of the meal, with two beers and two cups of sake down him, Nakata was loosening up. When the Japanese reach this state, they often switch from tatemae to hone, revealing the deep secrets of their heart.

Nakata wanted to talk about family history: his distaste for the strong-armed tactics of the Tanaka government, the loss of the family farm, the need to find an alternative means of livelihood in pachinko, his indebtedness and the obligation the family had incurred when borrowing to set up the Good Hour. Japan hasn't yet fully recovered from a bank crisis involving bad loans on property. Most of this property was insufficiently secured and used by the yakuza as a means of raising money—borrowing funds with inadequate collateral secured only by the overinflated prices of land. Frequently the interest rates were below two percent, not much different from the inflation rate, resulting in almost free capital for the borrower.

But the Nakatas' case had been different: with the pachinko had come yakuza-backed loans, loans that in practice could never be paid back. In the 30 years since the opening of the Good Hour, Nakata had repaid the equivalent loan value nearly four times over, with no end in sight. In a culture with no concept of grace and forgiveness, giri is strongly avoided, as payback terms are ambiguous. In fact, the unwritten understanding is that, in reality there can be no payback. Once in, once obligated, there is no extradition except by death. One has no recourse to leave the organization, although that's exactly what Nakata and Kanagawa had been in the process of attempting when Kanagawa's untimely death had intervened.

Alpha voiced the pertinent—and all too evident—question, "So does this comprise a possible motive for Kanagawa's death?" "Yes," replied his father-in-law without hesitation. "And a means?" "Yes. The yakuza, unless they want to make a strong statement, generally use means that make the deaths look accidental. A person dies from an overdose, falls from a window, or has a heart attack. Nakata could have been drugged anywhere prior to the time of death, brought to the Ichiban and tossed out the window. No one there would ever admit to seeing anything, even if they did."

Alpha pressed on: "Why wouldn't they just let him die? His days were numbered; he couldn't have had long to live."

Nakata replied, "Unlike you Americans, who believe in a god who metes out justice after death, we Japanese look at the situation differently. We cannot let a person go to his grave un-avenged; that's why the theme of revenge is so strong in the Japanese culture, in literature, and in movies. Since there is no powerful or moral god to do it for us, we are obliged to do it ourselves, during the lifetime of the perpetrator. Otherwise, there would be no meaning to the death; we would be letting someone off the hook by allowing them to go to their grave without due punishment.

"From the yakuza's standpoint, Kanagawa was guilty of trying to leave the organization. With our background influenced by Confucianism, with its strong tradition of loyalty, it is inconceivable to do something against the wishes of the oyabun or the Organization as a whole. And the worst thing that could happen in the eyes of the Organization, if my interpretation is correct, would be to let him die a natural death. I may be in the same boat as he. I was his confidant and employee for all these years."

The story of the 47 ronin flashed into Alpha's mind. More than 300 years earlier 47 samurai (46 actually—the youngest had been just a messenger and was forgiven due to his youth) who had lost their master (Asano) devised a plan to bring revenge on Kira, the samurai whose arrogant behavior had caused the whole incident.

The plot to avenge took two years to fulfill; when it was successfully completed, all 46 were required to commit harakiri or *seppuku*. To the Japanese this true story is the prime example of the bushido—the samurai code of ethics—with its stresses on loyalty, sacrifice, persistence and honor.

Alpha was distraught. Minimally, this meant that he, Alpha, was implicated in an overall plan in which his father-in-law and wife's great-uncle were in collusion. And he was coming to understand, too, that his parents-in-law still thought of him as a foreigner. He hated it when the Japanese say "we Japanese" or "you Americans." This inherent mindset is something no amount of language study, degree of familiarity with the culture, or amount of fluency in the language can alleviate.

The three salient aspects of crime—motive, means, and opportunity—were all present. The motive was certainly there: violating an inviolate rule, trying to leave the Organization and breaking free of its *kasuri*—the kickbacks—or the *moriryo*—the protection money that in effect only protects one from his "own" yakuza.

The opportunity too was present—a lonely, sick old man seeking company, someone to talk to, even in the context of that being provided by a Mama-san at a local bar. In all probability a local Mama-san had been adequately compensated to make sure Kanagawa hadn't left before he was duly under the influence, either of alcohol or, more likely, of alcohol in conjunction with barbiturates. Once the old man was drunk, a little sleeping medicine would have worked synergistically with the alcohol, and there would have been no fight left in Kanagawa. One inebriate carrying another around in Japan is so common a sight that no one pays any attention to it. The fifth-story window of the Ichiban had quite clearly provided the means. Suicide from a love hotel isn't at all uncommon.

When Americans visit Japan they are invariably surprised by the disproportionately high number of small bars in Japanese cities. Streets are roped off as inebriated individuals become too great a risk for traffic. On weekend evenings train station employees get ready to clean up the vomit and attempt to deal with all of the men who have fallen asleep on the benches and missed the last train home. The bar districts feature literally hundreds of bars; some buildings have several floors with numerous bars on each one.

Generally the bars in one major area—the mizushobai district, near a train station—have one mama-san each, as well as two or three attractive hostesses who in addition to the Japanese may be Philipino, Thai, Vietnamese or Cambodian. Frequent patrons have their own bottles of whiskey reserved for private consumption. This arrangement gives them bragging rights when they go for a drink with an acquaintance. They use their diamond rings to scratch a line on the glass bottle for a visual record of the amount consumed.

The mama-san's and hostesses' main goal is to rack up as high a bar bill as possible. She pours her patron a drink and then without his permission pours one for herself, in effect doubling the bar bill in one stroke. If a cigarette is brought out, she is quick on the draw to light it. If there is any complaint with life in general, she is the one who will listen and offer words of comfort and consolation—an instant enabler. While this is an expensive form of personal confirmation, Japanese men, especially those whose doting mothers have passed away or aren't psychologically present, look to the mama-sans as surrogate mothers. And they in turn play this role to a tee. While their affection, attention, and confirmation tend to be even more indulgent than those of a biological mother, they don't come with a low price tag. The tab for a company president and two or three employees can quickly extend from several hundred dollars to thousands. Such is the price Japanese men are willing to pay for surrogate motherhood, allowing them to retain their personal but immature illusions of power, of being right and of being irresistible.

When a man is already in an inebriated condition, any other sedative type drugs that are ingested have a synergistic effect on the central nervous system. In combination with alcohol they vastly enhance the effect of both. In such a condition Kanagawa would have offered no resistance to being taken to a love hotel and thrown out a window; he would, indeed, have been completely unaware of his impending doom.

Americans tend to soften death's blow by making the dead person look alive, by embalming, hiring a good undertaker, using funeral homes with reduced UV lighting (so the blood in the veins isn't prominent) and purchasing an elaborate casket. Not fully impacted by the reality of death, adjustment can take months and years.

Japanese law, in contrast, mandates cremation, and for this a simple cardboard or pine casket is adequate. Just before the body is inserted in the crematory oven, relatives and friends are invited to drive the final nails into the coffin. This is in no way considered to be impolite or insensitive. In fact, in a real way it's a more realistic response than the Western approach, amounting to a public declaration that the life of the loved one has ended. It's a quicker, sharper acknowledgment of death, while perhaps being initially more painful, ultimately allowing for a smoother readjustment. If it weren't for the Buddhist priests and their excessive fees for the *kaimyoo* and memorial services, Japanese funerals would require only a fraction of the cost of American ones.

Select members of the staff of Shinkinsei, along with Rie, Alpha and the Nakatas, visited the crematory. They were ushered into a small tatami room where both beer and sake were offered. Out of respect for Kanagawa, they drank Sapporo beer and Gekkeikan, the beer and sake he had favored when he was alive. After an hour the still smoldering bones were rolled out and metal chopsticks used to retrieve some of the major bones, especially the larynx, which is thought to represent the whole person. The rest of the remains are placed in an urn; the local temple has a *nokotsudo* where such remains may repose for centuries.

Of course, there is a mandatory donation to cover the temple expenses and funeral ceremony. Alpha, not being Buddhist, didn't especially appreciate the ceremony. The melancholic cries, the chanting of the Sutras and the customary sounds of despair all made him despondent. He sensed the lostness, despair and anguish of a life ending on so solemn a note. He wished there might be an uplifting hymn, like the kind that had been sung at his grandfather's funeral. Sadly, he couldn't remember titles or lyrics.

For the remainder of the day and evening Alpha tried to think of the personal implications of this death for himself and Rie. In reality, there was no proof of criminal intent and no known witness to Kanagawa's death. Only conjecture. And suicide being looked upon in Japanese society as an honorable means of personal redemption, the police wouldn't be searching for another, more sinister motive. Japan, with its already high suicide rate, would have a much higher one if the local police weren't as cooperative as they were with the grieving family. Facts are distorted to make numerous suicides appear to be something else.

The two men decided to return to Alpha's apartment. There was still enough sake and Asahi Lite, but Alpha's father-in-law, not wanting to impose, insisted they stop by the sakaya on the way home. Alpha wished again that Nakata would purchase some European wine; instead the older man selected another bottle of sake, of a higher quality than Gekkeikan, for 60 dollars. With an overabundant supply of drink he wouldn't have to stand on ceremony. Alpha knew it might be a long evening before the alcohol took over and conversation would no longer be meaningful. There would be a small window of opportunity, after the alcohol had just taken hold and before it began to skew the conversation.

It seems to be a reality the world over that daughters come to appreciate their mothers more after they have entered into a marriage and permanently moved out of the home, and this was the case with Rie. The two women, mother and daughter, had obviously enjoyed preparing the meal together. Rie's mother felt a tinge of envy when Rie expressed her feelings for Alpha—the younger woman was still in love, and her love was maturing and transitioning from the honeymoon, erotic type to the more sustainable kind that includes respect and voluntary self-giving. While the older woman's marriage had been satisfactory by Japanese standards, there had never been the degree of intimacy her daughter seemed to be enjoying with her son-in-law.

Most Japanese meals (except for the deep-fried ones) are undeniably superior in quality and nutritional value to most of the meals Americans eat. As soon as he sat down Alpha understood why connoisseurs rate Japanese food as among the best in the world—appealing to the eye, not heavy, and offering extensive variety in conjunction with good taste and nutrition. Indeed, the Japanese, although representing only about two percent of the world's population, comprise about half of the population that is over one hundred years of age. Alpha felt again that he was blessed beyond what he deserved to have a good wife who could also cook Japanese food and who related well to her own parents.

Nevertheless, no amount of food, sake, or Asahi beer could assist the foursome in their quest for an answer. With full stomachs and a now mutual inability on the part of the men to tolerate more to drink, the group called it a night. The futons were already spread on the tatami mats in the guest bedroom, and the bath had been drawn and heated to just beyond the right temperature. Ordinarily the guests would enter the bath first, being careful not to dirty the water in consideration of those to follow. While Alpha and Rie enjoyed bathing together, he noticed that his parents-in-law did so separately. Rie, with a baby in her womb, preferred to go last so as to avoid the more extreme temperature.

The parents-in-law looked for an excuse to postpone their return to Niigata for an additional day. With just a little urging from Rie, they decided to take Monday off to spend time with her. Her pregnancy indicated symbolically her independence from them, and they were beginning to feel some dissonance with the coming birth of a grandchild, indicating to them the arrival of old age. The ancient Chinese had looked at old age as beginning at 40, and the Nakatas were well beyond that. Rie was happy to talk to her mother in a way only mothers and daughters can, and some of the fears that universally accompany impending motherhood were being put to rest.

Alpha, though filled with anxiety about Shinkinsei, left for work later than usual so he could enjoy a leisurely breakfast with his in-laws. There would be numerous legal matters to take care of, he knew. Alpha wondered whether this would be an intestate situation, where one dies without a will and lawyers' fees can consume most of what remains. However, resorting to legal intervention is much rarer in Japan than in the West. Even with a will, in Japan inheritance taxes are very high, comprising up to one third of the value of the estate. Hence the saying "Die three times and the government gets everything."

Mr. Kaneda, the man Alpha had met on his initial visit to the company, held the position of office manager and was doing a capable job. Alpha would have to lean heavily on his expertise and knew that the future of the company was probably dependent on their maintaining a good relationship. With Kanagawa out of the picture, it was imperative for Alpha to find out what type of company Shinkinsei actually was. How deep was its involvement in other businesses that were functioning beneath the surface? Was its trading activity just a cover? Kanagawa undoubtedly had many of the answers. Alpha regretted that he hadn't to this point made more of an attempt to cultivate a relationship with him.

As it turned out Kaneda was in a mood for talking. He and Alpha were alone in the conference room, and green tea was brought in for both. Alpha didn't need to prime the pump. Kaneda began by launching into a history of his long relationship with Kanagawa:

"Your uncle [by this he meant Kanagawa] and I went to the same elementary school between the wars [WWI and WWII], but I was three years younger than he and was bullied [*ijime*] by the other students, on my way to quickly becoming an *ochkobore* [dropout]. Maybe that was because we were poor; I do not think anyone knew of my Korean ancestry. Already in the third grade there was a group of winners [*kachi-gumi*] who walked around as the elite gang, talking loudly, and a group of losers [*make-gumi*] The kachi-gumi bullied us, took our snacks, called us names, and generally made fun of us.

"School got more difficult, and life outside the classroom became deplorable. Your uncle and I hung out together, and we had three others in our clique. To this day I do not know where or how your uncle got them—he never told me—possibly from some American GIs, but one day he came to school with a pinup of Barbara Stanwyck. Later he got one of Rita Hayworth. Everyone wanted to see these pictures on the pinups—not just because they were women but also because they were foreign, and looking at such items was forbidden. Needless to say, they were also fun to look at.

"If you were a trusted friend of your uncle's, he would let you take them home for a night. Everyone wanted a turn at this—there was a lot of pride involved to be in possession of a pinup of a beautiful American woman. This became the well-protected school secret. Even the girls waited for a turn to take the pinups home. Soon our group turned the tables and became the kachi-gumi. It all started from your uncle's ability to get things other people wanted but could not get. Maybe that's where he developed his knack for trading."

The phenomenon of ijime is well documented in Japan. Newspapers feature articles on students who resort to suicide after having been bullied. In numerous cases the bullied students just retreat to their bedrooms, not wanting to come out even for meals. Alpha was surprised to hear of instances of this going back more than 70 years. He had thought of it more as a modern phenomenon, as a corollary to the conformist nature of Japanese society: you have to conform and keep the rules, both written and unwritten, or the conformists will make you pay the price.

Kaneda continued, "Because we had so much in common, even though your uncle was older, he took me under his wing. Sometimes he gave me money. When I finished high school just after WWII, he asked me to move to Tokyo with him. He was already active in trading with the Occupation Forces. He got things—coffee, sugar and cigarettes—that were very hard for most Japanese to obtain after the war. We have been together ever since."

Kaneda's voice tightened, as though he were having trouble speaking. Already most of Alpha's fears had been assuaged. He was beginning to feel he could trust Kaneda in the same way he had trusted Kanagawa.

While the causes of bullying in Japan are diverse, it often develops from something as minor as a speech impediment, birthmark, questionable ancestry, or lack of social power. Other times it may arise from religion (such as from being a Christian), social status, or ethnic background. There is a group of Japanese called the burakumin or *eta* that numbers around two million. Traditionally these people worked in occupations associated with death—

butchers, tanners, gravediggers and the like. They, in a manner similar to Koreans, are the object of much discrimination. Sometimes it isn't clear why some students become the objects of bullying while others do not.

Alpha felt both relief and a new wave of confidence. He couldn't help asking, without preamble, "Do you think my uncle committed suicide? Or do you think he was murdered?"

Not noticeably taken aback by the candid question, Kaneda reflected, "If anything, Kanagawa perked up a bit and didn't seem depressed in the days immediately preceding his death." His interpretation coincided with Alpha's. However, Alpha also knew of people whose depression had seemed to lift once they had made the choice to die on their own terms—after they had planned a time, location, and means for their own death. Alpha asked which scenario Kaneda thought applied to his uncle, to which the office manager replied unambiguously, "He was not the type to commit suicide. Things regarding a successor to the company were just starting to look up. He looked forward to you coming to the company. He had no uncontrollable pain and in all probability would have lived for months yet, maybe even a year or more. He confided in me that he did not have any more sex drive, so it was strange for him to be at that love hotel. So his untimely death does not make sense. Maybe he just wanted companionship."

"By a successor?" Alpha inquired. "Yes, you and Rie," Kaneda replied. Alpha was surprised to hear this from someone other than Kanagawa for the first time in his formal role in Shinkinsei. But as is the case with American companies, when one takes over a company they acquire both assets and liabilities. Alpha hoped that the former outweighed the latter.

Whether there has been a verbal *yuigon* (one's expressed last wish) or is a written will (*yuigon josho*), in Japan the desires of the recently departed are held in high esteem and strictly carried out. Perhaps this has to do with the Japanese concept of the spirit of the deceased lingering and returning periodically (during the Obon festival in July or August) after death. Or perhaps it's a factor of ancestor veneration; more likely it has elements of both.

Alpha didn't want to appear rash or insensitive, but he felt the need to ask Kaneda about Kanagawa's last wishes, as well as about the existence of a will. Kaneda seemed in no way offended, as though he had been anticipating the question as appropriate and timely.

"Your uncle was a very thorough person. While I do not know the details, he left a sealed binder to be opened upon his death. Since you, Rie, and her parents are the only known living relatives, I suggest we open it in everyone's presence."

With his new appreciation of Kaneda, Alpha wasted no time in phoning Rie. She and her parents were only an hour away, and they could all meet at Shinkinsei for lunch. Alpha ordered the delivery of three extra obentos, upgrading the standard menu with additional variety.

Alpha again recognized some of the differences between the Japanese and American cultures. The Japanese are externally driven. Maybe, he reflected, that comes from being dependent for centuries on the sea. It's the sea that brings food and life to the Japanese. What is your address? It is Japan, Tokyo, Shakujikoen. In American it would be all about me—my name, then my street, then my town. Some things were starting to come together. Alpha conjectured, That's why the Japanese often say, "Well it's time. Let's start the meeting." The external force of time necessitates that we begin. Americans usually just want to begin the meeting so they can finish it earlier and get back to work.

The obentos arrived. Green tea is always available at Japanese companies, and nothing else goes as well with meals. It's a healthy drink that aids in digestion. Kaneda was invited to join them. He was hardly a stranger to the Nakatas, and as they talked they found more common threads in their backgrounds. In Japan it isn't so much what you know as who you know; and knowing the same people, having a store of similar experiences breaks down even otherwise impermeable social barriers.

The meal was one of those situations in which, had the context been Christian, prayer would have been appropriately offered. The unknown, the mysterious, the fearful and the threatening—all of these encourage people of faith to look outside themselves to God for help. But the Japanese have no such custom. There is no formal prayer before meals in the sense of addressing a deity with a distinct personality. In a more formal setting a housewife may announce, "We have nothing, but please eat a lot." And they do say *Itadakimasu*—"I will receive." This is a standard phrase used in Japan before one eats a meal.

15

Where the Money Went

When threatened with the unknown, most people revert to what they are accustomed to. Routines become sources of reinforcement. After more than an hour of going over the same topics, questioning again and again whether Kanagawa's death had been self-inflicted or the result of a homicide, the consensus was that there was insufficient evidence to conclude there had been wrongdoing. The death would, in any case, have occurred by natural causes within a matter of months. All agreed that Kanagawa would have wanted them to carry on as though he were present, so they decided it would be business as usual.

This issue having been resolved, no matter how unsatisfactorily, the binder was opened. The list of assets included a small rented apartment about 20 minutes' walk from the company. There would be a couple of months' deposit money to be returned. There were also some current stock certificates and office equipment. Kanagawa must have made some pretty good money in his lifetime, but he had little to show for it.

Alpha, not wanting to appear greedy or impolite, nevertheless asked Kaneda where the money had gone. Again the office manager was forthright: "To North Korea—to feed his siblings and their children, his nephews and nieces. Those of us who came to and remained in Japan ended up being fortunate if we survived the war. There were tough times in Japan during the war, but it was far worse in Korea. The economy of North Korea deteriorated under communism, being badly mismanaged under the dictatorships of Kim Il-sung and Kim Jong-Il. Millions starved to death. We tried to smuggle the money in but later were forced to turn to bribery. So only half, if that much, of what he sent got through. The rest greased the palms of those along the way."

Alpha wondered whether, in his new role at New Morning Star, such bribes should continue to be sent. Kanagawa couldn't have formally stipulated this in his will, but Kaneda admitted that this was probably his implied desire. Alpha knew he might get into legal trouble if this practice were to continue.

More than likely Kanagawa's practice would fit the definition of money laundering—concealing the destination of monies, in while or in part. Some reform measures had trickled down into Japanese law after the Marubeni bribery incident, in which Lockheed paid a $22 million bribe. But bribery remains a way of life in the Orient.

Still, in this case there had been no intention of making a profit—only of providing humanitarian aid. Alpha knew of a doctor near Sendai who had forged birth papers in order to prevent abortions. With no black mark on her record, a young girl would still have high marriage potential, since there would be no legal proof she was not a virgin. Maybe this constituted a similar situation—a violation of the law in order to save lives that would otherwise be lost, in this case from starvation. If such a good end didn't justify the means, Alpha reflected, what would?

So much, then, for where the money had gone. But Alpha, Rie and her parents also wanted to know where it had come from. The only one who could answer that question was Kaneda. Alpha had gotten to pretty well know the accounts. What he didn't know was whether they were fully legitimate, as opposed to being front companies for the yakuza.

The luncheon was interrupted by Rie's cell phone. She noticed immediately that the area code was that of Niigata. Her parents, and her father in particular, disliked the use of cell phones for the interruptions they caused. Mr. Nakata had worked hard through the years. When he had a few moments to himself he wanted no interruptions.

Thus time, however, the manager of the Good Hour, Tanabe, was calling to inform him of a devastating fire and of the need to call the Niigata City Police Department immediately. Rie's father took the cell phone, and Alpha noticed his father-in-law's hands trembling and the color draining from his face. The call had the effect of making him instantly and fully sober, except for the fact that his hands kept shaking.

The conversation with the city police ended in less than two minutes. There had been a fire at the Good Hour. It had started at around at 3:00 that morning, fortunately at a time when there were no employees or patrons on the premises. The parlor had technically closed at midnight but had remained open long enough for the diehards to complete their games; this generally happened before 1:00 a.m.

According to current reports there had been no injuries. The fire had burned undetected for possibly 30 to 40 minutes before a local squid fisherman on his way home after fishing all night had reported the blaze. Due to the likely proximity of other buildings in Japan, a commercial fire almost invariably affects neighboring businesses. Were other buildings in any way damaged by the fire, smoke, or water? Had their businesses or sales been adversely affected by the fire department's response time? If so, the issues would require personal visits by Nakata, along with apologies, gifts, and the incurrence of giri—he would become obligated to the adjacent shop owners due to the inconveniences to which "he" had subjected them. Then there would be the usual concerns associated with a fire: any injuries? personal claims? cause? insurance adjustment, clean up, and possible rebuilding.

The Nakatas had no choice but to return immediately to Niigata. Within 10 minutes they were off, with Alpha and Rie accompanying them to the Bullet Train Platform in Ueno, about an hour away, not far from the park where Alpha had proposed just months earlier. There the older couple would pay a fee to change their tickets and then take the Shinkansen, the bullet train, back to Niigata. The 300-kilometer distance would be covered in less than two hours, and they would arrive by early evening. Alpha and Rie would come the following day to help out.

Travelers in Japan carry minimal luggage, as the crowded commuter trains are unforgiving with regard to extra baggage. In fact, luggage is usually sent on ahead; the airport baggage services will hold it until you come to claim it, or deliver it to your address. The Nakatas had little personal luggage, only one piece packed with their toiletries. It was still before the afternoon rush hour, so Alpha could carry it with them as far as Ueno. The bullet train, in contrast to local trains, has ample space for luggage, as it is intended for long distance travelers.

The Japanese attitude toward work is far different from that of Americans. Work for the former is the primary provider of both identity and meaning. Ask any Japanese person what he does for a living, and his first response will be not *what* he does but *whom* he works for—the company's name that gives him his identity. That's why the Japanese continue to work long beyond what is necessary, even if that means assuming a far more menial job after retirement. They crave the comforting identity of belonging—of doing rather than just being.

The Nakatas sat largely in silence as the bullet train sped toward Niigata, each pondering the future, wondering whether it would be worth the undoubtedly huge investment required to rebuild. Insurance, they both knew, wouldn't cover a major portion of the loss. Nakata purchased two cups of sake from the saleslady who walked the aisles with her cart, for which Mrs. Nakata chided him, knowing he'd already had enough to drink. His sardonic retort: "It isn't every day your business burns to the ground." Both, separately and side by side, longed for the former days on the rice farm where life, although more difficult from a physical standpoint, had brought more satisfaction with the predictability and enjoyment of planting, growing, and harvesting the rice crop.

Arriving at the Niigata Station, the Nagatas took a taxi to the Good Hour—or to what remained of it. In previous years they would have walked the 400-meter distance, but the stresses of a death and a funeral in the family, combined with advancing age and now the fire, were beginning to take their physical and mental toll. The scene was still crowded with police, who had cordoned off the area; accident and fire investigative teams; and two individuals, an older man and a younger female, from the family's insurance company.

Japan boasts among the best disaster response teams in the world, and no stone would be left unturned in analyzing, describing, finding a cause, and appraising the extent of the financial damages. Ultimately, the police report would be the main document by which everything else would be judged. Everyone on the investigative team remained close lipped; if the Nakatas were to determine anything from the formal report, they would have to wait for more than a week.

The Nakatas were devastated. The building and contents were a total loss. While part of the frame was still standing, the roof had collapsed inward. Japanese construction codes mandate the use of fireproof materials in exterior walls and roofs, to prevent the lateral spread of fire that had been so devastating in the fire bombing of Tokyo in WWII, when such fires were responsible for more deaths than the atomic bombs. So while the fire had not spread to adjacent buildings, the fireproof construction had acted as a vortex, a furnace with a strong upward draft, giving form to the spreading fire so it could burn longer while remaining contained and undetected.

The intense heat had melted much of the plastic surfaces of the pachinko machines; all of them, as well as most of the rest of the contents, were completely destroyed from the fire, heat, smoke, or water. Fortunately, collateral damage had been minimal. The store to the east had two second-story windows cracked from the heat and some exterior plastic waste plumbing blackened from the smoke, but it appeared that the business had not been unduly interrupted by the blaze. The fire, the fire department's response, and the extinguishing of the blaze had all occurred before the morning rush hour.

Immediately the Nakatas went to the adjacent shop, offering profound apologies and bowing deeply. Fortunately, their roots with the proprietors went far back, and it appeared likely that one or two more apologies, accompanied by a gift of 50,000 yen, would be sufficient to discharge the giri that had ensued from the fire. Nakata took it upon himself to call a glass company, paying for the pane himself, at least initially, until the insurance company could be dealt with. The glass company would come within two hours and replace the glass without burden to the store owner and without a night passing before the repair. Emotionally exhausted, the Nakatas returned home by another taxi.

Mr. Nakata felt the same way he had when the family's rice fields had been taken—helpless, devastated, and robbed of his main purpose in life. Along with this he felt responsibility for the nine employees at the Good Hour. Unemployment in Niigata was still higher than in those prefectures with large metropolitan areas, and unemployment forced by a fire would probably require some of the displaced workers to relocate to Tokyo, Nagoya, or Osaka. Rebuilding would require several months, more indebtedness, and a lot of energy—energy the Nakatas no longer had. And the heavy snowfall expected in the upcoming winter months precluded the idea of building prior to next spring.

The response to suffering and loss is not necessarily more difficult for Japanese people, who as a group have a cyclical view of history. A fire is looked upon much as an earthquake or flood would be. It happens, and there may be no significance behind the facts. Such events may in the short run even be harder on theists, people like Job of the Old Testament, who face a need to reconcile the loving and providential care of the God they believe in with their present circumstances when great personal loss is confronted.

The Japanese tend to react to pain, suffering and disappointment with what they call *gaman*—perseverance, patience and endurance—neither giving up nor quitting. Calamitous events for the Japanese are never interpreted as a wake-up call from God. They're just a part of existence, a matter of taking the bad with the good. Nature in this view is an indiscriminate force that can affect a moral person to the same extent it can an immoral person. Stoical endurance is the culturally ingrained response, and melancholy provides the psychological frame of mind. The Japanese protect themselves from falling into psychological potholes by this mindset, never allowing themselves to become inordinately elated with the fortunate and never getting overly despondent with the unfortunate.

So it was that the Nakatas had already defaulted to the Japanese nationalistic gaman mode by the time Rie and Alpha arrived around noon the next day. The foursome sat down together on the tatami floor at a low table. In a few minutes the ramen, a noodle dish with vegetables and a thin piece of pork, would be ready. The preliminary, unofficial report on the fire was already available, though only in verbal form. The Nakatas, having grown up in the Niigata area, were well connected and didn't have to wait for an official version. After lunch they would go to both the police and fire stations to find out as much detail as possible.

16

The Report

Nakata knew two former schoolmates in the Niigata City fire department who were now officers. He would have known more people except for the Japanese practice of frequent job transfers, usually as often as every four to six years. Added to that was the fact that retirement, due to an overabundance of elderly workers, often occurs at 55 or 60 years of age. If you stay on beyond that, your pay decreases, often by more than half. The frequent job transfers provide two functions: more versatility that comes with cross training and a minimizing of the number of illegal activities, such as embezzlement, that can develop more readily in the case of long-term assignments. Because the Japanese tend not to make friends easily, most families choose to remain behind rather than go through the upheaval associated with a move. The husband becomes in effect a corporate bachelor, returning home, depending on the distance, possibly only during holidays. Tanshin funin—starting a new post without one's family—is a common Japanese expression for the practice.

So it was that Nakata, using the familiar level of Japanese grammar reserved for close friends, asked an old schoolmate for a verbal report on the details of the fire. In most companies, as well as in most public buildings, each section has an area where, if invited, one may sit down and drink green tea with the section head. The three sat down together. Coffee was offered for Alpha, but Nakata took the initiative by stating that Japanese blood, if not in a physical sense, at least in a metaphorical sense, flowed in his son-in-law's veins and that he would prefer green tea. Perhaps it was the sight of an old friend or the rare visit of a foreigner that resulted in this courtesy not typically extended to visitors. At any rate, Nakata got what he wanted—an upfront, unofficial but probably more accurate report of the fire than the written version that would follow in a few days.

Tanaka got right to the point, inquiring about the official cause of the fire. Miura, the section head, replied, "We could find no official cause. There is no evidence to suggest that it was the work of an arsonist—no evidence of either an accelerant or a break-in. The fire started somewhere on the pachinko floor and had just reached the more remote staff kitchen when we arrived. That is the only place gas is used in the entire building, so we can rule out a propane leak. It started somewhere near the center of the main floor and spread outward from there. So by the process of elimination we have to conclude that the cause was electrical in nature. However, it is very unusual for a fire to begin in such an area.

"We checked camera records from tollbooths on the expressway and were able to determine that two black Mercedes Benzes arrived in the city limits at around 8:00 p.m., just minutes apart. One of them appears to have returned around 4 this morning; the other we have no further record of."

Alpha understood why the man had mentioned the two Mercedes—purchasing such vehicles had become an affordable way for the Japanese yakuza to show both extravagance and proof of their presence in the vicinity. While initially the yakuza had preferred large Mercedes models, recently the trend was also to modify Japanese luxury cars by installing oversized, low-profile tires and lowering the chassis to be nearer the pavement.

Nakata expressed gratitude for the information, and he and Alpha rose to leave. The fire and police departments in Japan have the highest percentage of solved crimes of any developed country; at the same time, the cause of every fire has to be ascertained, even when the conclusions goes beyond known facts. In this instance the electrical wiring would be blamed by default, in the absence of any other proof. On the way home Nakata remarked to Alpha that these two recent developments—the death of their distant relative, Kanagawa, and the fire at the Good Hour—might be related.

Nakata related that the Japanese yakuza had lost nearly half its members in recent decades. Now, he stated, most oyabuns didn't want to see further erosion of their power and its corresponding income. He went on, "So it could be that these two events were in response to Kanagawa's and my action to terminate moriryo [protection money payments] to them two months ago. They would allow us to do that but wanted severance money instead—what is called *en-kiri-ryo* [money paid to cut off one's connection with a yakuza]. They demanded high sums from us, nearly a quarter of a million dollars for Kanagawa and $150,000 from me.

"We—that is, Kanagawa and I—thought that now was the time to make this move if we were going to save some money for the future. I am sure they don't look favorably on anyone trying to extricate themselves from monthly 'protection' payments—what they also call *mikaijime-ryo* or *shoba-ryo*. The irony of the whole situation is that they inflated our degree of indebtedness and, like a moneylender, charged exorbitant interest and made it so we could never in reality break free of our connection with them. In effect, they wanted a big payment to sever a relationship we hadn't wanted for many years. I believe they took the attitude that 'if I can't have it, I don't want you to have it either.'"

Alpha asked, "Why can't such people just be content with a little less?"

Nakata replied with a wry smile, "They wouldn't be Japanese if they were that way," to which Alpha retorted, "Well, aren't they at least Buddhists, and shouldn't they thus be content without worldly entanglements, material possessions and the like?" Nakata wasted no time in his comeback: "If you insist on that definition of Buddhism, there are no Buddhists in Japan. Even the temple priests would not qualify!"

Alpha resisted the temptation to bring up his college days and the study of various philosophies. But Friedrich Nietzsche, the German philosopher, sprang to his mind. He had believed that the primal drive in all humankind is the will to power and that this thirst for power unites all people and activities in the universe. If Nietzsche were at least partially correct, he mused, his explanation might provide a clue as to why the Japanese work so hard to amass economic and social power. Not being people of faith, it is money, not faith, that for them provides a guarantee against an uncertain future.

That, he concluded, is why fads come and go in Japan with such intensity; not to have the latest and greatest would be an admission of helplessness, of lacking the means to have the best, of not having power. This, he conjectured, is another reason the Japanese sacrifice so much to the company. Their personal economic power is tied up with that of their company; if their company is well off economically, they'll share in the resulting economic power. The delusive nature of such power may be the reason the yakuza oyabuns attempt to hang onto power even in their dying moments. While they leave this world as empty-handed as the next guy, they at least die with the illusion of power. And they have very elaborate funerals, often televised on TV and visited by thousands.

Nakata spoke further: "The oyabuns get a cut on everything. They call it *kasuri*. They take a percentage of the cost of construction. They get a part of every prize we give out when somebody wins at pachinko. They get monthly protection payments. Kickbacks on everything. And there is no letup. We have a saying that 'there is no *kusuri* [medicine, something to alleviate the pain] for kasuri.'"

Alpha was taken aback by Nakata's bluntness. The Japanese always present themselves in the best possible light. Twist one's ankle, and along with the excruciating pain a smile emerges, a tatamae smile. Strike out with men left on base, and the humiliated player offers a tatamae smile. This defense mechanism, used proportionately to the amount of embarrassment or pain one is experiencing, has become a means of coping with a cruel world.

The Japanese are so good at this, and this approach is so ingrained in them, that they can operate on both levels simultaneously. While the casual observer may interpret this response as dishonesty or deception, in reality it is not. It's merely a type of grease, a lubricant that makes resistant, frictional elements of a crowded society work together with greater compatibility and less interference. Alpha thought of the disarming smile he had seen so many times on Japanese faces and reflected ruefully that confrontations in Western society would often go a lot better if tatamaes were used more effectively.

Confession is good for the soul, and Nakata's spontaneity provoked a similar response in Alpha. Not that it had bothered him—indeed, he saw no connection—but Alpha finally brought up to his father-in-law his visit to Akihabara with Rie some weeks earlier. He divulged the interest shown by a man named Suzuki in a chip whose exact part number he couldn't now remember—a chip that was an integral part of the American-made pachinko machines Kanagawa was importing. The chip that had been included in Alpha's first translating assignment.

Nakata probed, "Was there any other response from Suzuki? Did you have any further connection to or response from him?"

"None, except that we couldn't find the copy in our apartment that I'd made of the spec sheet. I thought maybe Rie mistakenly threw it out, but she said she didn't. We thought at the time someone may have stolen it. But they would have had to break into our apartment to do it. Nothing else was missing, and there was no sign of a forced entry.

"By the way," Alpha continued, "why were you in the process of purchasing American-made machines that cost a lot more than the ones made in China of Japan?"

Nakata's reply was succinct, to the point: "We anticipated trouble, as we were breaking our ties with the yakuza. The pachinko industry is both very competitive and very controlled. If you don't have the latest model with the newest features, your clientele will soon vanish. That is why we had to quickly switch to the new pachi-slo machines as soon as they came out. It only takes a few weeks for your customers to know about and expect them on the floor. And the yakuza controls both the supply and the cost: no kasuri, no pachinko machines. Pay a higher kasuri each month, and the purchase price for the new machines may go down, especially if you stay in the yakuza's good graces. That means your days of doing good business are numbered as soon as your machines become dated, unless you find an alternative source of supply. In order to force you out of business, the yakuza needs to do nothing other than prevent you from buying updated machines."

He continued, "Your Uncle Kanagawa, before his death, found a new manufacturer in America. Not only I, but many other pachinko parlor owners were ready to jump ship, if we could lock up this supplier. We first wanted to try them out on Americans at the base, as this is a community relatively isolated from mainstream Japanese society. There are numerous Japanese employees on bases with the Department of Defense and so forth, so they could also try them out. So we wanted to do this limited and isolated test run in the relative privacy of the American base. And we were willing to pay higher dollars to do this. What we paid extra in purchasing the machines would soon be recovered in what we would save by not paying kasuri."

Alpha inquired, "If the American and Oriental made machines perform almost identically, why would there be such an interest in one chip?" Nakata was pensive and waited a moment to reply. "I don't know. But I think Kaneda might. There's not much more we can do in Niigata for the next few days, until the formal report of the fire is made public, so let's go back to see him tomorrow."

Alpha was struck by how readily the Japanese are willing to travel. Perhaps the long commutes to which they are accustomed predispose them to it. Indeed, with the Shinkansen they could move from the western side of the country on the Japan Sea to the east side on the Pacific in less than three hours, easily returning to Niigata by nightfall. Alpha also wanted to stop by his apartment to see whether there was any mail or messages, and Rie wanted him to fetch another change of clothing so she could stay a bit longer with her mother. Now that she had become a wife and an expectant mother, she had begun to empathize more with her mother, to share the emotional burden Japanese women carry around.

The Japanese culture is too repressive of emotions to allow for their free and uncalculated expression in all but the most extreme cases, resulting in their lifelong suppression. Only when people are vulnerable can one gain insight into their honne, and Rie didn't want to waste a moment of opportunity to get to know her mother better on the honne level.

Alpha contacted Kaneda on the cell phone; he would order in lunch and await their arrival. Travel by train in Japan is usually very predictable, unless there is a natural disaster or a suicide on the tracks. Most Shinkansen tracks are inaccessible to people on foot, and desperate people usually resort to easier measures than attempting to climb up the platforms to jump in front of the fast moving trains. Departures are generally within seconds of the schedule.

By 12:30 the pair had arrived at Shinkinsei, and, true to form, Kaneda had their lunch, Japanese obentos, waiting for them. Men in Japan are by habit among the fastest eaters in the world. Kaneda and Nakata were finished within five minutes but graciously sipped their tea until Alpha could catch up.

The conversation that ensued moved quickly in the direction of the pachinko machines recently imported from America. Kaneda offered his explanation: "There is a new chip in these pachinko machines, actually one chip with four layers, each stacked on top of the other. They were developed out of a cooperative endeavor between a Silicon Valley company and a Las Vegas casino game manufacturer. Your uncle had a lot of foresight in being the first to tie up an exclusive five-year contract with these American companies. These chips are heavily protected by patent, and most of the gaming world wants to know their technical details so they can try to develop something similar that sufficiently deviates from what is patent protected in order to avoid patent infringement. Each layer of the chip is in itself a complete pachinko hardware package.

"The only thing the other three layers do is change the odds of winning a fever. Pachinko must operate like any other business, making a profit, or its days are numbered. Typically the house takes about 11 percent—some more and some less. This means that, over the long run, people on average will leave with about that percentage or less of money. If we can change the odds corresponding to the customer's degree of belief in his invincibility, we can make more money. Just after a fever is won, this chip automatically increases the house's take, correspondingly decreasing the odds of winning another fever."

The customer, Kaneda went on to explain, barely notices this during the time it takes for the effect of winning a fever to wear off. Japanese society is perhaps the most predictable in the world, explaining to a large degree why pachinko is so popular. It provides an element of risk, of unpredictability, of adventure that is lacking in everyday life. As such, it's a positive influence, providing excitement and adventure that otherwise would be denied to these buttoned-down workers living an all too predictable lifestyle. If not for affordable pachinko type gambling, Japanese society would in all likelihood fall prey to a host of much worse gambling vices.

Kaneda went on to explain that the whole basis of gambling depends on what is called random reinforcement. Compared with periodic reinforcement—such as one's monthly salary—a combination of luck, skill, and house policy [how the machines are set] determines when and how much a player may win—the amount of random reinforcement he'll get. After someone wins a fever or jackpot he is particularly vulnerable. For an hour or more he'll over-rely on his ability, believing more and more in his invincibility and mentally minimizing the odds that are against him and maximizing his ability to beat those odds. During this period the house can usually win back a significant part, if not all, of its payout.

That, Kaneda explained, is why this chip was so valuable: it automatically switches to a different layer of the chip after a fever. The software in this new layer makes it more difficult to win; in fact, the odds become quite a bit lower. If even a small pachinko parlor takes in $80,000 a day, they would ordinarily clear about $8,800 prior to expenses. If this chip can make just a 10 percent differ-ence, that's almost a thousand dollars a day, or about $300,000 a year, significantly increasing the profits of the pachinko owners. If everything gets really fine-tuned, it would even be possi-ble to pay out more in winnings and still end up taking more in profits—assuming the winner keeps pushing his luck and stays in the game until the adjusted, more difficult odds predictably take their toll of his new winnings. The purpose is to have him win more in the short run, as long as he then loses more than he has won. It can work in the opposite direction with the novice—giving him greater odds of winning when he, due to his lack of experi-ence, would ordinarily lose. That way he gets hooked.

"We don't know at this point if this chip will have to be regu-lated by the National Gaming Commission," Kaneda conceded. "We do know that its presence is hard to detect. You would either have to have a copy of the specs to determine whether this chip has been installed or have a pretty good idea of what you are look-ing for. The software in this chip can also be changed remotely and automatically. If a pachinko establishment, for example, does not like one of its customers (maybe he is dirty, or smelly, or an intimi-dating member of the yakuza), it can remotely program the ma-chine to reduce his odds of winning, in the long run discouraging his further patronage. You kill two birds with one stone: you make money from his gambling losses and get rid of him as he seeks other establishments looking for better odds."

17

An Obvious Conclusion

Alpha didn't want to volunteer the information that, possibly due to his and Rie's visit to Akihabara, the information on the chip and the machine specs in general may have been compromised. But Nakata took the lead in announcing, "Their apartment was broken into, and a copy of the specs is missing."

Kaneda restrained his response, obviously kicking into the tatemae mode in the realization that he couldn't amend the situation by affixing blame. He also knew that Alpha was the individual now running Shinkinsei and that his own future in part depended on their relationship. So he steered the conversation in the direction of loss control:

"What would be the worst case scenario? The other side would gain quite an advantage in their attempt to learn our machine's specs. And they might feel sufficiently threatened to take measures to stop us from acquiring them or selling them in Japan. In the Tokyo area alone there are more than 1,500 pachinko parlors. Each one has at least two to three hundred machines—some thousands. So you have the potential of making a lot of money. Perhaps we can do business with a yakuza front company and sell the machines that way. But this may pit one yakuza faction against another and would probably be a short-lived arrangement."

As the conversation continued, Alpha noted wryly that the situation wasn't all that different from the results of an alcoholic intervention—when all the facts became known by all the relevant parties, the conclusion became obvious—some drastic steps needed to be taken. Kanagawa's death and the fire at the Good Hour were related; the "accident" that had destroyed the imported pachinko machines was no more accidental than the death was a suicide, and both were intended to send a clear message. Alpha asked, "If that's the case, why doesn't the yakuza communicate more directly? Why don't they just send an unambiguous message and tell us to drop this endeavor? Or offer us an opportunity to do it in cooperation with them?"

Kaneda volunteered an explanation: "The yakuza does not believe in empty words. You have a saying in English that faith without works is dead. Similarly, the yakuza has a saying that words without muscle are meaningless. So they intended to convey their message with a sufficient degree of force to show that they are serious."

Alpha thought aloud: "How will this affect our future—mine and Rie's and Shinkinsei's?" His father-in-law was the first to respond: "It is hard to fight an enemy you cannot see. The yakuza has a thousand faces, each different in appearance. You often cannot know who they are ahead of time. But they do have a moral code. Remember when we first talked about it at the onsen? Part of that code is that normally family members—wives and children—no matter what happens, are exempt from any of the yakuza's activities, whether preemptive or retributive. But you yourself could become vulnerable if they decide that you or your work—Shinkinsei—has the potential of eating into their profits or carving up some of its territory. Shinkinsei could become very vulnerable."

At the risk of sounding naive, Alpha verbalized something he ordinarily wouldn't have: "But I'm American. My father worked at the embassy. We still have good contacts there. If anything were to happen to me, it could result in international attention, including FBI involvement."

Nakayama replied automatically, as though no forethought was necessary: "It would just be an accident. Maybe your being an American would provide an extra degree of protection, but maybe not. Maybe that is why Kaneda was initially quite favorable to the idea of your taking over the business. Maybe he thought he could pull this off with the added influence of your family background."

Alpha replied slowly, "But I'm not accident prone."

To which Nakata rebounded without missing a beat: "You don't need to be."

18

Retirement

One of the courses Alpha had taken in international business before dropping out of his graduate program had included a module on risk assessment. He had never expected to have to apply the material personally but now found himself unconsciously running through one of the models, tossing it around in his brain to determine whether anything he had learned might shed some light on the situation. First he thought about the identification step, but it was almost impossible to apply a quantity or percentage to the probability of identifying various yakuza reactions. Next he tried to map out the social scope of the issue—Nakata, Rie and himself were the players of interest. Nakata was probably at this point considered to have been duly chastised, leaving only Alpha and Rie and their soon-to-be-born baby.

Alpha didn't know whether his foreign status would provide any degree of insulation or protection—probably not in the case of an alleged accident. But if he himself were not the object of the yakuza, then Rie or the company he had just inherited would most likely be at risk. The next steps—defining a framework, followed by analysis and mitigation—seemed too remote and irrelevant to be of any help. The situation boiled down for Alpha to the two basic responses—fight or flight.

The Clark family had never been known to flee from challenges. On the contrary, their DNA included a stubborn and persevering trait. Alpha's great-grandfather had founded Hokkaido University at a time when foreigners were rare in Japan. His grandfather had worked in intelligence during WWII, and his father had worked at the Japanese Embassy—all jobs that had required tenacity, facing struggles head on, and coming out ahead. Fleeing for Alpha was out of the question. He decided to hang in, knowing that time would work in the direction of bringing things to a head, of providing additional clarity.

The family business in Niigata City, the Good Hour Pachinko, wouldn't, he knew, be rebuilt. His father-in-law didn't want to incur any additional debt at his age. Rebuilding would be costly, and if Nakata could get out now he could depart with at least some money on the black side of the ledger. If the fire had been the result of arson, he hadn't been the only one negatively affected. He would no longer pay any kasuri—there was no longer anything to pay for or with. The older man clearly felt as though the Organization that had helped him long ago, when he had possessed no voice, at this point was functioning like a vaccine that had gone awry. At first it fights the disease, but in too large a dose it actually *becomes* the disease. For more than 10 years he had wanted an out; now there was no alternative.

Alpha and Rie could do nothing more than offer a bit of comfort to Rie's parents. Japanese society is highly specialized, and the cleanup of the burned out Good Hour would be handed over to a demolition contractor, after which a real estate agent would put the land up for sale (despite the bursting of the economic bubble in Japan, it was still quite valuable). The Nakatas' insurance company would step in to recover the losses, so there was little more for the family to do. After all accounts were settled, the Nakatas would retire from active employment. Their house was paid for, which is no small matter in Japan. They would begin to receive Social Security (quite generous in Japan, even though the economy is heavily burdened by having to support the largest proportion in the world of elderly people drawing benefits).

Maybe this still healthy couple could start climbing some of Japan's mountains or discover some cross-country trails. Maybe they would travel with a group to Hawaii or even to the American mainland. Possibly, if Alpha could arrange it, they could go as far as Arizona and visit his own parents. For the time being they just wanted out of the entrapments of doing business in Japan.

Alpha, anxious to get back to work, took the Shinkansen back to Ueno, followed by two local trains back to their apartment in Shakujikoen. Rie had decided to stay on a few more days in Niigata, to be with her parents, both of whom were for the time being still feeling very down. Given her position as the oldest daughter, her parents would lean heavily on her.

19

A Message Sent

Kaneda was looking after Shinkinsei. Alpha felt privileged to have him there and had no anxiety about leaving things in his capable hands during his own absence. While they were in Niigata, a fax had come to the company from the Department of Defense, Base Affairs Bureau, to the effect that DOD wanted the new pachinko machines installed within the next 30 days. Since the machines were now modified to Japanese voltage, it would be a simple matter of transporting them no longer than two hours by truck, if done after 10:00 a.m. Traffic moves at an average of only eight miles per hour in the Tokyo area, so commuters have to plan around rush hour and other predictable traffic jams, such as those caused by construction.

A transport company was enlisted, and the move was scheduled for the following Thursday morning. In all probability the usual route would be followed—going from the city of Sakura, entering the New Airport Highway, turning onto the Tokyo-Chiba Highway, and finally traveling on the East Kanto Highway. The term "expressways" in Japan is a misnomer, as only in the remote countryside do speeds ever approach 100 kilometers per hour.

Usually these intended thoroughfares resemble huge parking lots, with stop and go conditions until late into the night. Too few roads, too many tolls, and too much traffic make for trying vehicular travel conditions. Rest areas in Japan are located quite close to one another, as it is time traveled more than distance that determines their need.

While entering a curve on the Tokyo-Chiba Expressway, the truck transporting the pachinko machines was sideswiped by a large black car and overturned. The car, driven by an older man, was an aging Lincoln Town Car. Such foreign-made vehicles are expensive to own in Japan; as in America they also depreciate quickly, even though they may have fewer than 50,000 miles on them. It is, however, a sign of status, or indulgence, to drive around in one. Since the intrinsic appeal is in these cars' size and newness, however, few want them after they are a few years old. For one thing, they won't fit into most of the car park elevators that provide parking. Most are black with white lace on the seat covers, and one type of client more than any other—the Japanese yakuza member—bothers to maneuver them through Japan's narrow streets.

The air bags deployed on both vehicles, and there were no serious injuries to either driver. All of the cargo, however—the pachinko machines—was irreparably damaged. Most likely the driver of the car would incur four to six points on his license and face a fine of one to two thousand dollars. If he had a past record of accidents, his license might be suspended. The moving company carried insurance, so Shinkinsei would in time be compensated for its loss.

While Kaneda and Alpha were discussing the implications of the accident, the salient point was that the insurance policy would cover only primary damages. While it would pay the full invoice value of the machines, it wouldn't cover secondary losses, such as Shinkinsei's inability to fulfill its contract with the Department of Defense. Since the bid was mainly to acquire new business and was in actuality a loss leader, Shinkinsei would incur the substantial loss of all future business.

A much less ambiguous aspect of the accident was the message it was intended to convey. Legally, an accident report enters the public domain after about two weeks, and it includes the name of the driver. Beyond that there is typically little or no relevant information. With an adequate payment, however, perhaps in the area of 500,000 yen, it might be possible to ascertain a great deal more. There are an estimated 10,000 detective agencies in Japan. Their quality varies immensely, as there is little government control and no formal licensing.

The detectives, given sufficient funding, will do just about anything to earn their fee. Kaneda wanted to determine whether the driver of the Lincoln was in any way connected to any yakuza. He felt that it was worth the 500,000 yen to find out. Alpha realized it was technically his responsibility to approve this unbudgeted expense. In the way Japan has worked for centuries, no formal measures would be necessary. The Japanese, who more or less intuit harmony—they talk things over until everything meshes together; they often do not formally vote at board meetings, see no need to make such decisions overt. Alpha only had to say "I think so, too."

Almost everything in Japan is done by referrals. Kaneda had his favorite hangout—the Vatican Grill—where he had spent tens of thousands of dollars over the years in drinking and eating. He didn't know the significance of the name. Italian restaurants are popular in Japan, and possibly such a name afforded an impression of legitimacy. It was possible the owners of the Vatican Grill, the Itohs, had visited Vatican City. At any rate, he would go there and ferret out the name of a reputable detective agency.

Itoh knew of two he thought to be dependable. Frequently in Japan, because of extensive connections and obligations, one company can't accept work that another, with a different set of social obligations, can. True to form, the first company declined Kaneda's request without offering any formal reason. The second, Kimura Detective, accepted. The initial payment would be 400,000 yen, plus expenses, plus another 200,000 yen when all documents had been handed over.

It took Kimura only four days to come up with the first report on the driver of the Lincoln. He had the driver's name (Saburo

Sasaki), date of birth (September 13, 1943), address, and employment history over the last 30 years (all for the same company). There was a smaller yakuza, limited to the Tokyo area, called the Morishita-kumi. Morishita was the boss, the oyabun, and Sasaki had for the past 30 years been a kobun—an assistant.

Reaching retirement age in his mid-sixties meant that his position was more versatile than that of younger kobuns—he could do time, if necessary; have his driver's license suspended, if it came down to that; or spend months recovering in a hospital if injured. Records showed that he had very recently purchased the Lincoln from Morishita for 100,000 yen.

Older luxury cars are cheap in Japan. As are older people.

20

Disappearance

Alpha conceded to himself that there was too much going on to be the result of coincidence. What would be next if he continued with the attempt to import pachinko machines . . . or, indeed, opted to continue on with Shinkinsei?

All things, as folk wisdom would have it, come in threes—and there were now three mishaps. Alpha began to feel increasingly vulnerable. There was no visible enemy, but there were interests to protect. And there are inviolable laws by which the underworld abides—laws that were broken when someone attempted to become independent of a yakuza's grasp. This "game" reminded Alpha of the hanafuta—try as one might, they couldn't determine the size or quality of their opponent's hand.

Arriving home just after 5:00 p.m., Alpha phoned Rie. Everyone there was okay. The Nakata family would enjoy an early dinner, followed by a bath and an early retirement. Rie would stay two more nights, leave Thursday midmorning, and arrive back at their apartment early Thursday afternoon. This would in all likelihood be her last major trip, as she didn't want to compromise the health of their baby, whom she could now feel kicking in her womb.

On Thursday Alpha decided to work for only a half day. He ate lunch quickly at the office before departing for home. On the way he purchased some carnations for Rie. With a bit of luck he would arrive ahead of her, make some arrangements for supper and place the flowers in a vase. He knew she would be tired from the trip.

Indeed, Alpha did arrive before Rie. He aired out the apartment, placed the flowers on the kitchen table and cooled a bottle of Chardonnay, even though Rie would drink only a small amount because of the baby. It was now after 1:00 a.m., and Rie wasn't yet home. Alpha decided to call her mother and find out which train she had boarded. She reported that the entire family had slept in and gotten off to a late start. Rie had indeed boarded a later train, one that had left Niigata at 10:15 and was due to arrive at 13:09 in Shakujikoen. Alpha decided to hurry down to the station to surprise her.

The 13:09 train, however came and went, with no Rie disembarking. Perhaps she didn't feel well or had stopped at some station along the way to buy something for the baby. The next possibility was the 13:59 train. In the meantime Alpha decided to walk to the park where they had enjoyed so much time together. He would have less than 10 minutes before he would have to return in order to meet Rie. Soon, he thrilled, they would welcome the third member of the family. Alpha looked forward to pushing their baby in a stroller in the park, proclaiming himself to be a father. In less than two years their baby would begin to speak, and the challenge would be on. Rie would teach their baby Japanese, and Alpha English. What a privilege their child would have, Alpha reflected, to grow up naturally bilingual.

Alpha returned to the station with more than five minutes to spare. He was getting impatient and, aware that Rie would have some luggage—presents for the baby—decided to purchase a 140 yen ticket that would allow him to enter the station. He was standing on the platform when the 13:59 train arrived, less than a minute late. Rie wasn't on it.

Again Alpha phoned his in-laws in Niigata. No matter the circumstances, Rie should have arrived by now. Her parents had no explanation but would inquire as to whether anyone had become indisposed along the way. The Japanese rail system is excellent for providing update information on people who may have become ill. There are a lot of drunks on weekends who fall asleep in train stations or in trains, and they are treated with patience, as children who know no better.

Alpha tried phoning Rie. There was no answer, so he left her a short message. She could be absentminded at times and may have forgotten to turn on her phone. Maybe, on the contrary, she was preparing a small surprise for Alpha that was causing her to be late.

Not knowing what else to do, Alpha again phoned Rie's parents. They were concerned but had no further information. All three acknowledged that Rie had an independent streak; they were all too accustomed to her frequent digressions from the path most travelled. No one matching Rie's description had requested assistance en route. The Nakatas could only confirm that their daughter had been in good health and spirits when she had boarded the 10:15 train in Niigata. Alpha decided to return to the park and arrive back in the station in time for the next train. Rie didn't materialize, however, from the 14:59 train either.

Deciding to return home, Alpha plugged his cell phone into the charger to make certain he didn't miss her call. Still not frantic, he was beginning to get nervous.

He decided to walk down to the local police station. There was a *kooban*, a small local police post, on the far side of the tracks. The Japanese police force is efficiently decentralized—each community has a local office, usually near the train station, where the most people gather and where assistance is most likely to be needed. They even make attempts to visit each family in the neighborhood at least twice a year and so have at least some information on all residents in their jurisdiction.

The Shakujikoen police force did indeed know of Alpha and Rie but had no recent information on Rie. They took Alpha's cell phone number and assured him they would call or stop by if they heard anything. Alpha knew the police would not intently search for Rie in the immediate future.

Such matters as husbands disappearing from wives and vice versa are common events in Japan. Given the priorities of natural disasters, tax dodgers fleeing the law, suicides, homelessness and abductions by North Korea, missing persons tend to remain missing.

It was by this point becoming alarmingly late. Alpha phoned again, with the same result. Ruefully he remembered Einstein's quip, "A fool is one who does the same thing over and over and expects a different result." Nevertheless, he jogged down to the park, only to find "their" bench unoccupied. He dropped by the kooban once again but gleaned no new information. At this juncture he ran home—not knowing why he was in a hurry—only to arrive at an empty house.

Alpha began thinking about Hachiko, the dog at the Ebisu station that had accompanied his master to the station every morning. But that story had a happy ending. On the day Hachiko died, the now 16-year-old Yasuo had been befriended by Ando, a renowned artist who wanted to carve a statue of the famous dog. The statue, like the dog, became celebrated. And through that experience Yasuko met the girl he was to marry 10 years later.

Alpha checked his cell phone and email for messages. Nothing from Rie.

He tossed and turned throughout the night. At last light dawned, but still with no news. He decided to file a formal "Missing Person's Report" and took a recent photo, along with Rie's personal information, with him to the police station.

Not ordinarily one to worry, he felt as though he were grasping at straws.

After filing the report, he again jogged down to the park, sat down on their bench and cried.

21

Strange Encounter

Japan has 6,000 islands, only 420 of which are inhabited. The four main islands are Hokkaido, Honshu, Shikoku, and Kyushu. Next in line in size and population is Okinawa, with about 1.5 million in population, followed by Sado Island, located 30 miles off the Niigata coast with a population of 60,000.

Some commercial fishing boats, dropping their nets in the Sea of Japan or in the bays west of Niigata Prefecture, make Sado Island their home base, and ferries, pleasure boats, and high-speed hydrofoils connect it with the mainland in and around Niigata City. The slower ferries make the trip in five hours, the hydrofoils in one, and the three to four daily flights require only 20 minutes.

Sado Island is due east of North Korea. The 38ᵗʰ Parallel, dividing North and South Korea, intersects Niigata Prefecture and Sado Island near its small airport. While the island is easily accessible in modern times, its remoteness in ancient times resulted in its being used as a place of banishment for difficult or politically problematic people.

As early as A.D. 722 a poet was banished there for criticizing the Emperor. And in the late thirteenth century the Buddhist monk, Nichiren (the founder of *Nichiren*, a type of militant, intolerant Buddhism), was exiled there. The term "banished to Sado Island" had come to mean a one-way ticket, with no return possible. While this sounds harsh, it was in fact also merciful. Those banished there were not put to death but allowed to live out the rest of their days, provided they did not return to the mainland.

Two days had passed since Rie had boarded the train from Niigata to Tokyo—two days of nearly intolerable anxiety and sleepless nights for Alpha. While the local police near their apartment in Shakujikoen were accommodating, it was not their habit to pursue missing persons with much passion. They would file a missing person's report, upload it to a common police file to which every police station has access, and wait for some news. The suicide rate in Japan is very high, so high that the World Health Organization places Japan tenth in the world, with 22 suicides per 100,000 persons annually. The actual rate is probably much higher. With the passage of time most of the bodies turn up in some remote place.

As there continued to be no word about Rie, Alpha's apprehension increased. Feeling desolate and solitary, he called the Nakatas in Niigata two to three times each day, and they in turn called him every evening. The outcome was always the same in both directions—no news, no response, no updates.

In his helplessness and hopelessness Alpha began to pray in a manner in which he had never previously done, except possibly when he had been four years old and his pet dog had died. Alpha couldn't have articulated his reasoning, other than a desperate sense that reaching out at a point of human extremity might provide an opportunity for divine intervention.

Then, at 9:30 a.m. on the third day after Rie's disappearance, a call arrived from the police on Sado Island. They had located a young lady who matched Rie's description. She was incoherent and disheveled but had offered up the contents of her purse. Finding her address and Alpha's phone number, they had contacted Alpha immediately.

Alpha, utterly relieved to know that Rie was alive, called the Nakatas and relayed the joyous news to them. The fastest way for Alpha to get within proximity of the island would be the Shinkansen—the bullet train. This would still require five hours. The Nakatas, from their side, would depart immediately, taking some of Rie's clothing and changes of underwear with them; they would take a taxi to the Niigata Airport, purchase two tickets, and fly to the airport near Ryotsu, in the center of the island. With a bit of luck they could be reunited with Rie in less than two hours.

As it turned out, they were fortunate. Upon their arrival at the airport they learned that a scheduled plane, with three vacancies, would be leaving in 15 minutes. Thus the anxious parents landed in Ryotsu, the main city on Sado Island, just after 11:00 a.m. Another ten-minute taxi ride to the Police Station, and Rie was released into their custody. Though ecstatic about the reunion, the Nakatas were devastated by their daughter's appearance and demeanor. Rie had soiled her pants, was zombie-like in her actions, and barely responded to them.

The family checked in to a nearby hotel, booking two adjacent rooms with a connecting door. They prepared a lukewarm bath, and Rie's mother scrubbed her down and helped her get into the tub and soak. Rie was compliant and slowly became a little more coherent and responsive. The Nakatas disposed of her soiled clothing and, thinking correctly that some nourishment would help, used room service to order in some *okayuu* (soft-boiled Japanese rice) with seaweed flavoring, some miso soup, and Japanese tea. They were asked to check with the police before leaving the island but decided to spend the night. Even though it was now approaching noon, Rie wanted to sleep.

She manifested symptoms of retrograde amnesia: she was able to remember very little of what had happened since boarding the train from Niigata to Tokyo. All she could recall was a feeling of wooziness—like being hung over, dizzy, sluggish, and uncoordinated—but she had no memory of tangible facts. How she had gotten from the train to Sado Island was a complete mystery to her.

Alpha was not as fortunate in terms of his journey to the island. The last flight of the day had already left by the time he arrived at the airport, although there was one last jet hydrofoil, which he managed to board with no time to spare. The one-hour trip seemed like an eternity.

At long last arriving at the hotel via taxi, he found his wife sleeping restfully. Other than some pallor, Rie showed no external effects of her ordeal. Late in the afternoon when she awoke, she wanted Alpha to sit in bed next to her.

The Nakatas ordered in four meals for dinner, not wanting to go out in public with Rie before she had recovered. Some delicate questions needed to be asked, which Alpha tried to do despite the awkwardness of the situation. No, thankfully, Rie had no vaginal soreness, and there was no sign that she had been violated—nothing on her old underwear other than her own urine. And the contents of her purse were intact.

Rie experienced uncontrollable tremors in her hands and remained incontinent throughout the night. Her mother, in her usual resourceful manner, had exercised the foresight to purchase some feminine napkins at a drugstore near the hotel. Three had been soaked with urine before the sun's early rays had awakened the four. Despite unusual hunger and a mild headache, Rie otherwise wasn't far from normal.

Discussion over breakfast inevitably turned to an attempt to make sense of what had happened. What had been done to Rie was clearly more than sabre rattling. It was a clear warning, as banishment to Sado Island historically meant no return—ever. The implication was that an attempt to do so would result in death. Yet the relieved foursome rightly perceived a degree of mercy in the harsh decree. Something a lot worse could have happened. Typically one didn't get a warning.

The yakuza was without doubt the only group that could have pulled this off—or would have had reason to want to. Affiliates of the North Korean yakuza control the pachinko industry in Japan. And as the 38th Parallel intersects North and South Korea, it felt ironic to Rie and Alpha that, at exactly the same parallel on Sado Island, their lives were being intersected by the same forces. The pachinko interests didn't want their turf invaded, either by New

Morning Star Enterprises, an aspiring young American entrepreneur, or a Japanese family.

Rie had been drugged, possibly with GHB (gamma-hydroxbutrate) or a similar central nervous system depressant. GHB is sold both as a liquid and as a light colored powder that dissolves easily and is virtually undetectable when mixed in with a soft drink, tea, or coffee. Her symptoms were consistent with GHB ingestion. The hot tea Rie had drunk on the train may well have been the culprit. But she had no recollection, beyond that of beginning to feel a little dizzy. Her first thought had been that this was a sudden onset of morning sickness. GHB is detectable in urine for only 6–12 hours after ingestion. And it requires a sophisticated lab test, GS-MS (gas chromatography-mass spectrometry), to detect. The island's low population and relatively low level of drug use hadn't justified investment in the expensive equipment required for such testing.

The Nakatas, preferring to have Rie recover quickly, as opposed to trying to find out exactly what she may have ingested, opted not to submit urine samples to the police for drug testing.

If it indeed were the case—and it was obviously was—that Rie had been "banished to Sado Island," then the yakuza had violated one of its own cardinal rules—not to mess with family members. An infraction would have to be considered very serious to warrant such a drastic measure. This was perhaps why Rie was getting off with what amounted to a slap on the wrist—albeit a hard one. The statement was unambiguous; it spoke louder than the fire at the Good Hour Pachinko Parlor, louder even than the mysterious death of Kanagawa. Alpha and Rie were being directed to leave the firm that he had just inherited from Rie's uncle and to return to the States.

How long did they have (if, in fact, they had any time at all)? Without their compliance the next step would be death—designed, of course, to look accidental. And there would be no trail back to the perpetrators.

How could they fight an invisible enemy? One that never shows his colors, let alone his face? Alpha called All Nippon Airways

(ANA) and inquired whether there were any available seats to Phoenix. There were, but since one can only fly to Hawaii from Niigata, there would be a surcharge of more than $400 dollars per ticket to use the ANA vouchers that Alpha's parents had sent as a wedding present. It was still the high demand season when seats were at a premium, but there were two available on the following Tuesday, a low volume travel day.

The ANA vouchers, which Alpha carried in his wallet, fortunately applied toward this fare. Another $430 each, with a three-day stopover in Honolulu, and Rie and Alpha would soon be in Phoenix with Alpha's parents. Alpha wanted to introduce Rie to some of his college friends from the East-West University who had remained in Hawaii after graduation, so the short stopover wouldn't be unwelcome. In fact, it would help Rie to make a full recovery before arriving on the mainland.

The couple would remain on Sado Island until Tuesday morning, take the jet hydrofoil to Niigata, and proceed by taxi to the airport. In the meantime the Nakatas would travel to Tokyo, pack some of Rie's and Alpha's belongings, and return to Sado Island in time for their departure to Hawaii.

Rie's parents thoughtfully prepaid for two rooms in the hotel through Tuesday, even though they wouldn't use the second room for the entire time. Rie didn't want to venture out, choosing to remain in the hotel room with Alpha and rely on room service. She still required a lot of sleep. But by that evening her tremors had almost completely subsided.

The Nakatas returned from Rie and Alpha's apartment late Monday afternoon with four suitcases. The two couples finally ventured out for dinner, Rie somewhat reluctantly. Sado Island is noted for its fresh sushi, and they visited a noted sushi house near the hotel. The mood was somber, and the delicious food did little to alleviate the apprehension they all felt.

This, they all knew, would be their last real meal together, and it took every effort on the part of Rie's mother to keep from crying. Alpha realized that her cheerful mood was purely tatamae—that if her true inner feelings were to come out there would be no end to the weeping that would ensue. Yet there is something valuable, something functional and useful, in this aspect of Japanese culture. The use of tatemae enables people to cope with difficult emotional situations with an element of grace.

No one slept well on Monday night. The hotel offered a typical Japanese breakfast—green tea, rice, miso soup, seaweed, tofu, and several embellishments. Alpha was thankful for the lightness of the Japanese fare on a morning like this, when no one felt much like eating, despite needing the nourishment. The four checked out and shared a taxi.

The Nakatas remained fairly composed at the airport. They had brought with them a colorful envelope with 500,000 Japanese yen, or about $5,000, for Rie and Alpha. Apparently they hadn't found, or taken, the time to change the money into US dollars. There were plenty of banks in Honolulu that would happily do so.

As Rie and Alpha cleared final security, Rie's mother did begin crying—something uncharacteristic for a Japanese female to do in public. Rie was able to board the plane before her own emotions got the best of her. As it lifted off, she thought she could see through the window the silhouette of her parents on the observation deck. Her father was supporting her mother.

Glossary

abeku	adapted from the French word *avec*, or "with"; refers to a two- to three-hour romantic liaison.
ainu	Japanese indigenous minority.
amae	literally, "sweetness," an assurance that another party won't take advantage of an individual, that the person can unload excess psychological baggage on someone else without fear of reprisal.
amaeru	literally, "to be mothered," implying that a relationship has developed to the point of mutually indulging each other without fear of retribution; being "in."
anime	animations.
burakumin	Japanese citizens of low social status; outcasts.
bushido	the samurai code of ethics, involving stoical indifference to pain and hunger, loyalty and sacrifice.
cho-me	east-west; used in terms of the east-west coordinate of a basic single-block area.
chorei	a morning gathering at which a manager exhorts everyone to do their best for the company.
chotto	"A little," "not much," or "nothing important."
deji-pachi	digital pachinko machines.

ema	a painted wooden plaque in an ornamental frame, often depicting a horse.
en-kiri-ryo	money paid to cut off one's connection with a yakuza.
eta	traditionally an outcast group composed of those with occupations considered impure or tainted by death, such as executioners, undertakers, workers in slaughterhouses, butchers, or tanners.
fu-ka-koo-ryoku	a force impossible to resist.
fusuma	used as room dividers in Japanese style buildings, including houses, onsens, and hotels.
gaijin	informal for foreigner; often with a –san suffix (literally, "outside person").
gaijin-san	outsider, non Japanese person.
gaikokujin	formal for foreigner (literally, "outside country person").
gaisha	a foreign-made car.
gaman	perseverance, patience and endurance.
gawa	the pure form is kawa (as in Kawasaki); the form when it is not the first character in a word is gawa, as in Kanagawa, the prefecture where Yokohama is.
geta	traditional wooden sandals worn with a yukata at an onsen following ritual bathing.
giri	obligation, generally strenuously avoided by the frequent exchange of gifts, e.g., a gift is a payment for the obligation incurred.
Golden Week	April 29 (Hirohito's birthday)–May 5 (Children's Day), including Constitution Day (May 3). One of the three major extended holidays in Japan. The other two are New Years (January 1) and Obon (August 15).
gomen ne	"Please forgive me."
ha-ji-me-ma-shi-te	"Nice meeting you."

hai   normally translated "yes." It is written by joining charac-
                   ters for the left and right hands; it has a broad range of
                   meaning, far greater than our English word for yes. It is
                   an acknowledgment that you have heard what the other
                   person has said, but in some contexts it does not imply
                   agreement.

hamon   notice of excommunication from the yakuza.

hanafuta   flower cards; a game played with a deck of numbered cards
                   with elaborate floral artwork on opposite side.

harakiri   suicide.

hentai   erotic.

hinamatsuri   Girls' Day, celebrated on March 3 (the third day of the
                   third month, or the "Double Three").

hiragana   one of two phonetic Japanese alphabets; this one is used
                   to add sounds, declensions, particles, etc., to numerous
                   Chinese characters.

honne   one's real intention, one's heart, as contrasted to one's
                   tatemae, the face one presents to the outside world.

hooji   Buddhist memorial masses for the dead, conducted
                   periodically for each individual.

hoshonin   guarantors who help entrepreneurs establish credit and
                   take responsibility for their behavior and character.

ijime   bullying.

inazuma   lightening; also "rice plant wife" (implication: behave,
                   or else; "if I can plant rice plants, I can do a lot more").

inkan   name chop with which a couple stamps their names
                   at city hall in order to be married; this is the only legal
                   requirement.

irezumi   artistic tattoos often identified with yakuza members.

itadakimasu   "I will receive," a standard phrase used in Japan before one
                   eats a meal.

jamamono	an obstacle; a thing in the way; often used of Japanese husbands after they retire.
ji-riki	self-strength, self-reliance.
ji-satsu	suicide.
jieitai	Japanese self-defense forces.
jo	north-south; used in terms of the north-south coordinate of a basic single-block area.
Jopok	North Korean mafia.
jukyou	Confucianism.
juryo	the second highest division of six ranked sumo wrestling divisions; only 28 wrestlers are at this level at any time.
ka	excessive.
ka-nai	Japanese word for "wife" that literally means "inside the house."
kabuki	a theater where traditional Japanese plays called noh are performed.
kachi-gumi	a group of dominant students or "winners"; the elite gang at a school.
kai	association or club, similar in meaning to kumi or gumi.
kaimyoo	according to Japanese Buddhism, a posthumous name a temple gives to a deceased person, who supposedly goes on to become a Buddha upon his death.
kaizen	continuous product improvement (not applied to buildings, to which little maintenance is done).
kame	turtles (one of four animals considered by the Japanese to be divine).
kamikaze	special military attacks, or suicide attacks.
kane	gold or wealth.
kanji	Chinese characters (hanzi) used in the modern Japanese writing system.

karoshi	premature death from overwork, usually by a stroke or heart attack.
karoshi jisattsu	suicide on account of overwork.
kashikomairimashita	"I heard your request and will comply with it."
kasuri	periodic payments to the yakuza, similar to protection money; kickbacks.
katakana	one of two Japanese phonetic alphabets; this one is used primarily for writing foreign words.
kigyo shatei	literally, a "little brother" company, a front company for the yakuza.
kin-yoo-bi	Friday; literally, "wealth-day" or "gold-day."
kobun	"surrogate child" role; a follower of an oyabun.
kodoku	pity for a person whose days are numbered—one who, in spite of material success, is essentially empty and alone.
koinobori	carp-shaped flags draped on poles like windsocks at an airport in conjunction with Children's Day or Boys' Day on May 5 (the "Double Fifth"); the largest represents the father and each of the smaller ones his children (usually only the boys).
kooban	a small local police station or post.
kusuri	medicine; something used to alleviate pain.
love hotel	a hot-sheet hotel where rooms are rented by the hour (usually 2–3 hours at a time for sexual liaisons). Lately, due to multigenerational families living under one roof, some married couples have begun using them.
make-gumi	a group of school "losers" picked on by the kachi-gumi or elite gang.
makuuchi	the top division of sumo wrestling; only 42 wrestlers are at this level at any time.
mikaijime-ryo	monthly protection payments to one's yakuza.
miso	a traditional Japanese soup consisting of a stock called "dashi" into which softened miso paste is mixed.

mizuko	literally, "water child"; refers to an aborted fetus.
mizuko jizo	miscarried and aborted fetuses.
mizuko kuyo	"fetus memorial service," a ceremony for those who have had a miscarriage, stillbirth, or abortion.
mizushobai	literally, "water of entertainment," a reference to the entertainment or "water" industry, involving night clubs, mistresses and drinking partners.
monism	a worldview that looks at all reality as blending together in a harmonious whole. In contrast to dualism (e.g., Christianity), adherents do not differentiate a creator from creation.
moriryo	protection money that in effect only protects one from his "own" yakuza.
muga	the Buddhist concept of self-renunciation, the annihilation of self with the extinction of all desire.
mukooyoshi	a groom who, in the absence to a male heir, is adopted into the bride's family, assumes their family name, and thus maintains the family lineage.
Mukuchi	used in conjunction with Mr.; literally, "Mr. No-Mouth," a taciturn individual who seems to blend into the woodwork.
musubi	the undifferentiated coexistence between man and nature.
nakodo	a go-between for a prospective bride and groom.
NEET	acronym for Not in Education, Employment, or Training, i.e., unemployed.
ni-sei	a second-generation Japanese girl born in a non-Japanese host culture.
Nicheren	a type of militant, intolerant Buddhism.
nip-pachi	the two months of February and August, the slowest times in the Japanese fiscal year and thus the best times to take a vacation.
nokotsudo	a bone repository of cremated remains. Since most people in Japan die Buddhists, *nokotsudo* are mainly Buddhist; but Christian churches also have them.

obento   a Japanese packaged lunch, usually consisting of rice, fish and vegetables.

Obon   August 15, a Buddhist (and national) holiday when the spirits of departed ancestors are believed to return home. As Golden Week signals the beginning of summer, Obon indicates its end.

ochikobore   school dropout.

ohigan   the other shore; the alleged destination of the dead.

oicho-kabu   a game that uses only three hanafuta cards.

ojisan   uncle.

okayuu   soft-boiled Japanese rice.

okonomiyaki   Japanese pancakes, often eaten for lunch or supper, usually cooked in a restaurant in front of the patron and topped with sauce.

okozukai   pocket money given by wives to their husbands in steadily decreasing amounts in recent years.

omiai   an interview with a supervisor with a view to an arranged marriage with an interested male employee.

omiai kekkon   arranged marriage.

oniyome   literally, a "devil bride"; a strong-willed wife who answers to no one and does as she pleases.

onsen   Japannese hot spring baths.

osewa   help or assistance.

osewa ni narimashita   (You) have been a help, or rendered assistance.

oshibori   a wet towel, usually hot in the winter and cold in the summer.

oyabun   an individual who serves in a parent role: the boss or leader (usually of a yakuza gang).

pachi-pro   a pachinko professional or frequent player.

pachi-slo   pachinko slot machine(s).

pachinko	onomatopoetic term for Japanese pinball machines; now usually electronic but imitating the original sounds of steel balls bouncing off rubber bumpers.
ro	labor or work.
ronin	used to describe a person who has no master to serve, no duties to perform, and no group to belong to.
sakaya	a liquor store.
sake	an alcoholic beverage made from fermented rice. Usually occurs with an honorific "o" prefix, thus *osake*.
samurai	members of a frightening and deadly sub-society that emerged in Japan some three hundred years ago.
Seishi-kai	Youth Ideology Study Association.
seizen-kaimyo	a kaimyo (posthumous name) conferred upon a Buddhist while still alive.
sekihan	rice boiled together with red beans and eaten on festive occasions, such as New Year's Day or a wedding.
seppuku	suicide by disembowelment. Usually performed by making a horizontal cut in one's own bowels, followed by a vertical cut. An assistant usually accompanies this painful procedure to complete the process.
shabu	meth, methamphetamine.
shacho	company president.
shi	death; also the number four (these words are homonyms).
shibui	a type of beauty in perfect harmony with nature.
Shinkansen	a network of high-speed railway lines operated by four Japan Railways Group companies; also known as the "Bullet Train."
shoba-ryo	monthly protection payments to one's yakuza.
shochoo	a young woman's first menarche or menstrual period
shokaijo	letters of introduction that will open the right doors at the right time to the right people.

so desu ka	"Oh, this is new information to me," "Is that so?" or "Now I get it."
so desu ne	"Yes, I agree," "Yes, I was aware of that," or "Yes, I already knew that."
soba	Japanese buckwheat noodle.
sooshikaimei	process by which a foreign name (often Korean) has an additional character added to it so it will appear to be indigenous (e.g., Kim, or in Japanese, becomes Kane; adding results in Kanagawa, a native Japanese name).
soozai	Japanese food that includes the basics (rice, fish and soup), embellished by a number of side dishes.
ta-riki	literally, "someone else's strength"; grace (as opposed to ji-riki, or self-strength).
tai-an	a day designated to be particularly lucky.
tanshin funin	taking up a new post and leaving one's family behind.
tatami	straw mats, each measuring three by six feet, provided to onsen guests.
tatemae	façade, or external appearance, often with relation to one's true thoughts (honne). The face one presents to the world. An example is to smile when one is hurting.
TCK	a third-culture kid, a person raised during their developmental years in two cultures so that their personalities reflect a composite of the two.
tekiya	street stall operators.
tenugui	a Japanese bath towel.
tobiori jisatsu	literally, a death leap; suicide by jumping.
udon	Japanese noodles.
wa	harmony, peace, or peaceful.
yakuza	Japanese mafia.
yasuraka ni nemutte kudasai	"Please sleep peacefully."

yubizume   the practice of cutting off the tip of one's pinky finger to show regret for a failure by a kobun with regard to his oyabun.

yuigon   a person's verbally expressed last wish.

yuigon josho a written will; the desires of the recently departed are held in high esteem in Japan and strictly carried out.

yukata   a casual summer kimono or robe.

zai   side dish.

About the Author

Dr. Robert A. Cunningham, a native of Michigan, and his Swiss wife have parented two adopted children from Japan. He has studied at seven universities in the USA (Cornerstone University, Calvin College, Grand Rapids Community College, Trinity International, Northern Illinois University, the University of Illinois at Chicago Circle, and Rutgers), as well as at the University of Strasbourg in France, in private German studies in Switzerland, at OMF Headquarters in Singapore, and at the Japanese Language Centre in Sapporo. Dr. Cunningham holds four degrees, including two masters and a doctorate (D.Min.).

His professional career has included social work on Chicago's Skid Row (1968–9); pioneering an in-resident alcoholism recovery center in Sapporo, Japan (1973–84); and developing a anti-drug abuse educational center in Chiba Prefecture, also in Japan.

In 2010 he completed the development of Shalom Springs, a self-support living center for highly functional developmentally disabled adults located near Grand Rapids in Wyoming, Michigan. Since April of 2013 he has served as president of Hokuriku Gakuin University (HGU) and Junior College—a historic university founded in 1885 and located on the west coast in Kanazawa, Japan, near the Sea of Japan.

In writing this novel Dr. Cunningham drew on his extensive business background and over 40 years of experience associated with Japanese companies and the Japanese government.